Airships

from the

North

George Beckman

Book 2 of the Wolfskill Series

ISBN: 978-1-7366485-9-9

No characters in this book are anybody you know. The story takes place in 1896, and they all died years ago!
smile

Other Books by George Beckman
(In Order)

Members of the Cast

Partway to Wolfskill- poems of the canyon

The Ship from Wolfskill (Book 1)

Books from Graestone

Dedication

This book is dedicated to all the kids I taught through the years. For years my 6th graders wrote six chapter "books." It seems only fair that Mr. B. do some writing. I hope all of you are happy and doing well.

Acknowledgements

Without Ruth, I cannot imagine writing. She not only gives me time to write, but encourages my work. We are a family of writers and our children, Rachel and Matthew make me proud.

I want to thank my critique partners and beta readers, especially Mark, Abby, and Harlow. To all my #LineByLineTime friends on Twitter, please know that your support is a powerful force in my writing.

And to Donna, who doesn't seem to mind reading a manuscript over and over, pointing out a comma here and a quotation there. If you find grammar and punctuation mistakes, they are probably not her fault—I seem to introduce errors as I make corrections. Sigh.

The parasol and vial images are courtesy of
https://olddesignshop.com/

Content Advisory

I write wholesome books. While the main characters are wholesome people, Freebooters aren't. *Airships from the North* is the second book of a trilogy, and the characters are now New Adults. The war against the enemy becomes more violent.

Table of Contents

Cloud Queen's tired crew seeks

Respite at Eagle's Crest's hearth

While Freebooters plot

1

José rang for Slow high above the water, the Santa Monica pier shimmering in the distance; a perfect day—except for the soldiers.

I directed the telescope toward the colorful promenade along the structure and invited Mrs. Mortimer to take a look. "Remember the small adjustment here."

She oohed and aahed.

We had received the third letter. The third warning, Finn called it. We were to surrender the *Cloud Queen*; the Army wanted our airship. The letters came to Dad, and he sent them to us, keeping our whereabouts to himself. We never spent long in any one location. The novelty of a flying riverboat and the Army's appetite for her secrets forced us to be elusive.

Laura brought a tray of lemonade. Mr. Mortimer sat in a deck chair next to Mr. and Mrs. Thomas puffing a smelly cigar. Laura, behind them in her maid's outfit, wrinkled her nose and rolled her eyes.

I refocused the telescope, one hand behind my back. Three Army wagons stood near our sign, "Flying Riverboat Excursions." I nodded to Laura and swung the telescope to the west.

"Mrs. Mortimer, there is a fine view of a red tailed hawk sitting on a high branch." The big bird surveyed the land below him. Mr. Mortimer dozed.

Mr. Thomas joined her, guiding her hand on the focus knob.

I went aft, catching a glimpse of myself in the passageway mirror. I took off my captain's hat and put it under my arm. Laura joined me.

In the engine room, Finn adjusted the boiler injector pump. The smooth oscillation of the steam engine and the dynamo whirr always comforted me.

"What's going on out there, Will?" Finn asked.

"The Army is back." I waved my hat toward the ceiling. "We are having a quick meeting in the pilothouse."

Finn checked the gauges, and we climbed the steps. José made a subtle turn of the big wheel.

I stood by the engine order telegraph. "Let's keep an eye on our guests. We will have to join them if they begin to wander."

Laura's face showed her displeasure. "As long as Mr. Mortimer dozes, I think Mr. Thomas and Mrs. Mortimer will be more than happy to be fascinated with the telescope. Mrs. Thomas is either a fool or doesn't care."

Benny glanced at the deck below and pulled at his steward's collar.

"Three Army wagons are waiting by the flat," I said. "There are fourteen horses." I admired Army discipline; they tied their horses in a row.

"We cannot give them the *Cloud Queen*," Finn said. "Even if we gave it to them, they will hound us to learn more about Levitrite."

I had no intention of telling the soldiers how the airship worked. If we gave up the ship, it would not take long for them to come for Finn. As Engineer, he knew every inch of the *Cloud Queen* and how she worked.

José, always practical, asked, "How much money do we have?"

"Nearly thirty-three thousand." Laura glanced down at the guests. "Hopefully, Mr. Mortimer will press a large bill in my hand when they leave. I shined that man's shoes this morning!"

Flying Riverboat Excursions had been disagreeable work, but we had paid off the mortgages on our parents' homes and farms. And we had plans underway. Big plans.

"We'll have to stop for fuel—when we leave—run." Finn looked from face to face. "We are running, right? To Eagle's Crest?"

Everyone nodded.

Three years earlier, after we drove the Freebooters back, it became apparent the Army was interested in our airship, and they demanded a demonstration.

A self-important Major Stephens had come aboard strutting like a rooster. He swaggered around the pilothouse, barking orders. He pulled me aside and whispered loudly, "I see you have a 'Messcan' driving."

I said nothing, and José pretended not to hear.

The major demanded to see how high we could go, and we took him up until his ears must have been ready to burst. I wasn't about to suggest he work his jaw to relieve the pressure.

The silliness became serious when he hollered into the speaking tube, "Let her down. Let her down fast!"

Finn had ignored the order.

Major Stephens squared off in front of me. "How fast can we drop?"

"Like a rock," I assured him.

Laura winked.

I went down to the engine room. "Benny, hang on. We're going down. Let her go, Finn," I said quietly.

Finn slid the lift lever to twenty percent. We were expecting it, but it was impressive when the ship started to fall. My stomach rolled, and I pulled up on the railing surrounding the engine, pressing my feet to the floor. The airship listed to the starboard, Finn trimmed the lifters, and the *Cloud Queen* righted herself.

"Good enough, Finn." I hoped it was good enough for the Major.

Finn opened the lift lever to forty-five percent. We continued to fall, but Finn controlled our descent, watching the altitude gauge. The needle wound down to five hundred feet.

I started to the wheelhouse when I met Laura and a pale Major. He vomited at the bottom of the stairs, and I was sorry we would have to clean it up.

At three hundred feet, Finn began to talk to José, and we settled gently to the ground.

The Major tried to put on a good face and said he would meet us later in the afternoon.

I suppose what we had done was childish, but the *Cloud Queen* had driven the Freebooters back, and this was how the Army thanked us.

Laura helped the Major off the deck, and with some amusement, we watched him wobble away. He leaned on a wagon and lost the rest of his breakfast.

Soldiers milled around the airship. A private with a dirty uniform pulled himself on board.

"We would rather you stayed off the airship, sir," I said. I was nineteen at the time, and he glared at me.

I poked my head into the engine room. "Finn, give us a shake."

Immediately the ship raised a few inches and dropped back with a thump, sending the soldier over the railing. Something fell and broke in the forward cabin.

I snapped open the gate and reached for Laura's hand, pulling her aboard.

The Major gagged an order. A young sergeant shouted, "To your rifles, men! To arms!"

Laura waited with big eyes at the engine room door, the blower whine increasing as the engine spun up. Soldiers stumbled around, the sergeant pulling a pistol from his holster. Air and smoke whistled up the stack.

"Go!" I yelled. "Get down, get down! Go, go!"

I flattened myself on the deck. Wood creaked, and we lifted at a terrific rate. Gunshots drifted up from below, but the hull protected us.

In the engine room, Finn grinned. "When Laura told me what was happening, I waited for the engine to reach two-hundred-forty revolutions. When I pulled the lift lever, we were gone before they realized we were launching."

"Our own Army shot at us!" Laura was angry. "I'd like to dump some water on them, and not fresh water!"

I had laughed that day, but was also troubled. The Army did not behave like the Army in the history books at school.

We learned our lesson well: the Army, at least a part of it, was not to be trusted.

After our quick getaway, we had a reprieve. The Army was called to Sacramento, and we began offering air excursions to those willing to part with their money. We converted the *Cloud Queen*'s single smokestack to two black pipes with fluted tops. With a fresh coat of paint, the *Cloud Queen* appeared to be a flying Mississippi riverboat. Our reservation book was full of folks eager for an overnight adventure, and our ledger showed the profits.

Operating along the coast was a popular run. None of us liked the job; most of our guests were rich and spoiled. We played our roles well: Finn the engineer, José the pilot, and Benny acting the part of steward. Laura was a skilled pilot, but it was soon apparent that our customers liked a pretty young woman to coddle them.

She was beautiful with a white apron over her blue dress. She only went along with it because we needed money in a hurry.

I moved to the forward window of the pilothouse. Below, Mr. Thomas left his hand on Mrs. Mortimer's elbow a little too long. She turned to him and cooed something that made him smile. Mr. Mortimer's head had fallen to his chest.

"So, how do we do this?" José asked. "We have to get our passengers off the ship safely."

"Maybe we could leave them in a field, somewhere," Finn suggested.

"No, I want a nice tip," Laura said. "If I must pretend to be interested in what Mr. Mortimer babbles about, I want that old goat pushing folding money into my hand."

I tapped the window sill. "What if we gave them the thrill of their lives?" I gestured toward the pier. "We offer to drop them at the far end of the promenade. We hover and let them walk down the forward gangplank."

"I would like Mr. Mortimer to walk the plank. He pinched my arm!"

I had not seen Laura this frustrated. After seeing women mistreated when we fought the Freebooters, she had no patience with men who took liberties.

"Mrs. Mortimer wants to pat my cheek every time she sees me." Benny rubbed his jaw. "She pats hard."

"Can we do it?" I wondered. "Can we hover off the end of the pier long enough to let them off?"

"The wind usually shifts about this time," Finn answered. "For the next hour or so the air will be still, with slight movement out to sea. Yes, we should be able to do it. We have nestled next to a coal car enough times."

I turned to José. "We have to be sure. We can't take the chance of anyone getting hurt."

"If it is too risky, too much wind, we will abort," Finn said. "But it's worth a try."

José stepped away from the window. "It can be done."

2

Laura was perfect. She tightened her apron, making her waist even tinier. "Follow my lead. Mr. Mortimer is going to pay for this." She leaned close to José. "Keep us over the water so we can see the pier from the front deck. Finn, be ready to give us a slight tip to starboard. José, I'll give you a signal. Will, you come with me." Laura winked.

She arranged a tray of iced tea and cakes, and I followed her to the front deck. The airscrews quieted, the ship hanging motionless.

Laura touched the dozing Mr. Mortimer's arm. "Would you like some tea, Sir? I have some of the little cakes you like."

"Oh, that would be splendid, dear. How thoughtful."

Laura poured the tea and remarked how peaceful seagulls were as they hung in the air off the bow. She mused about the colors worn by the people on the pier, and Mr. Mortimer had to get up to see. Laura stood close and laughed at something he said.

She gave Mr. Mortimer her radiant smile and laughed again. I stood to the side, chest out at attention, playing my part in my captain's coat and hat.

Laura glanced up at José and wiggled her hand. When the *Cloud Queen* shifted, Laura put her hand on Mr. Mortimer's arm to steady herself. "Oh! Excuse me," she exclaimed.

I stifled a laugh, turning it into a cough.

Laura floated her hand toward the pier. "I have always thought it would be such fun to be able to let our guests disembark at the end of the promenade. We could extend the bow gangplank." She gestured with a flourish. "The airship could hover at the end of the pier, just there," she sighed, "floating majestically, at the end. It would make a wonderful sight with the ladies in their finery coming down the gangway."

Mr. Mortimer squinted toward the end of the pier. "Could the airship do that? Dock at the end?"

"Oh, of course. Finn, our engineer, and José in the pilothouse are wonderful. They could land on a ten-cent piece if they wanted to." She giggled.

The gears turned in Mr. Mortimer's head. The soldiers continued to watch.

Mr. Mortimer beamed. "Captain Henderson. Your lovely maid just gave me the most wonderful idea. I wish to disembark at the end of the pier."

I put on my shocked and surprised look. "Oh, Sir. I—I couldn't. I—"

"Come come, young Henderson. Miss Laura has already told me it is perfectly possible and safe." Mr. Mortimer winked at Laura.

Laura looked flustered and reached back to adjust the ties of her apron, accenting her figure.

"Well, Mr. Mortimer, of course—it *is* possible. My crew could bring her to the end of the dock as gentle as a mother's kiss. But—"

Mr. Mortimer scowled. "But what, son?"

"Well, Sir, it's that we have orders to stay five-hundred feet from the pier at all times. It is the town fathers, Sir. There was mention of a fine."

"Well, well, I am sure we can cover the cost of a fine." Mr. Mortimer patted the breast pocket of his coat. "I am sure I can make it well worth your time." He flashed his teeth in a fake smile.

"But, sir, what if we lost our right to do business in Santa Monica? The landing site is on city property."

"Well, now. We know there are miles and miles of coastline. People will come to you, come to you! Why—we took the train from San Diego for this Flying Riverboat trip. I could set you up there—I have powerful connections." Mr. Mortimer brushed his smoke-yellowed mustache.

I wavered. "It would be taking a chance, Sir, a big chance. I am responsible to others with a part in the *Cloud Queen*. I must think of those good people, Sir."

"Enough. Three hundred should cover any inconvenience."

I was shocked. Three hundred was what we charged the couples for the two days and a night. Laura stood to the side and gave the tiniest shake of her head.

"I—er. I don't know, Sir. My actions might be seen as reckless."

Laura came close. "What is wrong, Captain Henderson?"

"Nothing, nothing. I—"

Laura tipped her head toward Mr. Mortimer. "Silly me. Sometimes my dreams cause me to make silly wishes. I suppose I spoke out of turn—I have put Captain Henderson in an awkward position. I *am* sorry, Captain Henderson." She lingered, looking toward the pier, her dark curls teased by a gust of wind. "It *would* have been *so* grand."

Mr. Mortimer rocked on the balls of his feet and put the cigar in his mouth. He reached for his wallet. "Let's make it an even five-hundred."

"Oh, my—five-hundred dollars!" Laura looked at Mr. Mortimer with her big eyes. "Is such a thing possible?"

Mr. Mortimer puffed up like a balloon and turned to Laura. "My dear. As pretty as you are, someday you will marry a man of means and have five-hundred dollars at your disposal."

Laura put her head down and leaned toward Mr. Mortimer. "I can still be impressed, can't I?"

I told Mr. Mortimer we would make preparations and that Benny would bring the luggage forward. "We can't be sure how long we will be allowed to dock," I explained.

In the pilothouse, we decided that José would steer. Laura would stay on the forward deck and ooh and aah as we came into the pier.

"We have a perfect wind. The air is slightly moving out to sea," Finn said.

"We will fly over the landing area and then turn out to the end of the pier," I said. "We don't need soldiers anywhere near the pier. When we turn out to the sea, we fly fast. José, bring us around tight. Then we try for a quick docking."

José's eyes narrowed. "We should call down to the soldiers. Tell them we are taking a last look for whales."

I nodded my approval. "Yes. We'll do just that, José." On the front deck, I relayed our plans to our guests.

"I am glad we will pass over the landing area," Mr. Mortimer said too loudly. "This will give everyone a chance to see this most auspicious event."

He was insufferable.

The airscrews bit the air, and we turned toward the soldiers. They tried to appear relaxed but drew their rifles close.

Finn and José worked well together, and we approached the field at fifty feet. "Ahoy. Sir!" I called through the speaking trumpet. "Please announce that Mr. Mortimer and company desire to take a last turn out to sea. The ladies wish to have one more opportunity to look for whales."

A young officer seemed confused. He was probably unsure who he was to tell, as we had no crew on the ground. But a crowd gathered, many running to watch the landing, and the young soldier addressed them. Mr. Mortimer and Mr. Thomas saluted the soldiers.

"It's always good to support the Army," Mr. Mortimer said.

"Yes." Mr. Thomas tightened his salute.

I gave a signal to José, and the engine order telegraph rang. The whirr of the airscrews told me he called for Full. We turned out to sea, and made good speed with the tailwind. We sailed past the end of the pier pulling into the turn.

Mr. Mortimer gave a grand wave and tipped his hat. He was getting his money's worth, and I wished we had held out for more.

José knew his craft well and brought her into the wind. Benny kept his head out of the engine room door, and I passed hand signals back to him. In the next few minutes, the *Cloud Queen* edged near the pier. Finn gave two short blasts of the whistle, and fishermen pulled in their tackle and backed away from the railing.

Our guests stood at the bow, Mr. Mortimer rocking on his cane.

We ran the gangplank out and down as we slipped in over the railing. When it touched the pier, a small boy started to run up. I stepped forward and held out my hand. "Halt, my good lad. Stand clear!"

The boy scowled, and a young fellow, perhaps a brother, pulled him back. When I turned around, Mr. Mortimer was already leading his wife down the walkway. I stepped off at the bottom and offered my hand to Mrs. Mortimer.

The Thomases were close behind, Mrs. Mortimer looked back

longingly for a moment, and Mr. Thomas smiled.

Benny lugged down two bags and set them on the dock.

"Will!" José stepped out of the pilothouse and pointed. Soldiers marched onto the end of the pier at double time.

Benny took two more bags past me and then hurried back up the ramp.

I strode up the gangplank as the clockwork gears eased it back.

"My parasol, my parasol!" Mrs. Mortimer squealed.

I picked it up from beside one of the deck chairs and went to the bow. Mr. Thomas stepped forward; I smiled and tossed it down. He caught it with one hand, snapped it open, and handed it to Mrs. Mortimer.

I waved gallantly, and the *Cloud Queen* rose. The blower speed increased, and the airscrews chopped the air.

In the pilothouse, José gave a mock salute. We sailed the length of the pier, thirty feet above shouts and applause.

The soldiers raised their rifles but thought better about shooting on the crowded pier. They watched with open mouths as we sailed over.

"Well, you gave Mr. Thomas a chance to thrill his damsel," Laura said.

"Yes, I did." I put my arm around her and signaled for us to climb.

"I am getting out of this costume."

"I thought you looked mighty fine, Mrs. Henderson. Mighty fine." I touched her arm the way Mr. Mortimer had. "Would you be so kind as to get me a warm cup of tea and another one of those little cakes, Dear?"

Laura batted playfully at my arm. "I don't think we will be seeing many more like that."

I gave her a light kiss. "You did look fine, and we are five-hundred to the good because of it."

We flew northeast toward the foothills and followed the mountains east. The breeze was still against us, but our headway was steady at Flank speed.

We met for a celebration snack in the pilothouse, as was our custom after a pleasure cruise.

"That was a perfect docking. José, Finn, well done," I said.

"How much did we get paid for that little escapade?" Finn wondered.

"Five hundred." I took the bills out and hung my captain's coat on a hook. "It is a shame you didn't all get to witness Laura. She played Mr. Mortimer, and he was more than happy to let her do it." I put the money in the strongbox under a hinged bench along the back wall.

Laura uncovered a tray of pastries, and José held one, little finger crooked, head held high.

Benny had replaced his steward's shirt with one of his new work shirts. "Boy! My tea has gone cold. Could you please get me another," he mimicked.

We were not the ragtag group we once were, but our hearts were the same. "We must make plans. Protect what is ours."

"I'm worried about the mine." Finn pulled his fingers. "If the Army is becoming aggressive again, they are bound to come back to the mine. I need time in the workshop."

"The loads of Levitrite already missing worry me," I said.

The low whine of the blower hummed in the twin stacks. We had discussed the moment many times. Each time it always came down to the same question. Would the thieves use the stolen levitating rock to build a flying machine? Finn believed it was inevitable; it was a matter of how soon.

It was good to be in the air again, without guests. We lounged on the rear benches of the pilothouse. The air was cool, and the days shorter. We kept the windows open and enjoyed the afternoon. Finn stared at the chaparral, deep in thought.

Laura had exchanged her maid's outfit for a dress, long duster coat, and a hat with goggles around the brim. The breeze tickled the hair in front of her ears. All was back to normal.

The sun was low in the west when Laura steered us into a canyon.

I rang for Half, and we closed over a clearing. A cabin and old barn stood close to the steep canyon wall, two wagonloads of coal in the yard. Smoke curled from the chimney of the log house.

A stocky man waved us down. "Welcome, welcome," he called. "I have the two regular wagons ready, as you can see. I can always get more if you want."

"You are a good man, Mr. Salsbury, but I am afraid we are on the run."

Mr. Salsbury's face showed his disappointment, but he smiled. "Well, we always knew you would have to be on the move, having a contraption like that. A curiosity is what it is."

"We could take a few minutes to give you a ride if you would like," I teased.

He put his hands up. "Not me. I prefer keeping my feet on the ground. But is there anything I can do?"

"The situation became dangerous this afternoon. We had trouble with the Army over on the coast. They cannot have followed us directly, but they know we went East. They could be along soon. They were serious enough to have rifles handy and appeared ready to use them."

"Not like when I served. Sounds like renegades. No better than Freebooters if you ask me. I don't know what this world's comin' to."

Laura came out with some of the leftover cakes. "These are for you. We hope you like them."

"Mighty pretty food—I'm sure I can get 'em down. You kids are always good to me." He gestured toward his barn. "I have the oil burner you wanted, Finn. Made up, exact to the drawings. The tank is there too. I made the wood for the stand myself. I have stove bolts to put 'er together."

Finn nodded toward the open doors. "Could I take a look?"

"Of course."

In the barn, Finn turned the burner, examining it from every angle. "This is well made and should work perfectly."

Mr. Salsbury swelled with pride. He showed Finn the tank he had bought. "I left it in the wagon. No sense lifting it twice."

Benny and I assembled the tank stand in the engine room while José opened the roof. Mr. Salsbury had the wood cut to length and bored holes for the bolts. He had even painted it white.

We used a block and tackle hung from the hay hoist on the end of the barn to lower the tank into the engine room. José guided it onto the wood stand, where we tied it down with cables and turnbuckles. José made short work of closing the roof.

Mr. Salsbury had a smaller kerosene tank in a third wagon to be pumped into the new tank.

"Anything else I can do for you young folks?"

"I have thought about that," I said. "After we convert the airship to burn oil, we'll need an extra supply. Any chance you could locate another wagon with a tank? We'll pay in advance."

"You always pay in advance." Salsbury looked at the wagons. "Paid and paid fairly. Sure I can have them here—keep them in the barn. How many gallons do you want me to have on hand?"

"What do you think, Finn?" I asked.

"It wouldn't hurt to have five hundred gallons at the ready."

Salsbury nodded. "I can do that. It will take a while. I get supplies for you in different towns. A fellow buying too much at one time tends to make people ask questions.

"Went about twenty miles away to have the work done on that burner." Mr. Salsbury smiled. "Tomorrow, I am going down to get the tin sheeting you ordered. I figure you want it here before I work on getting another tank?"

"Yes. Sheeting first. Thank you, Mr. Salsbury. We hope to be back soon. But if you were to ever hear we had been shot down or—well, sell the fuel and wagons."

"They better not shoot you down, or I may do some shooting myself."

Mr. Salsbury was older, but I wouldn't want him aiming a long gun at me.

"We'll load the coal—if that's alright. We want to fly tonight, so

14

we aren't seen. Hopefully, the Army won't get here before we leave."

"I have a dog in a shelter about a quarter mile down, on a wire that stretches the canyon. He lets me know if I have company."

Mr. Salsbury started for the barn. "I'll hitch the team and pull the wagon next to you. You can use your fancy chute."

The sun was behind the mountains when we finished loading the coal. We cleaned up at a spring behind the house.

We invited Mr. Salsbury to have supper with us, and Benny volunteered to serve.

"Benny, if you ever give up flying, you could get a job in a fancy restaurant," I joked.

"I choose flying. But, serving the crew is not bad."

We said our goodbyes to Mr. Salsbury in the cool night air, and Finn took us straight up.

4

I loved flying at night. Laura and I had the radiator on in the pilothouse and the windows closed. We sailed at Slow, hoping to land at the mine above Wolfskill by midmorning.

José poked his head in the door. "Benny will take the first shift. That kid is washing the dishes."

"He is a good crewman," Laura said.

"You want me to steer for a while till Benny comes?"

"Maybe that would be good." I was tired, and Laura was too. We went down to the rear cabin we used when we didn't have guests. Benny had changed the linens.

It seemed as if we had just gone to sleep when Benny tapped on the door. "Will. It's two. Do you feel like steering? The firebox has been stoked."

I staggered out of bed. "Sure, Benny. Thanks."

The moon was waning at a quarter, casting shadows below, the air calm. The altitude gauge read twelve hundred feet.

Laura came up as the eastern sky began to glow, smoke curling from the cook stove.

"We've made good time. We should be over the valley in an hour," I said. "We could get to the mine before full daylight. We don't need snooping eyes telling the Army where we are."

High over our valley, Laura spotted a red flag, waving left and right. "Will, that's at José and Benny's house. Something is wrong."

"Steer for the flag. I will get the guys up."

At the boiler, Finn tightened a bushing on the makeup water injector.

"Someone is waving a red flag down at the Rodriquez place."

Finn was never one to ask questions. He immediately increased the draft and stoked the firebox.

José and Benny were beginning to stir when I opened the door.

"Better get up, guys. Something is going on at your house. I'll meet you at the telescope."

Finn checked the oilers. Laura called for Full, and I tossed in another shovel full of coal.

On the bow, Benny peered through the telescope. "It's Papa," he said. "He is pointing to the south."

I went to the pilothouse and leaned into the speaking tube. "Finn, let's go to two-hundred. Send José forward."

Finn made a slow descent as I scanned the horizon in all directions.

"I'm going down to have a look through the telescope," Laura said.

The three took turns scanning the south. The sun inched down the sides of the mountains.

"Finn, take us to fifty feet." I rang for Stop, and we hung above Mr. Rodriquez.

José cupped his hands and shouted down. He listened and nodded.

Benny and Laura came up.

"The Army is coming." Benny kept his eyes on his father. "A telegraph message came, telling the people in town to watch for us and report where we are."

The Army was closer than we hoped.

"They rode hard last night. They got fresh horses in Pasadena."

Almost thirty-five miles. The horses would be about spent. "Do your parents want to come with us?" I asked.

"Papa says, no. He will stay and play the burro."

Mr. Rodriquez turned as his cousin, Primo, galloped into the field, the horse's flanks glistening.

Benny ran to the bow, listened, and shouted, "The Army is coming. They are a few miles behind the rider!"

I turned to José and Laura. "We have to turn them back. At least for a while. Finn, take us up."

I called for Half, and the *Cloud Queen* headed south.

Laura and José went down and used the telescope to scan to the south and the east.

17

"Finn, we have to make these guys understand that we are dangerous," I said in the speaking tube. "Then we dive at them like a hawk for a mouse."

"I have plenty of pressure. Send Benny back."

I opened the front window of the pilothouse. "Benny, Finn needs you."

Laura gestured up, never taking her eye from the telescope.

"Let's go to fifteen hundred, Finn."

Laura waved and pointed. I turned the *Cloud Queen* and signaled for Flank. "Give me all the speed you can!"

I set my course by the angle of the telescope. "Laura! Come up for a minute. Bring José."

In the pilothouse, Laura was distracted, trying to see the Army renegades with the hand glass.

"José, prepare some dynamite. I would rather that no one be killed, but we must get their full attention. We'll wait until they are in the open."

"Quarter sticks should impress them," José said. "We will drop two in front of them."

"Good. Then I will use the speaking trumpet to warn them."

"There." Laura pointed. "Coming around that rise. They will be along that dry wash for a mile or two."

"Laura, you steer. You know what to do. I'm going down."

The blower whine echoed in the smokestacks. The revolution counter showed the engine was running at two-hundred ninety turns.

"I checked the new propeller motor, and it's running cool," Finn said.

Benny leaned on his shovel, the chimney of the firebox glowing red.

"Finn, take us to five hundred feet," Laura called.

José and I went to the front deck. The renegade Army stopped, and some of the men shouldered their rifles.

"Fools," José grumbled. "We are a half-mile away."

"José, make your fuses for one minute. I will pass the word. Tell Benny to keep his head out."

I adjusted the focus on the telescope. The officer I called to at the Santa Monica Pier watched me through a small hand glass.

At two hundred yards, José made the throw. I gave Benny the signal, and the *Cloud Queen* rose quickly.

The explosion was behind us but made an impressive amount of dust high in the air. The *Cloud Queen* shuddered, but we were used to these concussions.

I gestured for Laura to hover, and the airscrews stopped.

Most of the Army rode back the way they had come. I pointed forward and immediately heard the blower whine increase.

I lifted the speaking trumpet. "That was a warning. We could drop one on you if we wished."

The young officer stopped and turned in the saddle as the last of his men galloped away.

"Do not follow us!" I tried to make my voice as deep as possible.

I wondered how much nerve he had. We were about a hundred yards from him when I gave the signal, and we began our dive. He turned and galloped away.

We gave chase for ten minutes and then turned for our valley.

5

We sensed that our situation had changed dramatically. It was no longer a matter of could the Army find us, but a question of how long they would stay away.

I called another quick meeting in the pilothouse. "I believe we must take our families out of the valley. It is time to move to Eagle's Crest. I know we planned to move later when things were ready, but—"

Faces were solemn.

"We cannot allow them to capture any of our family to be used as hostages to force us to give up the ship," I continued.

Laura shook her head miserable. "So, it starts again. But this time, we are the target."

It was true. But we had money and Eagle's Crest.

"We need time to convert to burning oil," Finn said. "This won't be easy or quick. I have the necessary steps worked out, but the firebox needs to be cool to make the change. We need all day tomorrow. If they come, we will be sitting like ducks."

I was doubtful. "Should we wait to make the switch-over at Eagle's Crest?"

Finn stood his ground. "We need to change over before we cross the mountains. Each trip uses coal. We don't want to use our supply at Eagle's Crest."

"But on other trips, we hauled loads of lumber and equipment," Laura said. "That uses more fuel."

"Yes, but we need to take the equipment from the workshop and all the family belongings," Finn said.

He was right. Our plans depended upon some of the specialized equipment still at the mine.

José gazed out the window toward our valley. "We take all our families to Wolfskill Lodge. Father can set some charges in the narrow part of the canyon below the lodge. If the Army comes, we blow the entrance. That will slow them down."

José was the strategy man. His family spent the last two winters at Eagle's Crest, working on the buildings, but I thought of Mrs. Rodriquez. She still did not like the flight over the mountains, nor would she be eager to leave her farm home.

Over the avocados and oranges at the Rodriquez farm, I said, "Bring us down."

Laura landed in the open area between the house and the barn. Mr. Rodriquez came near, and José explained his plan to his father.

"The airship is important to save," Mr. Rodriquez said. "I will guard the canyon, and then we go to Eagle's Crest. I will send my primo to get your father from the store."

We began to carry supplies to the airship. Mrs. Rodriquez had food ready, and Mr. Rodriquez brought tools and dynamite. The little ones couldn't wait to get on board.

We loaded two horses. With everyone working, we were ready in less than an hour. Laura sat with Mrs. Rodriquez in the forward cabin to keep her calm. The younger kids squealed and pointed as we took off.

We made a quick stop at Dad's house. His wagon came into the yard at full gallop as we landed.

"The Army—or Freebooters in Army clothes are close. We must hurry," I said.

"In town, the Army has taken over the jail and the sheriff's office," Dad said. "Something is very wrong."

We transferred the supplies Dad had thrown in the wagon. He grabbed a duffle by the door. "Leave the team—Jim will ride out to get them."

"Will Jim be safe at the store?" I asked.

"I believe so. He only knows that you have been doing pleasure tours. That much has been in the papers." He smiled. "There was a fair drawing of you and Laura on the deck of the *Cloud Queen*. You make big news. You looked very smart in your captain's uniform."

As soon as we were loaded, we set course for Wolfskill, flying at Full. Finn had a terrific head of steam, but the morning downwind was against us. It was midday before we landed in the clearing outside the lodge.

The headwind had been a drain on our coal, so we tossed armloads of wood on the deck.

Mrs. Rodriquez was no stranger to Wolfskill. By the time we unloaded what she would need, smoke curled from both the cook stove and fireplace chimneys.

"Dad, ride to the mine with us. You can bring the blasting detonator and wire back down."

The little ones begged to come along, but Mrs. Rodriquez held them close.

Finn had the engine idling to keep the blower running, and we had a terrific head of steam. The breeze had let up, and Laura cut the corners of the canyon. We were relieved to find the mine undisturbed.

Dad and I rode back down as far as Miner Tom's, and Dad took the horses on to Wolfskill.

Miner Tom glanced up from his sluice box. "I heard you come in. Trouble brewing?"

"Tom, the Army is coming, and they are determined to try to find us." I reached into my pocket. "Here is another fifty dollars for watching the mine. I think it's time to make yourself scarce."

Tom grinned and spat into the creek. "Your Jenny and I will head over to Oak Canyon. I have no hankerin' to be around the Army."

We shook hands, and I hustled back to the mine.

Benny had stopped stoking the boiler before we landed, but the firebox was still hot.

Drilling the hole for the injector pipe was the difficult part of the afternoon. Finn knew precisely where it would go in the firebox, but the iron was thick. My arms ached when we finally got the hole bored.

As we finished breakfast the following day, an explosion echoed through the canyon. We waited, the rumble fading away. A dragonfly buzzed past.

"Benny, you feel like running down the canyon and giving us a report?"

A second explosion rumbled through the canyon, and Benny waited.

"Finn, can we fire the boiler?" I asked.

"Yes, but the injector is not ready. We will have to fly on coal or wood."

"Laura and I will get up a head of steam. Benny, help Finn and your brother get all the tools and equipment from the workshop. We may not be able to come back again."

Finn was not happy but agreed.

In the next hour, we scrambled to make things ready. Between taking turns at the blower crank, Laura and I helped carry equipment. We managed to wrestle two workbenches onto the rear deck.

José said, "It is time to set the charges."

"Yes. I will help you get the dynamite from the side tunnel."

"It is good we have not heard any more explosions," Laura said. "Maybe the renegades are thinking twice about things."

I eyed the rim of the canyon. "I'm afraid the Army will go around and attack from above. I feel like a mouse in a barrel."

"Ask Finn if I can start the engine." Laura's face was red. "We have twenty pounds of pressure. The engine will take over the blower."

I didn't take time to bother Finn. "Disconnect the dynamo. Keep the engine at thirty turns."

She nodded, and the low whine of the blower echoed in the smokestacks.

I went to Finn in the workshop when a third charge rolled through the canyon. "You hear that?"

His voice was grim. "I heard." He handed me a box. "Pressure?"

"Twenty-five, and the engine is running."

"Good." He added a wooden box to the others stacked along the wall. "This will have to do. I don't think we can get the rest. We'll be heavy in the stern, and we still need to get everyone out of Wolfskill."

I was concerned about the extra load. It wasn't that the ship could not lift the weight, but extra pounds took extra coal to stay aloft.

It was mid-afternoon when we heard another explosion. It sounded closer.

"Laura, what's the pressure?" I asked.

"Thirty-five."

"Fifteen minutes, everyone. Sooner if we can," I said.

Benny ran with box after box, stowing them in the breezeway.

José and I helped Finn lug the drill press out of the side tunnel.

We all made several more loads from the workshop, and Finn nodded. "Good work, everyone. Better than I thought we could do."

Looking at the faces around me, I saw exhaustion. "Laura, you steer. José, sharp eyes up front. Benny will tend the boiler. Finn, you keep working on the burner injector."

I engaged the clutch, and the dynamo began to spin. "Let's make sure we are balanced."

José ran from corner to corner while Finn adjusted the lifters. When we were level, he called, "That will do."

I let us back down, and we stood on the deck as José took a lantern to the cavern. At the entrance, he looked back. "Ready?"

"Yes," we said in chorus. The engine began to spin up.

José lit the fuses quickly and was on the deck in one leap. Immediately the *Cloud Queen* rose, hovering two hundred feet over the cavern opening. The blast was muffled, brown dust and rock boiling from the mouth of the cave. The smoke hole in the cavern roof blew a perfect ring of dust as if to say goodbye.

Laura called for Full, and the *Cloud Queen* turned down the canyon.

The afternoon breeze started moving up the hills, and the trip back to the lodge took twenty minutes. We were all nervous. Laura kept us high, and José kept a steady lookout at the telescope. As we neared Wolfskill, another charge raised a dust cloud in the distance. Mr. Rodriquez galloped around the bend as we touched down.

Chairs and tables sat out in the clearing. Two stacks of wood lay ready, one for the boiler and smaller pieces for cooking.

Mr. Rodriquez reined in his horse as another explosion rumbled through the canyon.

"Long fuse." He smiled and then turned serious. "They'll come soon. I'll go and watch with your father. When we come, they will be close."

The little ones put the last of the chairs on the front deck.

Benny helped his mother on board, the little ones scrambling along behind. "Go to the rear cabin! Stay low behind the shields!"

We loaded wood. Both gangplanks were down, and we ran two wheelbarrows. The breezeway was cluttered with lab equipment, so we dumped wood on the deck and in the engine room, trying to balance the ship.

Mr. Rodriquez returned to the *Cloud Queen* at a full gallop. He rode the horse up the front gangplank and jumped off, handing Benny the reins. He went forward and lay on the deck, leveling his rifle.

José slid the side ramp into place as the first shot rang. Laura took her place in the pilothouse and swung the shields into position.

Benny and Maria loaded two armloads of wood onto the deck when more shots echoed. A bullet ricocheted off the pilothouse shield.

I cupped my hands. "Where is my dad?"

"He comes!" Mr. Rodriquez yelled. Several shots echoed from high on the side of the canyon.

Dad galloped into the clearing and onto the front deck. "Get down, get down!"

Mr. Rodriquez shot with careful precision.

The ship rose above the canyon while the gears pulled in the gangplank. Soldiers crept over rocks and rubble, struggling to find a path to lead their horses.

"I am going to fly west," Laura said. "I don't want to give them any idea about where Eagle's Crest is."

It was crowded in the pilothouse. We opened the doors and held a meeting. It still felt odd to be in charge when Dad was standing there, but I would be twenty in a few months.

"How is the *Cloud Queen* handling the load, Finn?" I asked.

"We are running the engine at two-forty, and we will have to run at Slow. This flight will use a great deal of fuel."

"We can't land at Eagle's Crest until morning anyway," I said. "So there's no hurry."

We decided to have Mrs. Rodriquez put the little ones to bed in the forward cabin after supper. Benny brought plates of food to everyone. Laura turned northeast, and the *Cloud Queen* climbed to clear the San Gabriel Mountains.

The air turned cooler, and we shut the windows and doors of the pilothouse. Laura held the wheel lightly in her fingers. We stood in comfortable silence as the mountains moved below us, an occasional cloud obscuring our view. We entered a mist, and Laura switched on the compass light.

"We need to move the wood inside," Finn said on the speaking tube. "We are headed into a storm."

"On my way." I turned to Laura. "Are you OK up here?"

"Yes. The wind is blowing us east. I'll have Finn take us to twelve-thousand. We don't want to run aground on Mt. Baldy."

Outside we worked carefully. The deck became slick from the mist, and I shivered each time I was outside. When the wood was stacked, we shut the doors and stood in the warmth of the boiler.

"Finn, would it make more sense to use the wood—lighten the load as quickly as possible?"

"I was thinking the same thing. If my calculations are correct, we will arrive at Eagle's Crest with plenty of coal and some wood.

I went to the pilothouse and sent Laura down to sleep. There was no sense in everyone getting their days and nights turned around. Benny took the first engine room shift. I called for Dead Slow and steered into the night.

About three in the morning, I realized José was not coming to relieve me. I called down to the engine room, and Finn had taken over for Benny.

"Do you want me to roust José out?" Finn asked.

"No, he ran with the wheelbarrow all afternoon. It is peaceful up here. If you are OK, I am too."

We chatted from time to time on the speaking tube, and twice Finn came up. I suppose we were checking on each other.

We had crossed the first range when the early glimmer of dawn came.

José pounded up the stairs. "Will. Sorry. I slept like a baby. You should have called me."

I clapped him on the shoulder. "Don't worry. All is well. Is anyone else up? Laura?"

"Only Finn and Mamá. Yesterday was a close call. Everyone is tired."

Mrs. Rodriquez was an early riser, and something smelled good.

Laura came up a few minutes later, her fresh dress brightening the pilothouse.

"Let's set up for a big breakfast in the forward cabin," she said. "Stop the airscrews and float. The men are starting to move around."

"Perfect." I lashed the wheel.

Breakfast reminded me of the meals we shared at Wolfskill Lodge when we fought the Freebooters. It had been three years, and yet it had the same feel. Community. Family.

I read from Psalm 5, the first eight verses, José murmuring the translation to his parents. The words seemed right for our current plight. We ate, laughed, and enjoyed being together.

The US Army going renegade as they had before made no sense. The faces around the table told me they were thankful we were safe, high above it all. Eagle's Crest was remote and well-protected.

Laura took a plate to Benny in the engine room. From time to time, the airscrews started as he trued us in the air.

"Well, the sun is out there, somewhere," I said. "What do you say we get to our new home?"

Laura and I went up to the pilothouse and rang for Half. José and Dad were at the bow telescope when the *Cloud Queen* slipped through the clouds into bright sunlight.

Laura's smile told me her spirits had lifted with the veil of cloud. José pointed along the length of the telescope, and I turned the *Cloud Queen* in the direction of Eagle's Crest. We had not drifted as far east as we feared, and I looked eagerly to the mountains in the north.

Eagle's Crest lay below us, an oasis deep in the mountains.

Progress was evident since delivering the last loads of lumber. The cabin roofs were complete, the main lodge inviting. The frustrations of playing host to the rich faded as we looked down on all we had accomplished.

Finn had reasoned the flat-topped mountain that held Eagle's Crest was an ancient volcano. His notion had proven true when we tried to drill for water and hit hot rock.

Finn harnessed the steamy mess to power an engine and dynamo that kept Eagle's Crest in electricity. We had warm and cold water and steam heat in all the buildings. The most impressive improvement was the greenhouse, with hundreds of panes catching the sun.

"Oh, Will. It's beautiful," Laura murmured. "Look! There's Mama. She has been hanging out wash, and she sees us." Letty was pregnant.

Our friends gathered to greet us when we brought the *Cloud Queen* down.

"Mary and Nathan look good together," Laura whispered.

When we rescued Mary, one thing was clear; even in her battered condition she was beautiful. What the Freebooters had done to her should never happen to any woman, but with time to recover at Eagle's Crest, she was radiant.

Hannah and Dolph had grown. They missed their father but were doing well. I saw deep sadness in Minnie's eyes. The toll of driving the Freebooters back had been heavy.

Later, we gathered near the lusty blaze in the grand fireplace.

"Beautiful job with the lodge," I said. "Well done, Nathan and Paul. Well done, Mr. Ryan."

"Will, it is time you started calling me Liam. We have come too far to be so formal."

It was hard for me to make the step between boy and man. I had known Finn's father for years. I reached out and shook hands. "Liam it is."

Mr. Rodriquez put out his hand. "Liam is right—you are no longer a boy. My name is Eduardo. Most everyone in town calls me Ed."

We shook. Times were changing.

"Will, you did not sleep last night," José said. "Your cabin is ready. You need to sleep."

"Thanks, friend." He was right—I was beyond tired. I kissed Laura lightly. "Wake me for supper."

"Yes, but you go right now."

I dreamed of flying. We soared high above the clouds, and the sun shone. It felt wonderful, but somewhere in the back of my mind, I knew there were Freebooters below.

It had become cool when Laura woke me, and she handed me a coat. We hurried to the warmth of the lodge. The long table was set, and the aroma of a banquet was in the air.

Minnie reminded the little ones to be careful when they carried hot bowls. Mrs. Rodriquez was humming, bustling about, glad the flight was over. I had to smile when Minnie asked Dolph if he had washed his hands.

I was about to sit down when Paul said, "No, Will. We want you to sit at the head of the table, near the fire."

I started to protest when Dad spoke up.

"Will, you have proven yourself a strong leader. You were the one who went and got the *Cloud Queen* when my brother died. You had vision and planned for this moment. You could have flown off, never to be seen again. Instead, you and your crew have paid the mortgages on all our land. You and your crew realized that the *Cloud Queen* would be sought after, so you've worked hard to provide this place. Because of you, we are safe here."

I was glad the lights were low as I am sure I blushed. Laura squeezed my hand.

When everyone was seated, I stood. "I am not sure I deserve

this place at the table, but I know I can depend on each of you. You have all had a part in making this moment possible. We have much to be thankful for and think about in the future, but in the meantime, we should eat before it gets cold. José, would you say grace? Spanish is fine; it makes no difference to God's ears."

We ate, talked, and laughed.

Benny got up to get more chicken. I supposed he had become used to waiting on others. While he was gone, Laura hid his plate in a sideboard drawer.

Benny came back and saw the empty place. "Everyone here is funny. Maybe I should sit and eat this whole plate of chicken."

We kept our heads down.

"Try looking," Laura teased. "We'll play 'Hot or Cold.' Maybe you can find your plate."

Benny pretended to be mad. "My food will be cold."

"That's why you need to hurry!" Mary said.

Benny began circling the table, Laura calling cold and colder until he started toward the sideboard. "Warmer. Warmer," the Rodriquez children squealed.

When Benny found his plate, Laura jumped up and cut a piece of pie. She brought it around, curtsied, and presented Benny with the dessert plate. "A piece of Minnie's berry pie, my liege," she said with an exaggerated flourish.

When Laura returned, her fork was missing.

She gave me a look, and I shrugged. "What's good for the goose is good for the gander," I said.

José slipped her fork back on her plate while Laura was giving me another one of her looks.

Minnie began to serve the pies, and they were her best.

After we finished, the little ones asked to be excused. They played at the far end of the lodge with the model of the *Cloud Queen* my uncle John constructed to prove Levitrite could bend gravity.

As we sat back and relaxed, I was content. We had escaped the renegade Army.

31

I had little interest in agriculture, but the Eagle's Crest farm was essential to our success. I joined Mary immediately after breakfast. She was anxious to show me the row crops and the greenhouse. The outdoor crops had nearly run their course, but it had been a good harvest.

I loved the greenhouse smell. A hint of frost was in the air, but Eagle's Crest's steam heat gave it a magical warmth.

"We will have tomatoes year-round," Mary said. A small orange tree grew at one end of the greenhouse.

In the barn, there were goats and chickens. Dad's milk cow, Clara Bell, chewed her cud, paying me no attention.

"You lazy thing. I threw hay to you and milked you for years." I rubbed between her eyes. "So, Mary, how is the supply of feed for the stock?"

"We will be fine for the winter." Mary rubbed a goat's ears with both hands, holding its head as if it were a small child. I thought of the little girl Mary had lost to the Freebooters.

"Yes. Good work, Mary," I said. "Excellent progress."

She smiled, scratching another goat's nose. "I grew up on a farm—working with animals. Having my hands in the dirt again—it's healing, you know."

Finn came from the greenhouse. "I checked the steam pipes and registers. Nathan's plumbing works as planned." He gazed toward the *Cloud Queen*. "We need to unload."

Liam joined us in the well-equipped shop. The tool and supplies had been purchased through Dad's store and taken by wagon to Mr. Salsbury. Our quarterly trips had stockpiled food, feed, oil, materials, and apparatus for Finn's laboratory.

The men placed the equipment according to Finn's directions. We left him happily organizing his instruments and tools.

Nathan and I stood outside the shop. Mary tied a goat to the milk stand.

"Mary has done a wonderful job with the animals and crops," I said.

"It is like that summer we spent at Wolfskill," he said. "She works and works." He gestured to where Mary milked the goat. "I think it helps her keep from getting too angry. Don't get me wrong, we are falling in love—but she lost her husband and child." He sighed. "It still has its effect on her. I can tell, watching her work."

Everyone had helped plant the crops, but each time the *Cloud Queen* returned, Mary was weeding and irrigating. While the men were finishing the roofing, Mary had been in the fields with her big straw hat and gloves.

The frame of a new airship stood in the hangar attached to the shop. The *Cloud Queen* was beautiful, perfect for excursions for the rich, but her riverboat design was not practical for speed or fighting.

Finn's new design was low and oblong, earning her the nickname *Pumpkin Seed*. She was one hundred-twenty feet stem to stern, thirty-five at the beam, the narrow bow designed for speed. All controls were in the front of the ship, in the helm. Wrangling the steam engine and boiler into the center of the airship had been difficult, even with the heavy engine in pieces. Finn had been careful with his engine selection, and all of us could recite the marvels of double-acting compound cylinders.

Liam showed me the control cables running back to the various devices. "We are about ready to put on the shell. It will be a big job, and we need more sheeting. We have finished putting heavier armor along the sides."

"I am afraid our schedule has been pushed ahead," I said. "Now that we all are here, we must double our efforts to complete this ship."

Liam rapped on the frame. "Everyone is eager to work. Mary

will continue tending the farm, but the men and your crew can start now if you like."

I pined to be in the air, but this new airship held great promise. The rough framing of the various rooms gave me a shiver as I imagined it as an ark, carrying us all to safety.

"Make a list of the things you will need," I said. "We will plan regular trips to Salsbury's for supplies."

Ed came in with José and Benny.

"It's going to be beautiful," Benny said.

José and Paul pried the sheets of tin apart, counting.

"I'll get Finn," I said.

In his laboratory, Finn bent over the oil injector for the *Cloud Queen*. Gauges, gears, and bearings were scattered on the workbenches. Out the window, Mary crossed the yard with a milk can on a cart. Mrs. Rodriquez met her. They would keep us in cheese and butter.

The airscrews for the *Pumpkin Seed* hung in the workshop. Built to specific plans, they were not the huge blades the *Cloud Queen* used but elegant six-bladed affairs.

"Finn, we are stepping up work on the *Pumpkin Seed*. Can you come back and line out the tasks for us?"

Finn slid his goggles onto his forehead. Dolph rolled up a sheet of plans, tapping the ends on the table.

Dolph pinned the plans to a bulkhead of the *Pumpkin Seed*, and Finn numbered tasks. One group would finish the interior while my group shaped the tin on the frame.

Putting the skin on the frame was not hard work, but the cutting was tedious. By evening we had over half of the sheeting in place.

"Benny, how many sheets are left?"

"Only six."

I went to the communicator, turned the dial to the lodge, and tapped out, "CAN LAURA COME TO THE SHOP" in Morse Code. Immediately I got a return, "BE RIGHT THERE"

When Laura came in, her eyes grew big. "That is starting to look like a mighty ship."

"Yes. And the inside cabins are also coming along quickly with everyone working."

Laura gestured to the remaining sheets of tin. "We need more supplies."

"I would like to go in the morning."

"We need to start training the new crew for the *Cloud Queen*." Laura was always practical.

"Yes." I had difficulty thinking about letting another crew fly the *Cloud Queen*.

Laura put her arm around me. "It will be alright, Will. It will be alright."

Liam was in the engine room, under the watchful eye of Finn. Mary stood at the wheel, being tutored by Laura. I didn't need to be on this trip, but I was concerned for Mr. Salsbury's safety.

Liam was a natural, having spent years working on locomotives. Mary was just plain smart. Early in the flight, I realized I was not needed in either place and decided to make lunch. I wasn't actually cooking because Minnie and Mrs. Rodriquez had sent plenty of food. I warmed the meal, feeling good about my efforts.

Laura came down and peeked her head in the door. When I showed surprise, she said, "Don't worry. Mary is doing fine. How are you doing?"

"Just warming things. I don't think I can get into too much trouble."

"We should all eat in the pilothouse. You want help carrying? "

"I can manage. I will get it up there."

She tossed me a kiss as she went out the door.

We ate a leisurely meal above mountains showing green from the early fall rains.

"The oil injector is working splendidly," Finn said. "We are using about a gallon and a half each hour. The fire is even and hot."

"The stack is not billowing black smoke anymore," I noted.

We snaked down the canyon from high in the mountains. When we began to descend, I didn't see Mr. Salsbury. Mary brought us around over the clearing, nose into the wind, and signaled for Slow.

"Bring us a little more into the wind." Laura watched the treetops. "Sometimes, I let her drift back before we come in. I find it easier to land moving forward than when slipping to the stern."

"Dead Slow?" Mary asked.

"Yes."

Mary swung the lever on the engine order telegraph, and the blower whine dropped.

"We are still too high," Laura said. "The treetops are not as close as you think. It seems so because we have been up so far."

"How much lower?"

"Call down for another fifty feet. They will be letting the sounding cable down."

The ship drifted east.

"You have to exaggerate your turns when the airscrews are running slowly." Laura made a turning motion with her hand. "There. Feel it. We have drifted back, so now you can call for Slow."

The ship hung over the clearing. These moments were magical —tons of weight suspended in the air.

"Sounding cable is down. We are at forty-two feet," Liam called through the speaking tube.

"Now you can tell them to take us down," Laura said. "They will land quickly but don't worry about that. Your job is to make sure we are centered over the clearing."

"Laura, take the wheel. I don't see Mr. Salsbury," I said. "Keep the engine speed up," I called down. "Something may be wrong. Be ready to go up, fast."

I stood at the upper railing. "Call for us to land, Mary."

The *Cloud Queen* settled to earth with a gentle bump.

The barn door stood open, and the wagon with the oil tank had the horses hitched to it. They were tied to a post with a bucket of water for each, but they had knocked them over.

"Keep a close watch—all directions. Close the shields."

I held a quick meeting near the speaking tube in the engine room.

"Finn, tend the engine room. Keep the RPMs up. Liam and I will check the cabin." I paused at the difficult command. "Laura, Mary, if anything goes wrong, you **must** take off."

Liam and I checked the rifles, and each took a pistol.

We sprinted to the barn and watched the cabin. "Should we call?" I wondered.

"I think so. If there are Freebooters, having them shoot while we are here is better than when we are halfway across the yard."

"Hello. Salsbury!"

One of the horses whinnied.

"Try the whistle!" I called.

Two long blasts echoed in the canyon. The horses rocked the wagon back and forth, snorting.

I was about to ask for another blast when Mr. Salsbury came slowly out onto the porch, a white cloth bandage on his head.

"Mr. Salsbury, what happened?"

"Nothing good." He eased himself down on a crude bench on the porch.

Laura took one look at the bandage and went back inside the airship.

"I was in town, about twelve miles west, gettin' oil. Soldiers came." Mr. Salsbury rubbed his knee. "Not real soldiers. Just renegades. They wanted to know what I was doing with oil. I said I was delivering it." He laughed. "Sort of true, I suppose."

"Anyway, they weren't happy with my answer, and we got into a scuffle."

"Did they follow you here?"

"One won't be following anybody. One of the renegades gave me a clout on the head with a cudgel. I shot him as I went down. I was out for several minutes."

Laura came with a bowl of water and bandages.

Mr. Salsbury brushed her away. "The man I was dealing with, Jones, from Pasadena Oil, got me inside, and I started to come around. He could tell those men meant me harm." Mr. Salsbury was laughing. "The young renegade fellow—well—I guess the next in command—if you know what I mean, banged on the door demanding to come in.

"This is where it got good. Jones went out and called for the undertaker. The Army fellows backed off in a big hurry. I guess they didn't want too many questions about why a soldier would club a civilian."

"When the undertaker comes in, I tell him I could give him ten dollars to carry out some old tools wrapped in blankets and to keep his mouth shut." Mr. Salsbury put a toothpick in his mouth. "And he did. Oh, he argued. Wanted to sell me a coffin for $15, and I told him I wasn't buyin' a box for broken tools—after all, they was only casual acquaintances." Mr. Salsbury chuckled.

"Silly fool. He got a stretcher, and they carried the 'body' out. I told him he could keep the tools if he made the death look good. I guess the Army thought there was no more they could get from me, so they left. I waited a day, and then Jones snuck me out of the place that night." He laughed again. "So, I didn't even get buried. But, I got your oil in the deal. It's in the wagon. I got home this morning."

Laura was mad. "These renegades are as bad as the Freebooters. Just Freebooters in nicer uniforms. This has to be stopped."

"We need to take you out, Mr. Salsbury," I said. "This is getting too dangerous."

He crossed his arms. "I'm not goin' anywhere. Maybe someday, but now I'm stayin'. You'll need more supplies."

"We won't force you." I met Mr. Salsbury's eyes. "You are welcome to join us. We have plenty of room in the mountains."

"I thank you, but I'm just an old miner. I don't have many years left, and I'm not goin' to spend them runnin'."

Laura stood over Mr. Salsbury, hand on her hips. "All right, you told your story. Now I'm going to unwrap that head and see how the wound is doing."

The old fellow put his hands up in surrender. "That you can do."

Laura and Mary worked on Mr. Salsbury while we loaded the sheets of tin. We filled the oil bunker on the *Cloud Queen* and put oil in several cans Mr. Salsbury had in the wagon. I admired his ability to plan.

The women convinced him to eat while we unhitched the horses and fed the animals.

Mr. Salsbury felt good enough to walk out to the *Cloud Queen* to watch us take off.

"I think you better come with us, Mr. Salsbury. I know how much you want to fly."

He laughed and waved me off.

Mary went to the pilothouse, and we were high in the air in moments. We were heading home, the airscrews spinning fast. Apparently, Mary didn't want to land in the dark.

"Building an airship is like building a house," Paul remarked. "The frame and walls go up fast, but all the finish work takes forever."

I stood at the wheel and polished the brass rim of the compass. The gauges were set in two panels on either side of the wheel.

Dolph put his hand on the levitation lever. "You can read the boiler pressure, burner oil pressure, engine speed, airspeed, altitude, and even water supply for the boiler from here," he said. "Finn thought of everything." His voice croaked on "thought," and José raised his eyebrow.

"You are growing up, Dolph. Your talker does not know whether to sound like a boy or a man." He ruffled Dolph's hair.

Dolph stood taller. "I can send code at 16 words a minute. Finn told me to slow down yesterday. I could receive even faster if there was anyone who could send faster." Dolph crossed his arms.

"Perhaps we should have a little contest," I said. "Fastest coder gets an extra piece of your mom's pie."

I peered in the periscope above the wheel. "Dolph, go out and walk around. I want to try the periscope."

The upper mirror could be rotated and moved up and down without the eyepiece moving.

José slipped out of the helm.

When my view showed the front of the ship, Dolph waved.

I went to the center window and waved back. Two other windows, on forty-five-degree angles, provided a splendid view to the front and sides.

Dolph made a gun with his hand, aiming up at me. I slid one of the iron shields in place and watched José slip up behind Dolph.

He grabbed Dolph, pinning his arms, and twirled him.

I faintly heard Dolph's squeals of delight. They disappeared around the side.

"I caught a prisoner, Captain Will. I believe he is one of their clever scientists." José put Dolph on his feet in front of me.

"Captain Will, I want to defect. I want to fly with you to fight the enemy."

"Good decision, young man. Your first assignment is to use that fast coding speed to call the lodge to see how soon we should come for dinner."

"Good kid," José said when Dolph was gone.

"You and Finn are good with him."

"We all are." José ran the shield back into place. "We all need to be good examples. The little ones are watching."

I slid back the cover for the ceiling glass port, giving a view of the rafters. There was glass in the floor as well. In the belly of the ship was a gun pod for prone rifle work through a narrow forward slit.

After supper, Laura handed us folded papers. "Each has a twenty-word message. Let's see if Dolph is as fast as he says he is." She winked.

Finn put one of the code keys at each end of the table.

Most of us held our own between ten and twelve words a minute. Finn sent sixteen and a half words. Dolph hammered out all twenty.

I only caught part of the message. "Wow, Dolph. You take the prize."

"Dolph, you will have to slow down for all of us," Finn said. "Well done."

Benny brought a large piece of berry pie. "Here you are. I don't know where you are going to put it."

"Watch me." Dolph picked up the pie and shoved the point in his mouth.

"That's enough of that, young man," Minnie said. "We eat with utensils at Eagle's Crest."

Dolph ducked and took a drink of milk. "Yes, Mother."

That evening, I walked to the shop and stood at the helm of the

"Pumpkin Seed" to familiarize myself with the controls. Big wagon brake levers controlled the airscrews and the levitators. I felt like a king in the high pilothouse of the *Cloud Queen*, but this ship gave me the feeling of stealth. With this craft, we would slip close to the enemy, fox-like.

November frost crunched under our feet when the *Pumpkin Seed* was ready for her first trial. Finn had tested and retested the boiler. I doubted he had slept that night. The breakfast Benny brought him sat untouched in the engine room.

The flash boiler did not need several hours to develop a head of steam. The ship was warm, and the pressure stood at fifty-five pounds.

Laura and I went to the helm.

"The pressure and water level read the same up here as in the engine room," I said. "So far, so good."

Laura went to the periscope and swiveled the upper mirror. "Everyone is gathering."

I took a turn. Folks stood in a semicircle, Mrs. Rodriquez with the baby at a distance.

Outside, Jose clipped a hose onto the speaking tube port. "Can you hear me, Will?"

"Perfectly."

I leaned toward the speaking tube connected to the engine room. "Ready, Finn?"

"Ready."

I reached for the big lever to the side of the helm and squeezed the release. The revolution counter showed the dynamo was turning at three hundred revolutions. I eased the control back. The airship had the eerie feeling of becoming lighter, as when we were flying the *Cloud Queen*.

"Anything, José?"

"She is shifting."

The twirling ball governor on the engine kept the dynamo

43

steady at three hundred revolutions. I pulled the lever another half inch.

"She is up, she is up. Let me check in back." In his excitement, José dropped the speaking tube, and the thump echoed in the helm.

José was back soon and dusted off the end of the hose. "Sorry. The back left is not up."

I eased the lift lever, and we stepped out to quiet applause. "We have some adjusting to do. We will let you know when we're ready for her maiden voyage."

Mary and Ed started for the greenhouse, and the others went toward the lodge.

By noon, the levelers balanced the airship, even when we attached heavy weights on one side or the other. It was time to test what Finn called tube fans. He designed the propellers with a shroud around each. The blower cages swiveled, allowing the ship to turn. The motors that powered the fans were impressive and could be reversed. Finn said the airship could pivot in mid air.

"Can we try moving a few feet forward first?" I asked Finn. "Or should we tow *Pumpkin Seed* outside for the tests?"

"Let's test the motors with the ship on the ground," Finn said.

I pulled the propulsion lever to Slow, turning the wheel right and left. In the periscope, I saw José chasing his hat across the shop, and I set the propulsion lever to Stop.

"Finn, everything ran as it should up here," I said.

"I think we are ready to lift and try to move."

I signaled to José to put the speaking hose to his ear. "Finn said we can try to fly the ship out. Disconnect the exhaust tube."

The exhaust tube ratcheted away, and José pointed up.

Light began to show in the observation window in the floor. Benny joined José outside the front window. The ship rotated to port. I corrected with the wheel and put the levitation lever back to zero.

"We are turning to port, Finn."

"I adjusted the motors. Try now."

The *Pumpkin Seed* moved toward the open end of the hangar. She responded to slight changes of the wheel, and I nudged the propulsion lever open further. José walked backward, watching both sides.

I thought of the first time we towed the *Cloud Queen* out of the cavern above Wolfskill. Here we had more room, and the *Pumpkin Seed* was under its own power. The morning sun brightened the helm.

Mary and Ed watched from their potato harvest. Mrs. Rodriquez held on to the little one while Maria sat in the shade of the building, reading her book.

I eased the propulsion and lift levers, and we settled to earth.

Finn opened the side door to cheers. Everyone had gathered, and we stood in a circle congratulating Finn. Long months of work were completed, and the first test of the *Pumpkin Seed* was a success.

The group became quiet, and Laura squeezed my hand. "They want you to say something," she whispered.

"Look at that sky. Look at this place. Look at our new airship. We have come a long way. All of you are a part of this." I didn't feel I had the right words, but many nodded.

"I have been thinking," Laura said. "*Pumpkin Seed* is not a noble name. What about the *Silver Seed?*"

The ship's galvanized skin gleamed in the sun, and Benny laughed. "It's a good name, *Silver Seed!*"

I beckoned. "Now is the moment many of you have been waiting for—time to see the inside. Paul and Liam will give you a tour."

Paul's finish work was beautiful. The polished wood and gleaming paint made the quarters inviting. There were rooms for married couples and general bunk areas for men and women. The rooms were not large but well planned. Beds, shelves, and a cupboard stood ready in each. Wandering the halls, the ship felt like a mansion.

There was a salon in the rear with windows at the stern and a long table across the beam. Cushioned benches around the sides showed Letty's skill as a seamstress.

Minnie came in with hot tea and coffee, and Mrs. Rodriquez brought the sweet rolls I loved. The others sat as we often did in the evenings, in twos and threes, chatting. I stood to one side, thinking, *"If only the world could be this peaceful. Cooperative. Loving."*

Minnie started to the lodge to bring the pies that were cooling but was back in moments, screaming, "There's an airship. It's dropping fire!"

12

My stomach clenched. A bullet whined off the hull, leaving a dent above my head. A shadow passed over us. *They've found us! They have an airship!*

Finn was already moving. "I can have pressure in two minutes."

"Get everyone away from the back windows until we lower the shields. Paul, Ed—man the rifle slots. Laura, Mary—meet me at the helm."

Benny shut the side door as more bullets ricocheted off the hull.

In the helm, Laura swiveled the periscope. "It is an ugly thing, I will say that."

I took a turn at the periscope and studied the dark airship. It turned awkwardly away from the lodge. The craft fought the morning breeze, and black smoke billowed from the stack. The hull swung from cables attached to a cube above the ship.

"Finn, there's a cannon on the front," I called through the speaking tube.

"I have pressure. Engine at two-forty."

I sounded the warning bell three times, and Nathan shouted, "We are going to fly. Sit down! Everyone, down!"

The other ship had turned toward the *Silver Seed*, but they were too far away for their rifles to be effective. The bullets that struck only rattled like pebbles on the hull, but I was worried about the cannon.

I pulled the levitation lever back, and we tilted to the stern. Mrs. Rodriquez cried out in Spanish.

Finn called, "Dad and I are making adjustments—the automatic levelers are beginning to do their job."

We were fifty feet in the air, but we needed to move. I pulled the propulsion lever to One-Third and turned the wheel toward the bunkhouses.

"José, run out the ramming rod."

The gears rattled, and soon the forty-foot pole was out in front of us.

We skimmed across Eagle's Crest and over the ridge that connected it to the rest of the mountains.

Laura scanned the terrain with a hand glass. "No sign of a ground Army—yet."

Paul came into the helm. "They're dropping fire."

Laura went with him to the salon. "Will, they are trying to burn the lodge!" she called into the speaking tube.

I spun the wheel over. Unlike the *Cloud Queen*, we turned so quickly that I heard cries of alarm from the back and glass shattering.

A ball of fire lay between the lodge and the shop. It had fallen on clear ground and would probably burn out. Another rolled off the tin roof of the lodge.

I put the propulsion lever at Half, and the *Silver Seed* began to pick up speed. Finn's design was certainly fast.

The enemy ship began a slow turn. They tried to run with the wind away from Eagle's Crest. One large airscrew churned at the rear of the airship, the hull listing to the starboard.

Laura returned to the helm. "Are you going to ram them?"

"First, we must stop their airscrew so they cannot fly back over our buildings. Then we can deal with them." I was aware that the *Silver Seed* was on its first test run and not a seasoned airship.

I pulled the lever to Full, and we started toward the renegade airship. Laura slid the shields over the windows, and José shot with precision from the rifle pod.

The *Silver Seed* bucked in the air bringing screams from the back. It was like sailing a tin can lid. I slowed the airscrews.

"We have to use the elevation rudders. Laura, can you do it?"

She sat in front of the large bubble level and adjusted the wheel. Immediately the ship flattened out. I loved that girl. I pulled the propulsion lever to ramming speed.

"Keep us level. I'll control the elevation," I called.

It took less than a minute to close the distance.

"Brace yourselves. Pass it along!"

Benny echoed the call for everyone to sit and be ready.

Another flaming wad fell from the ship, breaking up far away from the buildings.

The ramming pole tore into their propeller cage, shattering the propeller. The drive shaft bent up and to the right. Objects falling onto the deck echoed throughout the ship.

All forward motion stopped, and we swung behind the enemy ship. I gripped the wheel as the Freebooter's machinery tangled. A gearbox tore loose, churning in on itself. The steam engine tipped on its mounts, wrenching a steam line. A white cloud billowed into the air.

Finn ran to the helm. "They're going down! Retract! Retract!"

"All astern, Mary!" I yelled, and Mary threw the levers into place.

"Turn the wheel right, then left," Finn yelled. "We must pull loose!"

The renegade's engine lost power, the ship pulling our nose down.

"To the stern. Everyone not needed to the stern!" Finn called.

I spun the wheel left and right, the *Silver* Seed wiggling behind me.

The ramming pole gears growled in protest, our nose tipping dangerously.

I turned the wheel hard aport. "Mary, Full astern!" The tip of the spar broke, and the splintered pole tore from its tangle in the propeller cage. Slowly, the enemy ship fell away, landing in a heap at the edge of the slope behind the hangar.

"All stop, Mary."

The *Silver Seed* bobbed, and Finn called, "Give us a minute. Don't try to fly yet. We are making adjustments." The automatic levelers gained control, and the airship righted herself.

I went close to the center window, peering down. The ramming pole remained a splintered stinger, with a large sliver dangling in the breeze.

"Ready," Finn said.

I brought us around and made a quick landing. José and Benny manned the starboard rifle slots. Paul, Dad, Mary, and Ed were out the door with rifles the moment we touched the ground.

The sight was gruesome. Two men were alive, and one was able to walk. He started to draw a pistol when a shot rang out. He thought better of it and threw down his gun. His buddy had severe injuries and would not last long.

Paul and Ed carried the dying man to the lodge. We put a long chain around the other man's neck and tied him to a post.

Three men lay dead inside the renegade airship.

The open boiler door gaped toward the sky, coughing smoke like a dying dragon. Benny doused the fire, and we gathered around the wreckage.

"We made some mistakes," I said. "We were so busy congratulating ourselves about the *Silver Seed* that we let our guard down."

"The ramming pole was good in theory but a bad idea," Finn said. "Benny, Paul, get a crosscut and remove the rest."

José turned to the ridge. "We must expect more. But how did they find us?"

I was worried about Mr. Salsbury, but we had more pressing matters.

"We need to fly over the mountains while it is still bright sunlight. If the Freebooters come, we cannot let them catch us at night." I looked at Finn. "It will take too long to steam up the *Cloud Queen*. Can we use the *Silver Seed*?"

"I don't know why not. I will check the underbelly."

Benny and Paul made long pulls, chips curling off the saw blade.

"Papa should set some dynamite charges on the ridge. It would slow them down," José said.

"Good. Send Benny to help—I want you with us. We'll fly as soon as Finn has checked for damage."

I slid under next to Finn. "What's the verdict?"

"Dolph is bringing some wrenches. We can unbolt this mess, and the ship will be fine without it."

Nathan wheeled wooden blocks in a wheelbarrow. I raised the ship until they could set the blocks under the bow.

"Give us twenty minutes," Finn said.

Laura came out of the lodge. "He's dead," she said simply. "I don't think he ever knew we were trying to help him."

Mary glared at the remaining renegade. "His buddy can make himself useful." She held out her hand, and I gave her the pistol the man had tossed away.

I motioned to José, and we followed her to the prisoner.

"Well, aren't you a pretty thing? You can come visit me any time, darlin'."

Mary stiffened.

This man was no Army soldier. This was Freebooter in Army uniform.

José used his pliers to unfasten the chain from the post. He checked the chain around the Freebooter's neck and retied the man's hands behind his back.

Mary handed the pistol and shovel to José and took the chain. The renegade tried to resist, and Mary jerked the man off his feet. Having endured what Mary had at the hands of the Freebooters, I would not want to give her trouble. Dropping the chain, she grabbed the shovel.

The renegade lunged with his legs, catching Mary's foot, and she nearly went down. Like a cat, she made a quick hop, bringing up the shovel as she moved. It rang on the side of the man's head. Blood trickled from his ear.

"I do not think you should test her," José said. "She uses that shovel in the fields. To her, you are just another weed. She is not even mad—yet. You do not want her mad."

The man sneered, hooking Mary's leg with his foot. The shovel twirled, and the butt of the handle came down on the man's nose. There was a crunch, and his head fell back.

I got a bucket of water and tossed it in his face. "Wake up, you fool. You have graves to dig. Keep acting like this, and she may have you dig yours."

The man spluttered. Nathan and Benny had come, and Nathan jerked the man to his feet. He grabbed the chain and pulled his face close. "Don't ever, ever even *think* about acting like that with her again or—"

"After you dig," José said. He smiled at me.

Nathan jerked the man along, walking fast. The man tried to spin the chain around himself and lunged to snap it out of Nathan's hand. The prisoner stumbled and fell, but Nathan continued to walk. The man squirmed and rolled, trying to unwind his handiwork.

When the chain was only around his neck again, he choked and coughed. Nathan stopped and ordered him to stand, and the man scrambled to his feet. I had never seen Nathan so angry.

14

Finn declared the *Silver Seed* airworthy. We took time to load dynamite and rocks. We had taken down more than one Freebooter with stones.

We flew out over the ridge at Slow. Laura and I stood at the helm. She had the telescope trained on the crest.

"Anything?" I asked.

"Just some blue jays."

We inched over the rough terrain. José lay in the rifle pod, scanning the ground, while I watched through the floor port. After two hours, we felt confident that no Army renegades were hiking up the mountain.

"It's a full day of hiking from here, but we must watch daily," I said.

Renegades coming to Eagle's Crest was unsettling. "What if they couldn't cross the ridge?" I wondered.

"The cliffs are a tough climb. It is the only handy way in," Laura said.

"We blow the ridge," José said. "We can make it hard for the enemy to cross to us."

"I like it, my friend."

"It will take several charges," José said, "but Papa can do it."

When we arrived at Eagle's Crest, I surprised myself. "We are going to back the ship in." At the helm, I felt invincible.

I stationed Benny in the salon, and Finn ran the airscrews backward. I watched with the periscope, but the hull blocked the view of the ground. José followed with the speaking hose connected. The *Silver Seed* slipped into the hangar with only one correction.

"Benny, you don't know left from right when you are looking back," I teased.

He squinted at me out of the corner of his eye. "The right for you or the right for me? Which right is right?" he joked.

When we stepped out, the dinner bell at the lodge was ringing. As we settled in our places, Mary and Nathan arrived.

"Where is the prisoner?" I asked.

Mary sat down primly. "Digging."

"I looped the chain over a high limb twice and padlocked the end close to his neck," Nathan said. "He won't be going anywhere."

"He will dig if he knows what is good for him." There was a bite in her voice. I supposed anyone could be pushed beyond all patience with what she called "ingrates."

We were glad to be together in the lodge for supper, but my earlier bravado had faded. I no longer had confidence in Eagle's Crest as a refuge. The sudden attack from the air unsettled me, and I doubted I was the only one feeling uneasy.

After chicken, peas, and potatoes, we gathered around the hearth. The lodge was warm, but there was a chill in the air. Minnie and Mrs. Rodriquez took their children to bed.

"Did the Freebooter ship find us by luck, or did they know where to look for Eagle's Crest?" Finn wondered.

It was the question we all were thinking about.

"Their ship will not return. That will be a problem," José said. "If they knew where we are—flew here on purpose—they will come."

"*If* they knew. Maybe they only knew we went toward the mountains and found us while flying," Benny suggested.

"When we launched the *Silver Seed*, they immediately turned North." I wished I was sure about the next part. "Hopefully, they wanted to run with the wind and not head toward their base."

"I checked their ship," Finn said. "Not only is it of poor design, it lacks craftsmanship. The chances of them navigating to this spot are slim."

Liam nodded. "Finn is right. It is not nearly as sophisticated as the *Cloud Queen* and nothing compared to the *Silver Seed*."

"I am impressed with the idea of hanging the ship from Levitrite," I said. "That solved the whole balancing problem."

"But why didn't the hull hang true?" Laura asked. "The ship listed to starboard when they turned away."

Finn laughed. "Each rod that came down had a turnbuckle to adjust the length. Apparently, someone can't measure. On one side, the turnbuckles are hanging by a few threads—on the other, they were turned tight." He shook his head slowly in disbelief. "It was never going to hang true."

"The good news is that we were faster than their airship. Much faster," I said.

Finn pulled his fingers. "There is another upside. We will be able to salvage Levitrite, electric cable, a transformer, and the dynamo."

"What about weapons?" I asked.

"They had rifles, ammunition, and a small cannon." José jogged to the storage room next to the kitchen and returned with a rifle.

Paul examined the weapon. "This is a new Army issue. Not the '74s the Freebooters used. We found six that are undamaged. And lots of shells. We counted over a hundred."

"That's good," Benny said.

Paul smiled a sad smile. "Before you get too excited, remember the rebel army has these too. With train cars full of shells."

We passed the rifle from hand to hand.

"I don't like this," I said. "We know nothing about the enemy. The ship was a surprise. We only know that something is wrong with the Army. Benny, José, can you bring in the prisoner?"

José led the man in, Benny holding the chain from behind.

The rebel made no comments to Mary and didn't glance in her direction.

"What is your name?" I asked.

The man turned his head to the darkened end of the lodge.

"What is your name." José turned the prisoner's head.

The man spat in José's face.

José's knee came up so fast the Freebooter had no chance to try to turn away.

The man bent over, but Benny had the chain tight. Nathan stepped close and grabbed the chain with powerful arms, lifting the man by his neck. The man gagged and choked, finally putting his feet down.

José didn't bother to wipe the spittle off his face. He stood close, his voice lower. "I should adjust your mouth to stop that spitting habit you have. What is your name?"

The man panted a bit, and there was a tiny flinch in his jaw. "John," he said at last.

"Where did the airship come from? Where did you build it?"

The man turned his head away but thought better of it. He looked José in the eye. "Why should I tell you?"

"Easy one. You tell me because you like to eat."

The man closed his eyes, rocking slightly on his feet. I brought José a napkin.

José wiped his face carefully. "Thank you, Will. Laura, do you suppose there is more chicken in the kitchen?"

Laura brought the serving platter and stood beside José.

"This is the deal. You tell us, and you eat tonight. Or you tell us tomorrow and eat tomorrow. Or you do not tell us, and we eat." José took a large bite from a drumstick and returned to the bench. "What do you think? It is good chicken. But I can eat it all. I am still a growing boy." He laughed and took another bite.

"I think I could eat some pie," Finn said. "Anyone else?"

"I'll bring the pies," Benny said happily.

John watched José eating.

José gestured with the drumstick. "I do not think your friends are coming to rescue you." He took another bite. "You make the choice."

Mary moved to the end of the bench, where the rebel could not see her.

Nathan glanced her way. "Air is also important." He lifted the chain a little higher, and the prisoner coughed.

Laura began to serve everyone plates of pie, and Benny brought the coffee.

Mary stared into the crackling flames. I was startled when she jumped to her feet.

"Nathan, you should not have to hold that chain. Let me get a rope." She returned in a moment. "Benny, can you throw this over that beam up there, please?"

Benny coiled the rope and made a quick toss. The line arched gracefully over the beam. He took the end and quickly tied the chain, tugging until the chain pulled on the man's neck. He stood in front of the Freebooter, looking for a place to tie off the rope.

"Here, I can hold that for you, Benny. You eat your pie." Mary took the rope, looped it around her waist, and leaned back. The man went up on his tiptoes.

Mary faced the man, out of reach. "Did you know this Freebooter is a slow digger? He digs as if he has never worked a day in his life. You should see his hands. He had blisters in ten minutes. He only has one grave dug."

The man's jaw flinched again.

Mary leaned back against the rope. "Like a little boy's hands."

Nathan strode in with one of the anvils. I marveled at his strength.

When he had set it gently on the hearth, he turned to Mary. "You don't have to hold that fellow." He untied the rope from her waist and brushed her cheek with his thumb. He made a quick loop around the anvil, making sure the line was tight. He gave a pull on the rope. "What's that anvil weigh, Finn?"

"That's the two hundred pounder."

Nathan looked at the man. "Oh, you could probably drag that a little closer to you—with your neck. But you won't ever get to lie down. This could be a bad night for a man who is weak in the knees."

Mary sat at the end of the table with the prisoner's back to her. When Nathan sat down, she patted his back and put her head on his shoulder.

Her pain goaded, and I felt like cuffing the prisoner with the back of my hand, hard enough to leave a mark.

José finished his third piece of chicken, stood, and stretched. "Want to play some cards?"

We sat at the long table, playing. Laura sat knitting a baby bonnet for the Rodriquez's baby, Miguel. José had won a sizable pile of toothpicks when the prisoner spoke.

16

"What do you want to know?" There was defeat in the Freebooter's voice.

José laid two pair on the table and pulled the toothpicks to his pile. "Now we are getting somewhere." He stretched and stood. "Where did you build the ship? Tell me, and we will let you sit."

Benny brought a chair.

"There is a canyon in the hills above Alta Grande." John hesitated. "We have a—shop there."

"This is good." José slid the anvil closer and pulled the chair over. "Keep going, and you get to eat."

The man's eyes flared, looking from person to person. "We will destroy you," he growled. "This was the first ship, but there will be more."

"How many ships?"

"Two."

"Why is the Army fighting the people it should protect?"

"We are the Army—of the United States of America. It is good to support the Army of the United States of America."

"Mister. You are going to be here a while. That shop better be there. We may change your eating habits if we find out you lied."

"Can I eat? Maybe have a cup of tea?"

José looked thoughtful. "You get to eat. I think we will only let you have water."

Benny untied John's hands, and after the prisoner ate, Nathan led him outside.

For the first time that evening, I felt like eating my pie. "What do you think?"

"Hard to tell," José said.

Nathan came in and took off his coat. "I chained him to the flywheel of their steam engine. There is a sheltered place in the wreckage where he can sleep." He looked at Laura. "We gave him warm blankets."

"Can we believe this fellow?" Paul asked. "Do you think that ship was built in San Gabriel Canyon?"

"It better be true," Mary said, "or he will be answering to me."

"It makes sense that they wouldn't want to haul the Levitrite far," Finn said. "But it seems odd that no one noticed. The canyon is not that far away from town."

Dad had been quiet. "Once the trains started running again, it would be easy for the Army—renegades—to get materials." He put another log on the fire.

"The whole area is building up," Ed remarked.

"We need to know more. We need a spy," I said. "The only way to know for sure is to send someone in. We have to see for ourselves." I watched Laura's reaction. "I could go up the canyon. Posing as a miner."

Dad glanced up but kept silent.

"You and I can go," José said. "We will take two horses. It will be safer in pairs."

Finn paced in front of the fire. "What's your plan?"

"We will be careful," José said. "We wear ragged clothes—look dirty. No one will think anything of Will. Me? I am just another Mexican."

"Not to us," Laura said.

If I was going to spy on the Freebooters, José was the man I wanted with me.

"This can work," I said. "We ride up the canyon like a couple of young bucks trying our hand at mining. We won't talk any more than necessary."

"Let's all sleep on it," Nathan said. "It's been a long day. We will be able to think better in the morning."

Paul backed up to the fire. "We may want to question the prisoner again tomorrow. Liars often slip up when they tell their tale for a second time."

In our cabin, Laura was quiet, and I could tell she was not happy.

I put my arms around her. "I'll be careful."

She twisted around and grabbed me, hugging me hard. "You better be. I don't want to lose you."

"I know, but whatever is wrong out there—whatever is behind the Army behaving like Freebooters must be stopped."

She sat on the bed. "I loved history in school, so full of mighty deeds. Sometimes people have to stand against evil." Laura took a clip from her hair. "Whatever this is, Will, it is evil. I can feel it."

We slept well, but I sensed Laura was awake early in the morning.

"You have to go," she whispered. "I would go if I could. It has to be done."

"José will be key to our success. That guy has eyes in the back of his head."

José and I packed carefully, including quarter sticks of dynamite. We helped with the potato harvest and made sure our clothes took the worst of it. Dad had an old hat that was a little too big for me. Everyone agreed that I looked more like Huck Finn than the captain of the *Cloud Queen*.

On the third day, Finn called us to his shop. I was always surprised that Finn could create such marvelous devices in the chaos strewn about the long work table where we gathered. He knew where every tool and part was, refusing to allow anyone to tidy his space.

"This is something you must see." He handed me a small wooden box with one of the Morse Code keys attached to the top. A small crank came out of one side. "I read a piece in one of the papers a few months ago. An Italian has developed a wireless telegraph."

We waited in silence. Finn had amazed us before.

"It needs a wire stretched out, about a hundred feet. That wire sends a signal through the air. On the other end—the other box can receive the clicks sent out."

When I hefted the box, it was clear there was more of Finn's cleverness inside. Two knurled knobs were attached to wires.

"Does it work? Is this possible?" Dad asked.

Liam swelled with pride. "It will work."

"What do we do?" I asked.

"I already have a wire from the top of the shop to the lodge. It is connected to this unit." He led us to a larger box on an uncharacteristically clean table.

The excitement in the room was palpable.

"We have to test this in several stages. I have already made it work in the shop. Let us demonstrate."

Finn motioned to Laura, and I realized the invention was not new to everyone.

Laura placed the wooden box on the end of a workbench. "Paul, can you hold this wire out, please?" She clipped another wire to a water pipe.

"We'll send two metal stakes with you. The first is for the wire Laura put on the pipe. It must be pounded into the ground to make it all work," Finn said. "The second stake has this insulator to keep the wire from touching the ground. You only have to hammer it in far enough to hold the wire."

Paul peered at the roll of the wire. "This isn't going to shock me like when we installed the shop lights, is it?"

"No," Finn said, "but that was a good lesson, teaching us to disconnect the building power before fiddling with the electric wires."

Paul laughed and grabbed the wire, stretching it across the workshop.

Finn flipped a switch on the larger box. "Turn the crank as we practiced, Laura."

A soft whirring came from her box, and the code key twitched.

"You may notice that the key is already jumping a bit on both boxes. There is a lightning storm to the north. Big sparks are not the wireless's friend."

Finn sent a simple message, "Hi." Laura's key clicked at the exact moment Finn pressed his sender.

"It gets there fast!" José said.

"Instantly. Now, when operating Laura's box by yourself, the next part gets a little tricky. It's like rubbing your belly and patting your head, right Laura?"

Laura steadied the box with one hand, stretching her finger up to the key. With the other, she turned the crank. She tapped out TAKES COORDINATION.

There was an audible sigh.

"My box has to be set to the correct wavelength to be detected by Laura's box. We spent most of the day getting it right." Finn was in his element, experimenting.

"Time to take it on a little walk," he said. "Will, you and José go out to the point and stretch the wire to a tree branch so you don't have to touch it. It won't shock you, but contact with your hand will deaden the signal." Finn pulled on his fingers. "Then, send a message."

Paul wrapped the wire back on its spool, and Laura handed me the equipment. "You have to keep cranking. You can tell when the little dynamo is up to speed—you can feel the resistance."

As we walked briskly out to the ridge, José was quiet.

"If this works, we can send out messages while spying—or call to be picked up," I said.

"Down there, we need to get in, get out. Fast."

Near the ridge, we hooked a loop of the antenna over a limb. José unreeled the wire as he went down the side of the hill. I drove the stakes into the ground. When the wire was in place, I turned the crank and tapped, ANYONE THERE

We waited, the little dynamo whirring.

The key answered, FINN

José's eyes were bright. "Finn is a clever fellow."

The box clicked again, DID YOU RECEIVE

I quickly tapped out, YES

BRING IT IN STOP MEET US IN THE LODGE

Finn waited by the fire. "Good work. Dolph and I are making several of these keysets."

"How will you know that we are sending a message?" I asked. "Does someone have to wait here by the receiver the whole time we are gone?"

"The transmitter key can be linked to our existing system in the lodge and cabins. If I am not in the workshop, we'll have someone listening."

"I won't sleep well with you gone," Laura said. "If you send a message, I'll hear."

"We leave tomorrow morning," I said. "The *Cloud Queen* can be at the mine by noon. José and I will ride from there."

"One more thing," Finn said. He handed me three packets of powder. "These dissolve in the mouth. If you need a man out of commission for a few hours, give him one of these."

Laura and I held hands on the way to our cabin. "You must promise to not take chances. Listen to José."

"Yes." It was an easy promise. I had been listening to José all my life.

The *Cloud Queen* settled on a ridge above the mine. With the telescope, we saw no movement below, no sign of life.

We walked the horses down the plank.

Laura kissed me. "You come back to me."

"I will."

Laura patted my hat. "When you get home, we are burning these clothes."

"I thought I looked like a miner man."

"You look like a dirty man."

We led the horses down the hillside. The airscrews of the *Cloud Queen* beat the air, becoming muffled as she moved north.

As planned, we went to Wolfskill Lodge. I stretched our antenna. José sent, AT LODGE STOP UNDISTURBED STOP WILL IS TRYING TO COOK STOP

It was good to hear MR when the message was received.

We ate warm refried beans and rode down the canyon. Ed had done an excellent job of closing the canyon with the dynamite. We spent an hour leading the horses over the rubble and around a small lake that had formed.

We kept our heads down and rode in silence. No one challenged us. We reached the mouth of San Gabriel Canyon by mid-afternoon the next day. That evening José and I chose a bare flat above the canyon. No one would find us, but we kept our pistols near. We stretched out the antenna.

SAN GAB CAN STOP ALL GOOD STOP

ALL WELL HERE STOP I PRAY FOR YOU L STOP

In the morning, I woke shivering and stiff. True to his ways, José had a fire and breakfast cooking.

"Should we send a message?" José wondered.

"It will keep Laura from fussing."

We were getting good at setting up the transmitter and soon were in communication with Eagle's Crest. José told them we would not set up the radio again until we knew who and what was further up the canyon.

We packed the gear and followed a track along the stream. San Gabriel Canyon was a wider canyon than ours, and we rode quietly. Twice we passed miners. We touched our hats, keeping our heads down. The sun was high when we met a group of miners standing around a fire and pulled reins.

"Doin' much good?" I asked.

A man put his hand on a rifle near the sluice box. I held up my palms. "No harm meant. Only wondering if it was worth us trying up further?"

"You can try. Up about five miles, there is an Army camp. I wouldn't go near if I was you," the man said.

"Why is the Army in the canyon?" José asked casually.

"No Army I know," said the miner. "But they don't want to be bothered. They'll run you off. Shot a man a couple of weeks ago. Shot 'im dead. We leave them be when they come up and down in their wagons. Mean bunch."

We passed no other camps, but smoke hung above the canyon ahead.

"We should climb out of the main canyon," José said. "Up there, we will see them before they see us."

We found a deer trail to a ridge that formed a rough bluff. Riding in the thick scrub brush was tough on the horses. We tied them with long leads in a grassy meadow with a trickle of water. We each shouldered a bag, ducking and dodging up the hill.

Twice we worked our way out to a vantage point. Guards lounged around below. The second time we looked down on bunkhouses and a building larger than the shop at Eagle's Crest. Two men unloaded equipment from a wagon.

"How many you think?" José wondered. "Thirty men could sleep in the bunkhouse."

"Sixteen horses—looks like John was telling the truth. I can't wait to get a look inside that shop."

"In the dark, we will have a better chance," José said. "They are expecting trouble coming up the canyon. Only one guard is watching the upper canyon."

We worked our way north until we found a handy trail to the canyon floor. We chose a flat under huge oaks on the bluff and settled down to wait.

I chatted with Laura until my hand was sore from turning the crank. We decided to nap until dark.

When we woke, the moon cast a faint glow. We worked our way to the canyon floor with pistols and the pack holding the transmitter and dynamite. Once, a rock rolled down, and we waited to be sure no one had heard it. When we approached the shop, the guard sat asleep with his back propped against the wall.

I stood with my pistol ready as José crept forward until he stood over the man.

He beckoned for me to come and whispered, "He will have a headache tomorrow. He is drunk. His boss will give him a bigger headache."

I nudged the man's foot with my boot. He hardly stirred.

We went to wide barn doors and opened one slowly, José holding his candle high. Two airships stood in the gloom. The closest was nearly complete, its mast along the wall. The second ship was only a frame.

We slipped around the finished airship. A glance told us it was not ready to fly. The steam engine wasn't connected to the boiler, and the boiler's water supply was a work in progress.

"What should we do?" José wondered.

"I don't think they should know we were here. But we need to slow down their progress." I flipped open the oiler caps for the two main journals of the engine. I pulled the stuffing out and poured sand in the bearings. I stuffed the wadding back in and closed the cap. When I had dusted off the excess sand, I was pleased.

"Can we burn this place?" José asked.

It was a tin building. The timbers would need kindling to get them started. We were looking for oil or kerosene when I noticed a transmitter. It didn't look like the one in the shop at Eagle's Crest, but two wires, one connected to an iron stake, gave it away. I looked it over carefully, knowing Finn would be curious.

"Will, we can light the poles on fire." José shook a can. "Kerosene."

Voices made us douse the candle and retreat quickly. The drunk snored softly. José poured the rest of the whiskey on the renegade's shirt and left the bottle on his chest, dripping. As the voices grew louder, we slipped into the night.

Back at our camp on the hill, we were wide awake. "They have a transmitter," I said.

"Have they been listening to our messages?" José wondered.

"I don't think so. Finn said he and Laura had to work all day to get the signal right. But we have to figure out how to listen to them."

We quickly stretched our antenna, and Laura answered.

IS FINN THERE STOP WE HAVE QUESTIONS
WILL GET HIM

José started a small fire, and we huddled near it. I turned the crank while he warmed the beans.

FINN HERE

I told as much as we knew about the renegade transmitter.

CAN THEY LISTEN TO OUR MESSAGES STOP

NO STOP BUT WE MUST LEARN THEIR CODE FREQUENCY STOP CAN YOU GET TO THE TRANSMITTER AGAIN STOP

YES

After Finn gave us instructions, we slid down the hill and worked our way back to the enemy camp. The drunk guard was gone, and another man had taken his place. He was not drunk.

José slipped quietly into the shadows and rapped the man on the head with the butt of his pistol. He pulled the man's mouth open and emptied a packet of powders in his mouth, and held his jaw closed. "They cannot know I hit him. You check the transmitter—I will make this look like an accident." He lit the candle for me.

At the transmitter, my hands shook. Messages had been stabbed onto the pin of a message holder. I slid several messages off the spike and read through the latest few. There were requests for progress reports and talk of equipment arriving.

I pulled all the messages loose and stuffed several from the bottom in my pocket.

I stuck the candle to the table. Four screws held the side of the transmitter. I found a screwdriver on a cluttered bench.

I jumped when José whispered, "Stringers for the building were leaning back on the wall. It looks like one fell on him when he was sitting against the wall." He laughed.

I showed him the inside of the box. "You look, too. I see the coil Finn wanted us to check; it has many winds of wire. This slider touches it here—twenty winds from the top. Somehow it makes a difference. Count to the bottom winds too. I don't know which way is which."

I turned one of the messages over and sketched the parts inside. It was difficult because we had no idea what we were seeing. Morning glow began to show in the windows.

"I will check our friend," José said. "We don't have much time."

I started to put the side back on the transmitter when I heard men talking outside. They were changing the guard! I fumbled a screw and dropped it. It rolled on the tabletop, and I grabbed it before it fell into the dirt. I managed to get the threads started and gave it several twists with the screwdriver.

I turned to go out when a voice behind the building called, "Jack!"

José slipped in the door. He made a pinching motion, and I doused the candle. We moved with our backs to the wall toward a stack of lumber, where we crouched and waited.

"Jack, where are you?"

"Here he is. He's hurt. Help me. This corner post fell on him. He's got a knot on his head."

"I don't remember no post leaning here."

"Oh, you don't remember much of anything."

They tossed the wood aside and lugged Jack away. The door opened, and a railroad lantern made the dark workshop suddenly seem bright.

"Check the ship. I am going to get us a drink."

A bottle made echoing suction sounds, and someone lit a cigarette. The Freebooters sat on the edge of the ship's deck.

"Everything looks OK—let's go. It's time for morning tea."

There were more drinking sounds before the two went out the south door.

"Do we try to burn it, or do we leave?" José wondered.

"I think we have to hope the sand in the bearings slows them down. We don't want to destroy their radio."

José relit the candle. "It is a big chance. We do not need them coming for us."

"Finn is hoping to listen in on their messages." I patted my pocket. "I took messages off the bottom, but we can't let them know we were here."

I fumbled with the remaining messages, trying to slip them on the skewer without making a second hole. "Bring the candle close."

"Only the top few need to use the same hole." José grabbed a pile by two sides and slammed them onto the pin. "I am going to scout around."

After replacing the last of the papers, I scraped the wax off the table with my knife. As I turned to go, I tossed the screwdriver onto the clutter of tools.

José poked his head in the door. "Time to go. A guy in full uniform is coming from below."

The hair stood up on my neck as I ran. We scrambled up the canyon wall and watched the Freebooters filing into the shop. We gathered our bedrolls and took a last look.

"Whether or not to start a fire no longer matters," José said. "A fire would not have had a chance to harm the airship or the building."

Away from the canyon bluff, we ducked and batted our way through the low brush.

At the horses, we sent a message to Eagle's Crest. GOING TO HIGH GROUND FOR PICK UP STOP DONT START UNTIL WE CAN GIVE YOU A LOCATION

MR

We found our way up a side canyon, riding for several miles before it flattened into a meadow between low hills. A larger stream was in the middle, and we let the horses drink.

"This looks good to me," José said.

I agreed. It was late morning, and we had been up all night. We contacted Eagle's Crest, and the code box clicked: STEAMS UP STOP COMING NOW STOP

José started a fire, and we cooked breakfast.

We dozed until we heard the distant whisper of the *Cloud Queen*'s blower in the afternoon air. José tied a rag to the end of a long branch and waved it. Laura would be scanning the area with the telescope.

19

A speck of light twinkled in the dusk. Laura hadn't been off by much, and the steering cables creaked pleasantly in the wheel pedestal as she corrected our course. I stood before the pilothouse until I was sure a light pole had been erected in the middle of the yard. The tireless effort of our companions was comforting. Once Eagle's Crest lay below, our friends gathered, Nathan and Paul guiding us in. I fell into bed with no supper.

The following day, we considered our options.

When I told them about putting sand in the engine bearings, Finn approved. "Good one. Not sure I'd have thought of that. The engine will run, but the bearings will fail early. We might get lucky and have them lose the ship in the mountains."

José and I showed Finn the drawing of the transmitter, describing the parts as best we could.

"Here is the good news," I said. I laid out the papers I had taken from the desk. "Not much information here, but they write the time and date on each message. They send messages every morning and evening at seven."

Finn smiled. "This is working out better than we could have hoped. Now we know when to listen."

"They are not on long," I said. "From the look of these notes, they are not good coders. They resort to writing down the dots and dashes."

Finn studied a message. "Probably a group effort. One writing, one looking at the code chart."

"They do a lot of drinking," José said. "Tea and whiskey. They might have trouble even if they knew Morse Code."

Finn tapped the table. "From your drawing, I can see we need twenty-seven winds of wire in the coil. How big around was it, and what size of wire?"

I looked at José. He shrugged and indicated a coil two inches in diameter.

"Show us some different-sized wire—I think we can choose," I said.

We walked out to the shop and quickly agreed on a spool of wire matching the renegade radio's coil.

Finn glanced at the clock on the workshop wall. "Too late this morning, but we'll be ready to listen tonight."

Finn added numbers to our drawing. Dolph sat on a stool with a board clip, double-checking the numbers.

Finn noticed us standing behind him. "Out of here. We have work to do, and we have to have quiet." He swatted José's hand. "Don't touch that wrench. You guys have your own wrenches."

José held up both hands. As soon as Finn turned back to the transmitter, José touched the wrench twice and grinned.

"José, I know you are touching the wrench behind my back."

Dolph tried to wink at José.

When we were outside, we had to laugh. Finn was a great guy but had little humor regarding his workshop. José trotted out to the point to help with the dynamiting.

Back in the lodge, Laura studied the messages from the Freebooters. "They are talking to someone in Sacramento." She tapped a paper. "On the back of this sheet, we found 'Reguest "Sacmendo" to send more black powder and cannonballs.'"

She picked up another note. "Here is one with a curious reference: 'Ask Adjunct Leader for instructions for airship capture.' It was sent a week before the Army came to Santa Monica."

"You are better at history than I am, but I don't remember an Adjunct Leader in our school books."

"There isn't one. We have a governor—or had a governor. And for sure, the Army doesn't have Adjunct Leaders."

Mary stuck her head in the doorway. "We need everyone in the greenhouse. Time for seeding."

We had learned to move when Mary said it was time to work on the farm. "You like to eat—then you like to help on the farm," she had once teased when I was gathering wool instead of transplanting vegetables.

All adults, except the dynamite crew and Finn, worked in the greenhouse for the next two days. Many of the vegetables would stay in the greenhouse, but some were for transplanting outside when warmer weather came. The tiny seeds for lettuce and carrots were my job.

Occasionally a dynamite charge shook the greenhouse, and I wished Ed and his boys needed my help on the ridge.

Each morning and evening, Finn systematically experimented with different frequencies. On the evening of the second day, he and Dolph ran into the lodge.

"Found it. Got part of a message!"

Dolph smoothed the paper on the table, and we gathered around.

SKOUT SHIP NOT RETRNED STMP REQEST ODERS

"Then the reply came moments later."

SEND SINGLE SQUAD STOP DO NOT ENGAGE STOP REPORT ONLY

"The group on this end can't spell," Dolph said, "and even if they could, they can't code worth beans. Their message took forever."

"There was a two-minute pause," Finn said. "We thought they were done for the day when there was this nugget."

WIL SEND SQUAD IMEJATLY STOP THRE DAYS TRAVL BEFOR CLIME

"Finn, Dolph, this is excellent. Was that all?"

"We waited twenty minutes," Finn replied. "The good news is that we are close to completing a second receiver. We will have one for our communications and one that will be listening—all the time. Come with me to the shop. We have something new."

I held Laura's hand as we walked across the yard. It was a beautiful evening, cold, with a million stars.

Finn had cleared the end of one of the tables. A wondrous brass device with tiny gears and levers stood sentinel. There was a reel of paper tape that fed through the machine.

"This is a code recording device." Finn was smiling. "Dad told me that messages were originally received and put on paper by a device like this. This will save us from having to have one of us always watching the receiver."

Finn turned the machine from side to side for us to see. "I am particularly proud of this one. Dad told me what they looked like, and I have made some improvements."

"You don't have to wind it," Dolph said with boyish enthusiasm. "Finn made the tape advance with the electric signal."

Finn continued, "Anytime our renegade receiver begins to receive, this small paper tape will begin to mark the message. Maria and Hanna have been my helpers. They have cut yards of tape with razors. Will, you may want to give your razor an extra stropping before you shave in the morning."

Laura's eyes crinkled. "I gave them your razor—for the good of the cause," she teased.

"Finn—once again, you have amazed us all," I said.

"I'm working on a buzzer," Dolph said. "It will sense when the tape reel begins to move and ring that bell." He pointed to a red electric bell on the wall. "I've done all the wiring."

"Good work, Dolph. You are a right hand to Finn." I patted his shoulder. "Hopefully, we are staying one step ahead of the renegades."

José entered the workshop. "Two steps would be better."

"Or three!" Dolph chanted. He blushed and ducked his head.

Later, in the lodge, we passed the new messages from person to person.

"I'm guessing they will be coming from the north," Paul said. "Three days to come around the pass to the east and start up the mountains."

"You're thinking they'll bring troops over Cajon?" I asked.

"Just a guess. They could make it around in three days if they rode hard. I doubt they have a problem with appropriating horses or anything else they need along the way."

The uncertainty bothered me. "How would they know to look on the north side of the mountains? We are sure the ship we took down didn't have a radio."

"No transmitter," Dolph said. "We checked every inch of that ugly thing. I crawled into every crevice."

We sat in silence.

"I never liked Mr. White at the mercantile in Lancaster," Paul said. "He always asked too many questions, especially about the engine."

"No one followed the wagon," Nathan said. "I'm sure of that."

"We've always taken a spare horse, and I scouted back to make sure," Paul said. "If White spilled the beans to the renegades, they only know we were buying supplies."

"Then they can't know—for sure—how to get here by foot," I said. "Meanwhile, let's get the ridge project finished. If they come, I want them tired and with no large weapons."

"The work is getting harder," José said. "We are down to granite. Drilling rock is slow going, but the next blast will create a cliff."

"Good work, men. Ed, take your crew in the morning and finish the job."

20

"We can finish the greenhouse today," Mary said, "if you all work hard." She glanced at me. The slightest hint of a smile was at the corners of her mouth.

"Hey, I planted thirty rows of carrots, onions, and spinach."

Mary winked. "Yes, *Will*," She said with exaggeration. "You did just fine."

There was laughter, and I joined them. I wasn't the most enthusiastic farmer and was glad Mary felt like teasing.

By mid-afternoon, Mary congratulated everyone. "Good work. There will be plenty of vegetables next year."

I walked to the ridge with Dad. Ed and his boys knew what they were doing. Where there once had been a ribbon of ridge, we found a thirty-foot cliff. The chasm was wide enough that the renegades could not put a log across as a bridge.

"Our fortress is complete," I said, almost to myself. As far as I was concerned, those in the world who wanted war, killing, and taking could stay away.

"Will, José, all of you!" Dolph yelled, running on his lanky legs. "Finn says..."

Paul reached out and held the lad's shoulder. "Easy, Dolph, easy. Get your breath—tell us nice and slow."

"The message receiver was clicking. It was not on time. I mean, early—it was early—it's not when it usually gets a message."

"What did you hear?" I asked as we gathered the small tools, sledgehammer, and star drills.

"The code was terrible—'sendent the squawk buy trun.' or something."

Paul snorted, "Probably squad. Here, Dolph, help carry the shovels."

In the workshop, Finn had called everyone to join us.

"Paul's guess was right about them coming from the north," Finn said. He had pinned a map to the wall. "They take the Santa Fe line to San Bernardino and then north over Cajón." Finn tapped the map. "This could have them ready to climb a day early."

"I don't think we should watch them from the *Cloud Queen* or the *Silver Seed*," Laura said. "If they see the ship, it may help them know our general location."

José moved to the map. "We could fly far to the east. They will get off the train somewhere. We locate the Freebooters, let them see *Cloud Queen*—then lead them up the wrong canyon."

"What do you think?" I looked at everyone in turn.

"Why not eliminate them?" Mary asked. She moved to the map. "There are innocent people here—and here. These men cannot be trusted."

"The Freebooters are like ants in an anthill," José said. "You kick it, and they all come out. We should give them a trail of crumbs. If they follow us up the wrong canyon far to the east, they could be weeks tramping around the mountains before they realize we are not there."

Everyone was quiet. Finally, Nathan said, "Mary, we are going to get rid of these types, but we must be patient. If we are going to stay ahead of them, we must always know more about them than they know about us."

Mary hissed, "I know, I know. But while we are planning, they will continue their horrible attacks."

The fire popped a cinder onto the hearth, and José flicked it back with a twig.

Mary's eyes flared. "This is not a simple chat about war tactics." Her voice rose. "I lost my husband—was held captive!" She wrapped her arms around herself, turning away. "I lost my—baby girl," she sobbed.

Nathan touched her shoulder, but she flinched away.

I was ashamed of our cavalier attitude.

"I am sorry," Mary said. Her voice broke, her eyes red.

"No, Mary. We are sorry. And we will put an end to this." I turned away slightly so no one would see my own tears of anger.

I spent an uneasy night and was awake early in the morning. I decided we would eliminate, or at least capture, the squad of soldiers.

As we ate breakfast, Mary took a deep breath. "I have been thinking while I was in the greenhouse—you are right. We should lead the soldiers on a wild goose chase. Make them use as many men as possible while we make our plans."

"Early this morning, I decided you were right; we should eliminate them," I said.

Laura laid down her fork. "Or we could capture them."

Mary was insistent, "Then we have to guard them. I am already tired of our prisoner. He works half-heartedly in the crops and isn't to be trusted."

"It's true. We either have to watch him or keep him chained to something. He can't hoe weeds dragging a chain around," Paul added.

"I am sorry about my outburst last night." Mary pulled her coat tighter around her neck. "We have to get the *Silver Seed* tested. Finn needs time to finish his projects. Let's stick to our plan and not let them ruin what we have."

"We don't want to use one of the ships to go hunting," Finn said. "What about a drawbridge?"

"Like a castle?" Hanna looked up, eyes wide. "Like King Arthur? I like King Arthur!"

"Yes, Hanna, Eagle's Crest is not like what Arthur had, but it is our castle." I stood. "This is not a round table. But—we value the opinion of each one here. A drawbridge could keep us safe, but we wouldn't be cut off."

I stole a glance at Mary. "We have seen dark times in the past. Extremely dark times. I didn't sleep well last night. I can tell I am not the only one. We *will* prevail! And this place will not be ruined by whatever darkness is out there."

There was a moment of total silence.

"We need to move forward," I said. "Now that we are listening to the enemy, we may have to adapt our immediate plans from time to time, but Mary is right. With the greenhouse planting completed, we need to test the *Silver Seed*. At the same time, we must be prepared to lead them away from us."

"I have worked out a plan," José said. "Will and I go down again, like miners. We find the Freebooters when they get off the train. We act the fool— feeding them news. They will be eager for news. We talk about seeing a riverboat in the sky, going up the canyon."

Ed leaned forward. "Go on, mijo."

"When they go up the canyon, we send a message, and the *Cloud Queen* comes back to pick us up. Then we all fly right over them, up the canyon."

"They will search forever," Benny said. "We just fly off into the mountains, and they won't see us turn to come here."

"I threw away Will's terrible clothes," Laura said.

José chuckled. "Mine are gone, too. We will be classier miners this time."

"We need three teams," I decided. "One will stay here to help Finn and work on the bridge project. Another team will run tests on the *Silver Seed*. The third will meet our friends and lead them astray."

"Paul, Ed, and I have already gone over my sketches for the drawbridge," Finn said. "They can start immediately."

"Benny can steam up the *Cloud Queen*," Laura said. "Will, José, and I can begin testing the *Silver Seed*. I need to learn how to fly it. Then Mary flies the *Cloud Queen* to take José and Will down. It's only a day trip."

My face gave away my doubts.

"Will, Mary is ready. Maybe not for battle, but she can do this. Benny will be along. Liam can run the engine."

She was right. "Are we in agreement?"

"To work!" Ed said.

When I arrived at the *Silver Seed*, Liam had the pressure up to ninety pounds.

At the helm, Laura was practicing with the levers. I didn't disturb her until she finished her sequence.

"Shall we move it out for a little practice?" I asked. "It will be at least two hours before the *Cloud Queen* has a head of steam."

"Yes!"

When we lifted, the airship bobbed, and I made a note.

When we were in the open yard, I said, "Let's try straight up."

I went to the engine room and watched the levelers whirring and clicking, making adjustments. "Up faster," I called to Laura on the speaking tube.

Liam nodded. "Steady as a rock. Finn is a bright lad."

"Up faster, yet," I called.

"Will, maybe you should come forward."

My ears were popping, but I was surprised when the mountains were dwarfed below us. The altimeter read twelve thousand feet. "This is an amazing ship."

"Remember, the air is thinner. We don't want to get dizzy," Laura said.

Taking a deep breath, I felt the lightness of the air. "You are right. Take us down to six thousand, and let's try maneuvering this marvel."

Laura started the motors, and we moved forward as we descended. Immediately the ship nosed down, and Laura pulled the forward speed to Stop, her eyes wide in alarm. "If we had continued that fast we would have gone straight down.

I agreed. "Yes. You've operated the elevation rudders before. Let me steer, and you see how they react."

Laura was able to keep the ship level, but by the time I had the throttle at Full, we were first nosing up and then suddenly heading down.

"Slow down! This is scaring me. I only move the control a tiny bit, and the ship reacts too violently."

I pulled the levers to Stop and wrote more notes for Finn. "Liam, can you come up?"

Liam came forward looking pale. "That was some ride. Reminded me of a bucking horse."

I set the airscrews to Dead Slow and brought us about. I was surprised to see that Eagle's Crest lay far in the distance. "Faster than the *Cloud Queen* by two or three times."

"Yes, but almost impossible to control," Laura said. "We must do something about that before the ship is ready for battle."

We put the ship through its paces before we landed. Flying at Quarter Speed, the *Silver Seed* behaved beautifully, soaring high and low, executing tight turns.

Laura read through my notes and made additions. She corrected my spelling and winked at me. I never could spell "elevation."

"We have enough information to keep Finn busy. The *Cloud Queen* should be ready by now." I kissed her. "I will be careful!"

21

The *Cloud Queen* blower whined as Mary strode toward the airship in a tall hat, her duster flowing out behind her. José led the horses up the ramp.

Liam and Benny made last-minute preparations in the engine room while Mary and I went to the wheelhouse. I stood aside and waited.

"Ready to go," Liam said through the speaking tube.

Mary looked at me, and I nodded.

The *Silver Seed* was a beautiful, sleek airship, but the *Cloud Queen* had a majesty that called to me as we rose into the morning sky.

Mary set the engine order telegraph for Half, and we swung to the east. José brought up a map, pinning it to the side wall.

I pointed to a canyon west of Cajón Pass. "This one should do nicely."

Mary said, "I'll take us higher so we can get the lay of the land."

The map of the higher mountains wasn't very accurate, but the mouths of the larger canyons were well-marked.

José went down, and Mary turned to me. "Thank you for trusting me, Will. I won't let you down with my anger. I get..." Her green eyes looked sad.

"Yes, but you have a right to your anger. You work hard for our project and are turning into a fine pilot."

She rang for Full, and the airscrews bit the air.

I went down to the telescope and scanned to the east. The mountains gave way to the lower Cajón Pass, and I pointed to the beginnings of a canyon snaking north.

Mary brought us lower, and we followed the meanderings of the stream. She pointed to a tiny meadow in a side canyon. There were no cabins, and she brought us down gently in the glade.

"Very nice, Mary. Beautifully done. Tell Laura all is well."

"All *is* well, but you two be careful."

After we rode the horses off the *Cloud Queen*, Liam, Mary, and Benny stood on the front deck.

"You two look the part," Liam called. "I'm not sure you two are worth coming back for."

As we started working our way down to the main canyon, the *Cloud Queen*'s airscrews gained speed. She disappeared behind a hill, and I was aware we were on our own.

We passed several mining camps and a small farm along the stream, with fields in the rolling foothills. A young girl and boy worked on a fence with their father. The man tipped his hat, and we returned the gesture.

The three had a quick conversation, heads together, and then the man motioned for us to come over.

I looked at José, and he gave a slight nod.

"You might want to take care when you go down much further. A bunch of men in Army clothes were up here two days ago, but they are not Army. They looked like Freebooters but in Army duds."

"How far down?" I asked.

"They'd come up from the little settlement at the mouth of the canyon. Fred, my boy, rode down to take a look. Two of them were asking questions—asking about a flying boat. We've heard rumors of such a thing but didn't have anything to tell them. But they were pretty set on getting information out of us."

I exchanged glances with José. "What did they want to know?"

"They asked if we had seen such a thing in this canyon, flying over us. They got a little belligerent. Then they took some of our food—said they were authorized to take food in time of national emergency." The man stretched his back. "Never heard of any Army doing a thing like that."

José shifted in his saddle. "They threaten you?"

"Not exactly, but I didn't like how one of them kept looking at my daughter, Adeline. He was filthy and had a mean look about him."

Adeline moved closer to her brother. "He was not a nice man, I could tell." She was older than I first thought but was slight of build. The boy was a year or so younger.

José glanced at me, eyebrows asking a question. I nodded.

"We may need your help." I swung down off my horse. "If they were to come again, we need you to tell them that you have seen the ship—further up the canyon." I paused to see how the three were taking the news. "You might see such a ship one of these times. It is nothing for you to be afraid of. The ship is friendly to good folks—if you know what I mean."

The father tipped his head to peek under my hat. "You're the captain, aren't you? There was a drawing of you in the paper months ago. You're him."

José jumped down. "This is Captain Will. But those men must never know. I am José."

The man stepped forward. "James Thomas—Jim. Good to meet you. This is my son Fred and my daughter Addy."

We started to get back on our horses when Jim said, "We have stew. We would be proud if you stopped a bit. It will be dark soon."

A warm meal was welcome. Jim was curious about the ship, and we admitted to giving rides, as the paper had reported. We didn't mention Eagle's Crest.

22

We loafed around town for two days before we saw the Freebooters. They came from the west and milled about the mercantile.

José bought a bottle of cheap whiskey in the small saloon. "I will play the drunk."

Behind a building, José dumped half the whiskey on the ground, took a large swallow, and gargled. He choked and spat out the whiskey. "That burns. My nose is on fire. Ready?"

We wandered close enough for the Freebooters to overhear our conversation.

"I can't fergit that thing." José held the bottle to his lips and then pointed to the sky. "Like a shreemboat up in the air," he said loudly.

One of the men sauntered over. "What are you talking about?"

José looked at him, swaying a bit. "Flyin'." He gestured again. "Up the canyon. 'bout made me want to give up whiskey." He tipped the bottle again, dribbling some on his shirt.

The man motioned for his buddies to come closer. "Which canyon?"

"Right up there. Right where we're stakin' our claim!" José snorted, gesturing toward the hills with the bottle.

The man turned to me. "This Mexican know what he's talking about, or is he too drunk?"

"I saw it," I said casually, keeping my head down. "I wasn't drunk either. It was like magic. It floated up there, hanging in the sky like a hawk."

The men wandered off and stood in a ring in front of the mercantile. A few minutes later, they mounted up and rode toward the canyon.

José and I went behind one of the buildings and sat down.

"Good job, José. I almost believed you were drunk. How close do we follow them?"

"My eyes still burn." José put the bottle aside. "Not too close. We have to let them lead."

"I'm starting to worry about Jim and his kids. Sending those guys back up the canyon puts them in danger. Addy is a pretty girl, and we know Freebooters take whatever they want."

We rode quietly into the late afternoon. I wanted to keep the Freebooters in sight, but I knew the danger was too great. As we passed, José pointed to an overgrown trail leading up the side of the canyon.

Gunshots rang in quick succession. José urged his horse into a gallop, and I was close behind. The cabin lay under the bluff in the evening shadows.

The renegades were using a small mound as a blind. They shot toward the small house, and someone was returning fire. We took cover behind an outcropping of rock.

"Send the girl out, and we'll leave you alone," a Freebooter shouted. Several shots were returned.

A volley of shots came from the Freebooters. José and I peered around the rocks, shooting with our rifles. The cabin was quiet as Freebooter bullets ricocheted around us.

"I don't like the looks of this," I said.

Fred came out of the back of the cabin, running down the canyon.

A single shot rang out, and Fred went down. José was on his feet immediately. "Keep them busy." He tossed his rifle to me.

I worked the lever on the Winchester every few seconds, conserving ammunition. I fed it from a leather bag, sometimes not bothering to fill the magazine.

José ran straight for Fred. In one move, he scooped up the lad and turned toward the canyon wall. I fired quickly, sliding shells with trembling hands. I shot a couple of rounds with the pistol. There was little chance of hitting anyone at this range, but I hoped it would sound as if there were more of us.

I hadn't seen José coming from behind. He was hardly out of breath when he laid Addy gently down. She wore boy's clothes, and there was blood on her shirt. Her leg was bleeding, and she had a vacant look in her eyes. José made a quick tie with his bandana.

"Both rifles are empty," I said. I fired two more shots at the hill with my pistol. "José, we can't stay here! They will circle around us. No more rifle shells in my bag."

José leaned close to Addy. "What about your family?"

She stared ahead, her face blank. "Dead. Dead," she whispered.

My stomach rolled. I shot one more round, and the hammer clicked on the empty pistol chamber.

"Are you sure?" José slipped shells into his rifle. "We could wait or come back."

"Fred was shot right away. He died in my arms. A bullet hit Papa in the head." Addy took a shaky breath. "There was no chance."

José shoved the rifle toward me, and I shot three times.

José wrestled a quarter stick of dynamite from his saddlebag and lit the fuse. "We cannot hold them. Not enough ammunition. In ten seconds, yell retreat," he said.

He lobbed the dynamite toward the hill and picked up Addy. He tossed her up in his saddle and was up behind her in a quick jump. "We have maybe thirty seconds!"

"Retreat, Retreat," I yelled. It wasn't hard to sound afraid. I slung both rifles over my shoulder.

At my horse, I jerked at the reins twisted in the brush, tearing them loose. I followed José as the explosion echoed through the canyon.

It was almost dark when we reached a trail and rode up into the trees. The climb became steep, and we had to lead the horses. We slipped and clawed our way up, Addy leaning forward, her face in the horse's mane.

When we were near the top of the first hill, we stopped, and José helped Addy down. She was more alert and watched us warily.

We waited and listened.

"What kind of men are these people" Addy murmured. "They're animals."

"Animals are not so mean," José said over his shoulder.

We could hear the men starting up the trail. They cursed and scrambled through the brush. José lit a short fuse and tossed the dynamite over the hillside.

This time the explosion came much sooner, and there was a

shower of dirt and small rocks.

We listened for several minutes. Either the Freebooters were dead or had retreated.

"José, we need to send a signal. We have to move to higher ground."

José checked Addy's leg. "Are you alright? Can you ride?"

"You are drunk. I can smell liquor on you. Why should I go with you? You could be as bad as them." Her dark eyes flicked back and forth, accusing us both. "How do I know you aren't part of them?"

José moved back. "I am not drunk. I sloshed whiskey on my shirt to convince the Freebooters we were drunk. It was part of the plan."

Addy didn't look convinced.

Guilt overwhelmed me. I was responsible for the death of two people. "We had to get the men to go up the canyon," I said weakly, "but we never dreamed—never thought. I am so sorry about your family."

The simplest actions could cause so much suffering, and I hadn't considered the ramifications of our simple plan. I had hoped the last two years had curbed my impulsive nature, only to find that it remained with disastrous consequences. I quaked inside, the whole world trembling around me.

José offered his hand to Addy. "Let me help you on the horse."

"I am not getting on a horse with either of you."

In one quick move, José grabbed Addy and lifted her, kicking, onto the saddle. She tried to slide off the other side, and he grabbed her wrist. "You need to come with us. We own the airship. We can make you safe."

He took off his hat, his face earnest in the dim light. "I promise I will not hurt you."

"Listen to him—he rescued you in the middle of gunfire. We will keep you safe."

All the fight left Addy. She leaned forward and buried her face in the mane. Her muffled "I want to go home" tore at my chest.

23

"With the Freebooters in the canyon, no one is safe," I said. "But we have a home. It is a safe place—there are others—girls and women. They will help you."

José stepped up in the stirrup. "Slide back and hang on. We may not have much time." He swung his leg over the horse's head.

Addy didn't hesitate. She put her arms loosely around José, a quiet sob breaking the silence.

We rode without talking. It was getting darker by the minute, but the moon was on the rise. We came to a break in the trees and stopped.

"I will put out the wire." José slid down and looked up at Addy. "Will you stay—please? We do not have time to look for you. You do not want to be out here by yourself."

Addy sat up straighter. "I promise." She let José lift her down.

José took the spool of wire and moved quickly through the glade. I pounded the stakes into the ground.

"Can you turn this crank? It will make this go faster." I moved the box to where she was sitting. I gave it a turn. "About this fast."

Addy began to crank. "I have forgotten your friend's name?"

"José. He is a good man. You can depend on him with your life. I do."

"I shouldn't have been so mean to him back there. He saved my life."

"He understands." I began to tap out the message. "Keep cranking steadily."

NEED PICK UP AT FIRST LIGHT STOP HAVE YOUNG WOMAN STOP FAMILY DEAD STOP L AND M SHOULD

COME STOP

"This is like the telegraph in the train station," Addy said.

"Yes, but this one doesn't need wires on poles to send messages."

"Are you people magic?"

"Not magic. Sometimes I wish we were. I would say words that put an end to all this Freebooter trouble—that would bring back your father and brother. No, we are not magic, but we have inventions that seem like magic."

The key began clicking. WILL RAISE STEAM STOP L

EAST SIDE OF THE LAST CANYON BEFORE CAJÓN STOP MARY KNOWS STOP FURTHER DOWN THAN BEFORE STOP WILL FLAG.

LOVE L

LOVE W

I gave two tugs on the antennae, and José came toward us, winding the wire.

"Can we chance a fire?" he wondered. "There are big rocks over there. We can keep the fire small."

"I think so. Addy, let me help you get to the lee of that outcropping."

In a few minutes, José had a small fire of twigs. I went to the trees with the hatchet and brought two armloads of wood. It was cold, and clouds were moving over the moon. "Could be a bad night," I said.

José pulled a square of oilcloth from his saddlebag. He stepped two stakes into the ground and stretched it to the rock, making it fast with rope.

The fire felt good, and it didn't rain hard. José cooked eggs.

Addy flipped an unburnt end of wood into the fire. "How did you get eggs here in your saddlebags?"

"Packed in the flour tin I carry."

"Addy, you will learn from watching José," I said. "He'll be making tortillas in the morning if the ship doesn't come first."

José gave Addy a quick glance.

We rechecked Addy's wound. The bullet had torn through the side of the calf muscle, but it was not bleeding. José retied the bandanna. "Too tight?"

"No. Thank you." Addy shivered from the shock. We put her next to the fire, wrapped in a blanket, and José and I huddled beside the rock under the other blanket.

When I was sure Addy was asleep, I whispered, "José, we caused this. We sent the Freebooters up the canyon."

"Yes. But we did not kill Addy's family. Freebooters did that. We would not *be* here if there were no Freebooters." Jose took a deep breath. "Those guys were after Addy—they would have showed up sooner or later."

I wasn't sure I felt much better. However, in the business of fighting Freebooters, people died. We were in a war, but I didn't like being a soldier.

"You do smell like a drunk," I joked.

"I am sorry I said that," Addy whispered. "I should have known you couldn't run with me if you were drunk."

I was embarrassed to think Addy may have heard us. I once heard a Methodist Circuit Rider say, "Do no harm, do good, and stay in love with God." Apparently, one could do harm when trying to do good.

Twice we went for wood but found no dry limbs of any size. The clouds blocked the moon most of the night. When there was a break, we stumbled around and were able to keep the fire burning.

Later José found a dead limb deeper in the woods and dragged it close. He hacked it up with the hatchet. When the fire was burning well, I fell into an uneasy sleep. José tended the fire through the night. Twice Addy moaned, and both times José was watching. Once he gave her water.

There was only a glimmer of morning light when I heard the *Cloud Queen*'s airscrews. I was stiff and cold and scrambled to my feet. José was in the meadow, waving a bandanna on the end of a broken limb.

Addy sat up and stared in awe as the *Cloud Queen* settled gently in the meadow.

Benny hit the ground running and grabbed the saddlebags. "We'll have company soon. They were camping up on the mesa—maybe a mile."

Finn lowered the front gangplank. We were tossing the gear on the deck when the first shot cracked in the air.

José scooped Addy up and ran up the gangplank. I snatched the oilcloth, a rifle on the *Cloud Queen* returning fire.

Laura was in the pilothouse, her rifle pointing through the crack between the shields. On the side deck, Dad shot as well. I scanned the campsite to be sure we had left nothing and scrambled aboard.

Benny and José hurried the horses onto the ship, and the clockwork gears began raising the forward gangplank. A bullet tore into the hull as the *Cloud Queen* lifted.

I ran to the starboard to get a clear view of the meadow. I counted three renegades remaining and touched Dad's shoulder. "We can't kill them all. They must report that we are somewhere up this canyon."

Dad nodded and put the rifle aside.

"Come to the forward cabin," Laura called. "We have breakfast."

José had laid Addy on a bench, and Benny set up a cot near the stove. Addy sat up and insisted that she did not need to be babied. José stood to the side in a fresh shirt.

He came to stand by me. "We should ask Addy if she wants to get anything from her cabin."

"You ask her. You're her hero," I teased.

José said, "I am no hero." He grinned sheepishly.

In the following minutes, he paced back and forth. Finally, he clenched his fists and knelt beside her. "Addy, do you want to get anything from your house? We need to bury your papa—your brother."

Addy's eyes were moist. "Won't it be dangerous?"

"We will keep watch up and down the canyon. It can be done."

"This is important," Laura added.

"I need to find plants for her wound," José said. "They draw poison."

We ate a solemn breakfast at the big table.

José, Addy, Laura, and I went to the Thomas's cabin as the *Cloud Queen* floated above. José and I went in first to wrap the bodies in blankets and carry them outside. Laura helped Addy to the cabin.

Addy pointed to a wooden box. "Those are my mother's dishes—and the chickens. I know it's silly—but who'll take care of them?"

"The guys will get your chickens." Laura handed me some

90

clothes wrapped in a blanket. "Take these—you fellows stay outside and catch chickens." She went back into the cabin.

We found six chickens in the coop and had them in gunny sacks when Laura helped Addy onto the porch. Addy was in a dress, and her hair had been brushed. She glanced at José.

There was an awkward silence, and I finally said, "You look nice, Addy."

José came to life. "Addy, it would be better to bury Fred and your father in the meadow. Here in the canyon, it could flood."

Addy was quiet. I wasn't sure she had heard him when she whispered, "The meadow would be good. Papa planned to build a proper house up there. He always talked of living in a green meadow. In the spring, it is beautiful."

Laura began to help Addy back to the clearing.

We pulled and tugged until we got the cow up the ramp. She bawled, blowing steam in the morning air.

José brought two shovels from a small shed and put them on the bow deck. "Will, I am mad."

"I know. I am too."

"No. This must be stopped. There can be no more of this."

"I know, friend, but first, we must make them believe that our base is further up this canyon."

We started for the bodies when José held me back with one arm, and the *Cloud Queen* lifted. A Freebooter was sneaking out of the shadows along the canyon wall toward the cabin.

24

José charged, heaving a large rock that hit the man square between the shoulders. Surprised, the Freebooter turned in time for the butt of José's pistol to snap his jaw sideways. The Freebooter twisted, and José backhanded him with the gun. The fellow gave a muffled groan and sprawled in the sand. José held the unconscious man at gunpoint.

Two shots popped in the air, and the *Cloud Queen* came down quickly. "The Freebooters are coming up the canyon," Mary shouted. "Everyone, on board! Now!"

The *Cloud Queen* settled hard in the clearing. Dad lifted Addy onto the deck. Benny and José threw the Freebooter aboard, and I swung the box of dishes up and grabbed the chickens. The blower howled, and the deck pressed hard under my feet.

"They separated." Dad gestured toward the renegade on the deck. "We thought we had put this guy down. We had our eyes on the other two and missed him."

Liam shot twice from the port side as the *Cloud Queen* swung down the canyon.

I looked down the canyon with the hand glass. "We have to capture them or send them far down the canyon. We need time to bury Addy's family."

"I say we get their horses," José said with steel in his voice. "Having to walk will slow them down. It will take longer to bring the news back to their friends. No riding for them."

"José is right," I decided. "Those bums don't need horses. They probably stole 'em, anyway. They only need to get to the telegraph office."

We hovered over the canyon, watching from the bow.

"There." Mary pointed from the pilothouse door. "They are riding down the canyon." Bells rang, and the airscrews churned as Mary cut the corners of the meandering canyon.

José stepped to the winch controls. "I will have the chain ready if we can catch them in a wide spot." The motor whirred.

I went to the pilothouse and directed Mary to take us high enough to keep the chain out of the trees. The airscrews ran hard, and we made good time, the morning down breeze helping our speed. José joined us.

Mary pointed to a slope to the east. "The canyon turns up ahead. What if we flew on the other side of that hill? Could we get around them without their knowing it?"

Laura pounded up the stairs. "They are coming back on us now!"

Several shots rang from the canyon below.

"Fools cannot hit anything at that distance with pistols," José said.

"Let's get them. Mary, good job, but let Laura do this. You take care of the engine order telegraph and speaking tube—Laura needs to concentrate on guiding the ship. José, get the dynamite."

In the engine room, Benny was at the forward drop port, and Liam had a load of rocks in one of the chutes over the rear port.

"Lower, lower," Benny called. "Rocks! Rocks!"

Liam pulled the trapdoor in the chute.

"Ha! One is off his horse. The other went up the canyon."

Mary rang for Stop. Below, the Freebooter's head was bloody, and he didn't move.

We drifted several hundred yards down the canyon, and José tossed a quarter stick of dynamite with a slow fuse off the stern.

I went to the speaking tube and called to the pilothouse, "One down, and we dropped dynamite. Let's get the Freebooter up the canyon."

The *Cloud Queen* groaned into a turn. I was proud of the way Laura and Mary handled the airship. Laura had us low, running at Flank, but the renegade rode faster than we could fly.

Mary called for us to take the *Cloud Queen* up five hundred more feet. The canyon had a large bend, and Laura cut the corner, saving us a half-mile.

I spotted over the side, and José stood ready. We intercepted the Freebooter and swooped low, but not close enough. He turned and started down the canyon.

"Did the fuse burn out?" I asked José. "How long has it been?"

An explosion in the distance answered my question.

Laura brought us around.

"It is like a dog chasing a rabbit," José said.

"Yes, and rabbits get tired," Liam grunted.

As soon as the canyon widened again, Mary called for us to go lower. Benny spotted the chain, and I worked the control lever.

Mary called down, "The man has turned again. He is going to ride under us. Chain! Chain!"

I let the chain down and watched for the Freebooter. Willows snapped back in place as the chain moved along.

"Enough of this." José grabbed a rope and jogged to the back of the ship.

Three muffled shots came from the starboard.

"The chain missed," Benny grumbled. "He dodged to the side."

Mary rang for Slow and called, "Go out on the rear deck. You have to see this."

We crowded down the hall between the cabins. On the rear deck, José had a long rope on the Freebooter. It looped under one arm and around his neck. José had jerked the man off the horse and pulled hard on the line. The man stumbled to stay on his feet, trying to slip out of the rope. With lightning speed, José hauled the Freebooter in, hand over hand.

The man ducked out of the rope and scrambled up the side of the canyon, throwing the pistol aside. Liam shot below the renegade twice to encourage the speed of his climb.

"Now we get his horse." José swung onto his chestnut, and when we touched down, he was down the gangplank. The Freebooter's rifle was still in the leather slip. The horse spooked and ran back up the canyon, tail high. José urged his horse into a gallop.

The *Cloud Queen* sat two hundred yards from where we had knocked the first man off his horse. The gelding stood near the stream, eating grass.

While Dad and Liam went to check the Freebooter on the ground, I walked to the horse. He was a pretty Paint with blue eyes and allowed me to pick up the reins. I thought it odd that the blast hadn't sent the horse running in a panic. I slipped up in the saddle and gave a piercing whistle. The horse didn't even flicker his ears. I leaned forward and clapped my hands near his ears. The horse was deaf!

Liam and Dad returned from examining the Freebooter. "He may or may not wake up. He's sleeping pretty soundly," Dad said. "He won't bother us." He tossed two pistols and a gun belt on the deck. "The only other thing he had was a packet of tea. I don't understand all this tea. Perhaps the renegade army is more genteel than I thought."

We laid the Freebooter with the broken jaw in the middle of the canyon. Benny untied his arms but left his ankles tied together. "He will find his friend when he wakes up," Benny said.

José trotted his horse down the canyon leading the Freebooter's chestnut. "I gathered plants for Addy's leg," he said.

When the horses were on board, we hovered above the canyon. José made a poultice from the leaves, and Mary washed the wound again and wrapped it.

We took the *Cloud Queen* back up the canyon and slowed over Addy's cabin. There was no sign of the Freebooter who had climbed the hillside, so we loaded the bodies. José brought wooden stakes from the shed.

The *Cloud Queen* floated over the meadow, standing sentinel as we worked. Winter rains left the ground soft, and it wasn't long until we had two graves. José made two crosses and said a prayer over the graves. Addy's shoulders shook, tears running down her cheeks.

Laura stood behind her with her arms around her. "You let us know when you are ready to go."

Addy turned, sobbing against Laura's shoulder, and then let Laura and Benny help her away. The *Cloud Queen* settled to earth while José and I gathered the tools.

Addy sat silent, staring at the wall of the forward cabin. Mary wrapped a blanket around her, and held her close—whispering quietly.

I was heartily ashamed, but the morning's battle had driven my anguish away. We were fighting an enemy who would stop at nothing to get what they wanted.

25

Laura and I took the *Cloud Queen* high above the pines. "Will Addy be alright?" I asked.

"No, but yes. She is like so many we have seen in this world. Think of Mary and what she has endured. Eagle's Crest will be good for her."

"José saved Addy from what could have been horrible. You should have seen him. He ran, scooped her up, and was under the trees near the bluff in moments."

Below, the canyon twisted back and forth like a lazy snake lying in the sun.

"This is far enough," Laura said. "We haven't seen miners for several miles."

I went to the speaking tube. "We are turning for Eagle's Crest."

Laura set the engine order telegraph for Full.

Mary came up. "You two go eat." I lingered while Mary checked the compass and looked at me over her shoulder. "Go eat, Will. I know the way home."

In the forward cabin, we had a feast. Even Addy ate with some enthusiasm.

"Hey, Will, should I bring you a cup of tea?" Benny joked. "Your father found a tea packet on the Freebooter." He lifted his cup delicately with a crooked finger.

"The tea drinking is a mystery, I'll say that. Almost makes me want to give it up." I reached for a cup. The tension evaporated from the room while we ate. José and I took turns relieving Liam in the engine room as we relaxed after the meal.

The sun was low when Mary called down, "Eagle's Crest."

Laura and I went to the pilothouse. I always loved the sight of Eagle's Crest from a distance. Nestled in the dusk, lights aglow, it was an oasis.

Mary brought us down near the workshop. When we touched the earth, José and Benny made a chair of their arms and carried Addy across the yard to the main lodge. I stayed behind to help put the *Cloud Queen* to bed.

We were unloading the horses when Mary came down from the pilothouse. "I want to check the greenhouse."

"Would you believe the Paint is deaf?" I said.

Mary stopped. "He's a beautiful gelding." She rubbed his forehead. "Such beautiful eyes. You come with me, sweetheart. I will take good care of you." The Paint nuzzled her shoulder as they headed to the barn.

"Because of the attack from the air, I would like to put the *Cloud Queen* in the shop," I told Finn.

Bringing the ship in required Paul and Dad working with ropes.

Dolph came running breathlessly. "Captain Will! Finn! The telegraph is going. They are talking to Sacramento."

In the workshop, we let Dolph decode the messages for us. He carefully printed out each message. "I corrected their spelling," he said.

LOCATED CANYON WHERE STEAMBOAT HIDES STOP SENDING TWO SQUADS

WHAT ABOUT NEW SHIP STOP REPORT

ENGINE TROUBLES STOP BEARING PROBLEM STOP WILL POUR MORE BABBIT STOP WILL BE FLYING IN A WEEK.

FOOLS STOP SHIP HAS A NEW ENGINE AT HIGH EXPENSE.

MAYBE DEFECTIVE

WILL NOT TOLERATE FAILURE STOP DRINK LESS WHISKEY MORE TEA STOP

WILL BE READY TO FLY SOON STOP WILL MAKE THE RENDEZVOUS WITH OTHER SHIPS ON TIME

"Good job, Dolph," Finn said.

Dolph smiled, rolled up the tape, and put it in one of the small tins. He dipped a pen and wrote the date on a piece of paper. "Are you going to go destroy their ship, Captain Will?"

"Well, that is hard to say, Dolph. We may need to let it lead us to the other ships." I checked the faces of the others. "We don't know how many ships the Freebooters have."

"Will, I need our supplies from Salsbury," Finn said.

"Then we'll take the original crew down tomorrow. We can take the new horses to him."

26

In the mornings, before a flight, I was always restless, anxious to be in the air. I fretted about Mr. Salsbury's safety. He was a tough old codger, but I couldn't shake an uneasy feeling. At the first hint of dawn, I found Finn tending the boiler with a full head of steam. Mary insisted on keeping the Paint, so we substituted another. The horses loaded easily, and we sailed straight for Mr. Salsbury's cabin. When we were over the clearing, Mr. Salsbury greased a wagon wheel and gave us only a cursory glance.

"Something seems odd," Laura said. "He always waves us in."

"Bring us down. José, be ready with rifles," I called to the engine room.

Benny and José took up places near the telescope. Mr. Salsbury continued his work as we touched the ground.

"Good morning, Mr. Salsbury." I jumped down and went over to the wagon. "We came for our shipment."

"I didn't go down to get the things," he said. "Just didn't seem right."

I was stunned. "What do you mean, not right?" José and Benny took up places a few feet away.

"Well, it seems to me that you folks are fighting the Army of the United States of America, and we should all support our Army. I don't think I can help someone who's against the Army of the United States of America." Mr. Salsbury turned back to his work. "Just don't seem right."

"Last time we were here, you said you would fight them if you had to."

"That was before." He stood to ease his back. "You fellers

think you know everything. You're just Unenlightened fools. I know more now."

The word unenlightened struck me as unusual. Mr. Salsbury's speech patterns didn't include such a word. Our kind old friend was almost belligerent—condescending.

Finn joined us. "Are the items we ordered still in town?"

"Maybe yes, maybe no. I suppose your supplies might be there unless they sent them back."

Mr. Salsbury went to the rear of the wagon and lifted a cup. "I have a fresh pot of tea if you would care for some."

I had never seen Mr. Salsbury drink anything but coffee. We declined.

"Do you mind if we load the oil?" I asked.

"Took it back. Like I say, it don't seem right, you young folks going up against the Army of the United States of America." He handed me several bills. "Nope, we're done doing business. That ship of yours should be handed over to the Army." He glanced at José's rifle. "Ain't right."

I gestured that we should return to the *Cloud Queen* and gave orders to lift off. "Take us up the canyon to the flat."

In the air, I said, "Something is very wrong. It's like he has been hypnotized. He's not the same man."

"He repeats the 'Army of the United States of America' as if it is a prayer in church," José said.

"We need our supplies," Finn said. "How do we go about getting them? We have only the horses we were going to give Mr. Salsbury. We'll need a wagon."

Laura hovered over a sandy bend in the creek.

"The supplies should be at your dad's store," Finn grumbled. "I say we fly down and get them. This is costing us time."

I shook my head. "We can't chance landing in town to load supplies."

"Primo works our ranch. We can use the ranch wagon," José said.

"This will take two days," Finn protested.

"We're all frustrated, Finn, but no, we'll land at the lodge and ride down. It's less likely anyone will see the ship."

"After we let you off, we will take the ship to the high mountains," Laura said. "We don't know who is around these days.

This is spooky."

"José, Finn, and I will go into town," I said. "Finn, you will know what supplies to bring. We will leave the new horses at the Rodriquez ranch."

The sun was high when we turned the *Cloud Queen* east, sailing toward our canyon.

Laura knew the terrain well, and we soon hovered over the mine. Our dynamite blast had done its work on the mouth of the cavern, and there was no sign of the area being disturbed.

"There are only a few hours of daylight left," Laura said. "You better get started."

We made a quick landing at Wolfskill, and the lodge appeared untouched. We took only pistols and saddle packs. We spent an hour leading the animals through the rubble left from the blasting, with Finn grumbling the whole way. We trotted the horses to the mouth of the canyon and arrived at the Rodriquez farm near twilight. Primo thanked us for the horses and walked with José to check the crops.

In the morning, Finn was up early, anxious to get started. "I already talked to Eagle's Crest and the *Cloud Queen*. They are keeping the boiler hot above the mine."

It occurred to me that if Finn was in such a hurry, he might have hitched the wagon. José and I made short work of the task. We shivered as we trundled down the valley. The winter sun was bright, and we were glad for its warming rays.

"No unnecessary talking when we get to town," I said. "We don't need any questions."

"Let's load the equipment and get out of here," Finn agreed. "Get in the air and get home."

We pulled our hats low as we rode into town. The buildings appeared the same, but I sensed much had changed. Jim was sweeping the boardwalk when we stopped the wagon in front of Dad's store.

"Hey, Jim," I said quietly. "It's Will."

Jim glanced up and down the street and gestured for us to come closer. "Good to see you. Be careful. There are strangers in town, and they should be avoided."

Two men I didn't recognize chatted on a stoop, and a woman in a fancy dress stood at the corner, fiddling with a parasol. She caught Finn's eye and beckoned with a gloved hand.

I had never seen Finn show much interest in girls, but the

young woman was quite stylish.

"Young man," she called, "I cannot seem to master the mechanism of this parasol. The morning sun is simply a glare."

Jim hesitated, watching the woman. "Be careful," he whispered.

"Finn, we better get inside and check the supplies," I said.

"It will only take a second." Finn walked toward the young woman.

She struggled with the parasol and said something to Finn. He nodded, a silly grin on his face.

"Watch him closely," Jim said. "Don't let him out of sight."

José and I moved within earshot.

"Oh, my. I think it is something here on the end," the woman said. "It is like something is caught in the little hinges."

Finn examined the tip of the parasol. He jumped back, startled, and the woman leaned forward, laughed, and whispered in his ear. Finn listened intently, smiling.

Suddenly, the woman's parasol popped open. "Oh, my, you are wonderful! Silly me. I needed a smart young man." She put the parasol on her shoulder and gave it a twirl. She leaned forward and whispered again. She stood straight and patted Finn's cheek. "Thank you, young man. You are wonderful." She walked briskly down the boardwalk, Finn staring after her.

"Finn, come on. We have work to do."

Finn came as far as the storefront but turned to look back at the woman. "We have plenty of time."

"Finn, I think you are starstruck," José laughed. "You have love in your eyes."

"She is wise," Finn said. "A remarkable woman with insights into the workings of the world."

Jim folded his arms. "What did she say to you?"

Finn gave Jim a knowing smile as if Jim were a small child. "You wouldn't understand."

"We need to keep moving," I said.

Finn stared at me but not focusing his eyes. "I was thinking, we don't need anything. We have everything we need at Eagle's Crest. It is safe there. We can relax—let the problems of the world work themselves out. There is little we can do in the greater scheme of things."

José gave Finn a thump on the back. "Snap out of the dream,

Finn. We must get what we came for." José grabbed Finn by the jacket sleeve and towed him into the store.

"I have seen this before," Jim whispered. "He will be different. Half the town is different. Do not let him out of your sight. I've never seen this one with an umbrella. Once a woman wanted me to smell flowers she had picked, but I didn't bite." He started to move away and then added, "And no tea!"

"Tea?" Finn brightened. "A cup of tea would be lovely."

Tea? We could hardly get Finn to take time to eat.

Jim led us to the back room and showed us the equipment. "It's all here," he said.

"What do you think, Finn?" I asked.

He looked at the stack of gears and springs and shrugged. "Why don't we go down to that little cafe and have a cup of tea?"

"José, let's start loading the wagon." I reached into my pocket and handed Jim a wad of bills. "This should cover it. I don't know when we will get back this way."

Finn wandered behind the counter. "Where is your tea?"

"I will wrap some up for you, no charge." Jim winked at me.

José snapped his fingers in Finn's face. "Finn! Here, help me carry these tools out. These are for your lathe."

Finn took the box and walked to the wagon. José and I followed him with spools of electric wire.

"Do we take the sewing machine?" I wondered. "It's bulky if we have trouble."

José began to wrap it. "Letty is making all our clothes. She needs it and more cloth."

Finn shrugged and started toward the front of the store.

"He cannot be left alone. He may wander off," Jim said. "Get the rest of your supplies. I'll watch him."

The machine fit nicely behind the wagon seat, and José lashed the cabinet down. We made several more trips while Finn stood with Jim staring down the street toward the cafe.

I grabbed Finn's arm. "Finn, get in the wagon. We are going back to the *Cloud Queen*. Laura can make you a cup of tea."

The two men left the stoop and wandered close. Jim glanced at them and handed me a package. "Give him this blend. It is good for those who want to drink tea." He gave me a knowing smile. "No regular tea," he whispered. "Understood?"

"We would like some of that tea, storekeeper. You say it is good?"

Jim smiled. "Yes, sir! It is a new blend. It makes a splendid cup of tea."

"Thanks, storekeeper," I said.

Finn climbed into the back of the wagon and seemed happy enough to simply sit. José climbed up in the seat with me.

The woman Finn had helped stood across the street with her parasol closed.

I leaned close to José. "We need that umbrella. And don't breathe around the tip of it."

José jumped down and walked briskly across the street to where the woman struggled with her parasol. He bowed in front of the woman and appeared to offer to help. She pushed it toward his face and whispered in his ear.

José smiled stupidly and then grabbed her parasol and hugged it. The woman seemed startled by the speed at which José moved. He sprinted across the street and jumped up on the wagon in one leap.

"Whew, I have been holding my breath. A puff of air came out of the end."

I clicked the reins, and we rolled past the woman. She started to step toward the wagon when José called, "I must have this wonderful umbrella, ma'am. It smells so good." He hugged the umbrella, pretending to sniff the end. I coaxed the horses into a trot, and we drove quickly out of town.

I glanced back at Finn. He sat smiling, staring at the scenery. "We have to make sure he doesn't try to jump off or do something foolish."

"Will he be like this forever?"

"I don't know. Jim said no tea for him. Perhaps tea is part of the effect."

About a mile from the Rodriquez farm, gunshots came from behind us. I clicked the horses to a trot. Three men rode behind us on horseback.

"We should not go to the farm. It puts Primo in danger." José drew my attention to the Cloud Queen dropping from high above.

I turned the horses off the track toward an open field, but the *Cloud Queen* leveled off and flew over us. A stick of dynamite looped end over end as she began to come around.

José turned in the seat, leveling his pistol, but Finn pushed the gun aside. "We should not fight against the Army of the United States of America. You ought to know better. You had a talk with the beautiful woman. Didn't she give you the words of wisdom?"

José pushed Finn's arm away and shot two times before Finn batted at the gun again.

The dynamite blast was sudden, and the Freebooter horses skittered. The riders pulled reins behind a rolling cloud of dust. The *Cloud Queen* flew back over us, toward the far end of the field.

Benny came out on the back deck with a rifle, watched for a moment, and disappeared. With a crew of two, he would be busy in the engine room.

The *Cloud Queen* made a bumpy landing, and we rolled alongside. I looped the reins through a railing post.

Benny came onto the deck. "Hurry, the dynamite only slowed them down. They're coming."

"Benny, get Finn into the engine room," I called. "There's something wrong. Tie him up if necessary."

Another shot came from behind, and Laura returned fire with a rifle on the upper deck. The men slowed and took cover behind a clump of sumac.

Benny joined us at the wagon. "Finn is just staring at the engine. I told him to oil the bearings."

We lugged supplies, piling them on the deck, while Laura continued to fire.

"Leave the sewing machine," I said.

José stood in the back of the wagon. "No, Letty needs it." He drew his pistol and fired three shots into the sumac.

With a snap of his wrist, he cut the rope and lifted the machine to Benny and me. We wrestled it over the ship's railing.

José slapped the rump of the off horse, shouting, "Heyah." The team trotted lazily across the field, the wagon bouncing and rattling.

Benny went to the engine room, and we lifted straight up.

Laura brought the *Cloud Queen* around, and I went to the telescope. The men had crept around the brush. Only one was in uniform, and they were not shooting.

José joined me. "Do we give them some rocks?"

"I think they're mostly town's people. Leave them. We don't want to stir up any more trouble. It could be bad for Jim. Sorry the wagon and horses didn't get back to the farm."

José waved me off. "Primo will tell them we stole the wagon and horses. He is good at playing the fool. They will believe him. Besides, he has three new horses today."

I signaled for Laura to head back up the canyon. The *Cloud Queen* turned, and the airscrews began to churn the air. In the engine room, Benny adjusted the injector, eyeing his gauges. Finn stared at his beautiful engine with disinterest.

27

"He is not the Finn we know," Benny whispered. "He didn't even want to work the levitation lever."

"Something happened in town. A woman with this parasol spoke to him. This is a dangerous weapon—don't breathe near the tip." I gave the parasol to Benny. "I'll tend the engine. Handle it gingerly. Put it where Finn cannot find it."

Benny carried the parasol to the back cabins.

"Finn, do you want to have some of the tea Jim gave us?"

He brightened. "Yes, we should drink tea several times a day. It is good to enjoy a cup of tea."

I handed him the bag. "Why don't you stir up the cookstove fire and boil some water? Jim said this is a delicious new tea. I would like to try some."

"We can try it now." Finn went happily into the forward cabin.

José came in from the stern. "The men did not try to follow. They caught the horses and drove the wagon back to town."

"Finn is making some of the tea Jim gave us. Wait for Laura to set our speed—then come to the pilothouse." I checked the burner and pressure and went upstairs.

Laura put her hand on the Engine Order Telegraph. "I'm taking us far north. I don't want the Freebooters to see us." She rang for Full. "What's wrong with Finn?"

"While we were in town, Finn helped a woman with her parasol. He came away dazed. Since then, he has no interest in the ship and thinks we should not fight the Army."

Laura's eyes were big. "What did she do to him?"

José joined us.

"We are not sure, but it has something to do with her parasol. We have it. We'll examine it at Eagle's Crest."

"Finn would be the one to figure it out," she said.

"Finn is not figuring anything out." José shook his head. "He acts like a child who just woke up from a nap."

"José, when you were with the woman, what did she say?"

"She spoke quickly. She said, 'You enjoy having a cup of tea. Tea is good for you. Drink it several times a day. Go to Mr. Albertson at the bank for a meeting on the first and fifteenth of each month. Never hurt the Army. The Army of the United States of America always does good.' The next shows a big part of the Freebooter puzzle. She said, 'Obey any order from the Adjunct Leader in Sacramento. Always support and please the Adjunct Leader.'"

"Adjunct Leader? Sacramento?" This was bigger than we anticipated.

"Albertson must be part of this," Laura said. "He always seemed like a decent sort."

"If he is under the influence of a puff of air, he could be completely different," José said. "We cannot trust anyone."

"No wonder Finn didn't want you to shoot. The men following us must have been part of the Army, renegades, or—" I was at a loss for words.

I told them about the flowers offered to Jim. "Mr. Salsbury must have been given the treatment."

"This explains Mr. Salsbury's sudden support of the Army of the United States of America," Laura said.

I made a quick decision. "We will discuss this later at Eagle's Crest. Now we must get José and me closer to the renegade airship. I have decided we must destroy it. That ship can never be allowed to fly."

José agreed. "It is hard to tell what we are dealing with now. The Freebooter problem has become complicated. With that ship, they might attack the town or who knows what?"

"Yes, but first things first. We have to deal with Finn. Laura, in a minute, we will go down to the forward cabin. I'll send Benny up. We are going to have 'tea' with Finn. José and I will distract him. Get the tea we have in the cupboard and get rid of it. Finn is not to drink our tea."

"Now we know how people become Tea Drinkers," Laura

murmured.

"I am afraid so. Jim gave us some special tea. I don't know the difference, but he was insistent that it was the only tea Finn should drink."

"Do we dare trust Jim?"

"Yes, he appeared to be himself and warned us to stay away from strangers."

"Why would Finn talk to a woman? He's always so shy."

I grinned. "Well, she was stylish—comely. She charmed him off his pins."

Laura touched my chin. "We women have our ways." Her coat brushed the stairs as I followed her down.

Finn had set cups on the table and was pouring tea. He sat down with a satisfied look. "I am going to sit and enjoy a cup of tea. Join me?"

José and I sat down, admiring our cups. "It's good to have tea with friends," I said.

"It is good to enjoy a cup of tea," Finn intoned.

Laura slipped the tea tin out of the cupboard and stepped out. On her return, she emptied part of the new package into the tin.

"This tea tastes funny," Finn said.

"I think it has some jasmine mixed in." Laura gave Finn a dreamy look and took a sip. "Oh, I like this. Try it again." She looked him straight in the eye. "You will enjoy a cup of tea."

"Yes." Finn seemed undecided and then took a sip. "It is nice to be enjoying a cup of tea."

Laura leaned toward Finn. "I think it tastes divine, don't you, Finn?"

"Yes. It's divine." Finn gazed right through us.

Laura winked at me. "Finn, did we get all the supplies we needed?" she asked.

"It is all there, but I told Will we can get along without that stuff. We need to spend more time relaxing like this and less time worrying about the Army. The Army of the United States of America does what it does for our own good."

"Yes, Finn," I said, playing along.

She leaned toward Finn. "When we get back, will you finish the extra ship radios you started?"

"I was thinking I would take a few days off. I have been

working too hard."

Laura gave him one of her big smiles. "Finn, you could finish a couple for *me*, couldn't you? I'll make you some of the cakes you like. They would be good to enjoy with a cup of tea."

Finn sipped his tea. "I will make two radios for some of your cakes." He sat back. "They would be good to enjoy with a cup of tea." He took another swallow, looking at nothing in particular.

"Will, we are above the canyon," Benny called down the stairs.

I took the steps two at a time. We were several miles below the Army camp. "Good job, Benny. Trade with me. Man the engines. I'll give their camp a wide berth and go further up the canyon."

Finn came up and looked out. "I think I am going to go back and read. Maybe take a nap."

I couldn't remember Finn ever taking a nap. "Go ahead. After your nap, we can have a nice cup of tea."

"Yes, it is good to enjoy a cup of tea."

After Finn went to the rear cabin, we met in the pilothouse.

"It is like talking to a three-year-old who repeats himself," José said.

"Yes, but we have learned something," Laura noted. "Tie a request to having a cup of tea, and he seems more receptive."

"And we cannot mention the Army or our battle with them," I said.

"Try it the other way." José had a sly smile on his face. "If Finn questions our actions, we tell him we are helping the Army."

Laura was thoughtful. "Yes, but we dare not be too obvious. He isn't stupid—just stupefied by whatever was in the umbrella."

"How long will the effect last? Is this permanent?" I asked.

"The command to drink tea must have something to do with it," Laura said. "Finn was told he would enjoy a cup of tea for some reason. Perhaps it is the caffeine."

"Coffee has caffeine, too," I remarked. "Maybe something in regular tea enhances the effect."

"I was told to go to the bank twice a month," José said. "I do not think this lasts forever."

"The tea Jim gave us is terrible, but from now on, we all *enjoy* having a good cup of tea," Laura said.

José chuckled. "The things we do for this war."

I signaled for Stop and called Benny to the pilothouse. "We'll hover over this field until dark and tether the *Cloud Queen* with the anchor. José and I will check their progress."

"I will take the first watch in case we have visitors," José offered.

"In the meantime, I wonder if we can send a message while flying. I want to try." I brought out the transmitter. "Where would we put the wire out?"

"Could we hang it down from the front drop port?" José wondered.

I lamented not being able to ask Finn. "We can try grounding it to the boiler water tank."

José dangled the aerial wire below us, and I spun the generator crank. Laura clicked ANYONE LISTENING STOP.

We waited, surrounded by the engine's hiss and the fuel injector's gentle roar keeping the fire hot. WANT ME TO GET SOMEONE

The speed of the message left no doubt Dolph was eagerly taking his turn at the code station.

GOOD WORK DOLPH STOP YES GET AS MANY AS YOU CAN

I paced, burning off the excitement of talking to Eagle's Crest while in the air.

DOLPH SENDING STOP PAUL MARY NATHAN STOP

SENDING THIS FROM THE AIR STOP FINN NOT WELL STOP TEA BAD FOR HIM STOP HIDE ALL TEA STOP NO TEA FOR PRISONER

COME HOME STOP PRISONER NEWS

I was undecided. "What do you think? Can we be there by late evening?"

"We must leave Finn at Eagle's Crest. He is useless, and that means we are down a man. Liam can help man the engine room," Laura said.

I was anxious to check on the progress being made on the enemy ship, but I came to a decision. "Right, we need a fifth person. When José and I go into their shipbuilding operation, we need more than two on the airship. José, Benny, let's make speed. Three-thousand feet. Run at Flank."

COMING HOME, Laura clicked.

MR

I went to the pilothouse and set our course for Eagle's Crest. Laura opened the windows of the pilothouse, front and back.

"I am going back down to ask about Addy," Laura said. "I will make sure Finn is asleep."

We sailed over pine and oak. The whine of the blower told me we had quite a head of steam.

Later, Laura returned. "Addy is doing better. Her leg is healing, and she's limping all over Eagle's Crest. No infection, and she has an appetite. Mary has her helping weed the greenhouse. Mary says nothing heals the heart like getting your hands in the dirt."

Eagle's Crest was a place of healing, the perfect refuge from all the troubles in the world below.

"Do you think we could make more radios without Finn?" Laura asked.

"You and I think more alike all the time. Dolph probably knows how. If we open the one we have with us, we should be able to tell what parts we need."

The closer we got to Eagle's Crest, the better I felt. As the mountains passed below, it was remarkable how different the forest could be each year. It had been a wet winter, and the hills would soon be green with an early spring.

As evening shadow darkened the canyons below, we turned on the register and took turns sitting on it. We finally gave in and closed the windows.

Finn wandered up and stood looking out. The sun was still hitting the tops of the mountains, turning the snow a beautiful red. "I don't spend enough time up here. I am always cooped up in the engine room."

"Finn, we were thinking about the handheld code sender." I avoided eye contact. "Could you make two more for the *Cloud Queen* and the *Silver Seed*?"

"Why? We don't need them anymore now that we know it's not right to fight the Army."

Laura moved close. "But when we turn the ships over to the Army, wouldn't they be impressed if each had a radio?"

"We should help the Army of the United States of America whenever we can," Finn recited.

"The Adjunct Leader wants us to install radios," Laura said.

Finn looked up quickly. "How do you know the Adjunct

Leader?"

I was afraid Laura had gone too far, but she gazed into Finn's eyes. "He sent a letter. Jim gave it to Will at the store," she said.

Finn narrowed his eyes. "I didn't see a letter."

Laura didn't miss a beat. "The instructions were to read it and then destroy it. You trust the Adjunct Leader, don't you?"

Finn looked at Laura with admiration. "Yes. I will always do what the Adjunct Leader says. I wish he would send me a command."

"He did, Finn." Laura patted his arm. "That's why I am telling you this. He knew you had the ability to build the radios. He's depending on you."

Finn swelled with pride. "Of course. I knew he would find a way."

Laura casually stretched. "I would like a cup of tea. How about you?"

Finn brightened. "It is good to enjoy a cup of tea. I'll make a fresh pot." He went down the stairs.

I hugged Laura. "You are good. How did you know he would buy the idea?"

"It was a chance worth taking. If it didn't work, I figured we could handle Finn. Whatever is in the parasol makes him open to suggestion."

"Couldn't we tell him the other commands were wrong and turn him into the Finn we knew?"

"I am afraid that if he notices contradictions, it may cause more problems than it solves. We best use what he has been told to our advantage."

28

We tucked the *Cloud Queen* into her berth by midnight.

After breakfast, we met in the lodge. Everyone but Finn was there. He had insisted on building the radios, anxious to please the Adjunct Leader. After "enjoying" two cups of tea, he hurried away.

"Dolph," I said, "Finn is not well. We need you to go to the shop and help as usual. Don't mention his illness to him—he doesn't know he is sick. Tell us if he starts to do anything that doesn't seem right. Don't try to correct him; he may get the wrong idea. Don't say anything about us trying to defeat the Freebooters or the Army."

Dolph was all smiles. "Yes, Captain Will. I am the one for the job."

I liked that kid more every day.

We pulled chairs into a large semicircle in front of the fire, and I said, "So, Mary, in your message, you said that you have news about our prisoner."

Mary gestured toward John, sitting quietly on a stool at the far side of the room. He wasn't tied. She kept her voice low and said, "I've been making him work the crops. It is hard work outside. I have not been kind."

"Go on."

"About a week ago, John stopped constantly asking for tea, and there was a change in his manner. He's more cooperative. He didn't— leer so often." Mary blushed. "In fact, he has begun to act like a perfect gentleman."

"It is true," Liam said. "He has become cooperative. He doesn't fight us when we chain him to the wrecked ship." Liam shrugged. "I let him stay with me in the bunkhouse last night. It was cold, and we had snow. Sorry I didn't ask."

"We all must act on our best instincts," I replied, "and I hope we all offer each other leeway when something goes afoul."

There were murmurs of agreement.

"Go ahead, Mary."

"I am not asking to set him free or anything like that," Mary said, "but I think you should listen to what he has to say."

I nodded. "It can't hurt. Bring him over."

When John approached, I indicated that he should speak.

"My name is John Wells. I am from Kansas. I—I have been in a fog."

In the next few minutes, John told of being a barber in Kansas.

"I was coming back from the post office. A woman met me on the sidewalk and asked me to help her with the latch on her bag." John stopped and stared at the floor.

"Do you remember what she told you?" I asked.

"Yes and no. She told me that all people who are not Tea Drinkers are the Unenlightened—unimportant. The Unenlightened can be used for the work because they are ignorant. She told me to join the Army in California. She gave me a train ticket."

John stared at the floor, a vacant expression on his face. Mary indicated that we should wait.

The prisoner's head came up. "But this—this is not like remembering facts. It is more like remembering a dream—like when you try to tell someone about a dream, and it becomes faint and elusive."

"So you came to California," Mary prompted.

"Oh, yes. It was a pleasurable trip, sitting in the dining car, drinking tea with other men going to build airships."

"Why didn't you try to resist?"

"I am not sure." He struggled for words. "It's like, in a dream, you know what is happening may not be real or true, but you go along—you know—because it's part of the dream. You accept the parts that cannot be."

"John, here's a chair for you," Mary said.

He sat and stared into the fire, unmoving.

Mary prompted, "What happened next? What did you do in California?"

"We built the ship. Even at the time, I knew that the men

bossing the job didn't know what they were doing. They weren't part of the Army—or hadn't been." John sighed. "Maybe like me, new recruits. But they were part of the dream, too, so I didn't think anything about it. We built the ship according to plans we were given and flew over the mountains. If we found you, we were to destroy you."

"Tell them about the bottle," Mary suggested.

John furrowed his brow. "Oh! That's right. We pass the vial on the first and the fifteenth of each month. Everyone gets a chance to take a whiff of something smelling—like flowers."

John pulled in air through his nose and sighed a long wistful moan. "It's a beautiful crystal vial holding a delicate blue liquid that makes the tea taste so much better." John had a far-away look in his eyes. "It smells so good!"

I pulled out my watch to time the pause. John sat in a stupor for over fifty seconds.

"It is good to enjoy a cup of tea." He sat back, glancing at the table and then the kitchen. "What were we talking about?"

Mary smiled. "Smelling something?"

"There were little vials of bluish liquid." John pretended to hold something to his nose and inhaled. He gazed at his hand. "It's in a beautiful little crystal bottle. The stopper is pulled, and we each take a whiff as we have our tea."

"Why the fifteenth?" I asked.

"Oh, it's wonderful." John sighed, a silly smile on his face. "We all looked forward to passing the Blue Vial." He stared at something far away.

Mary snapped her fingers. "John, tell us about flying here."

John's eyes came into focus slowly. "It was almost funny, now that I look back on it. We were flying, which was wonderful, but the craft was cobbled together. The smokestack was lost in the shipping. The boiler smoked constantly, and we got lost." He gave us a wry grin. "We found you by accident. Blown here by dumb luck."

John became animated, speaking in bursts. "When you launched your ship—and came after us, we panicked. We tried to drop the fires. We were supposed to drop fire. Rags bundled and soaked in kerosene. One caught fire on the ship. We were trying to smother it and finally dumped it moments before you rammed us. I lived, thank God."

"Why should we believe any of what you say?" José asked.

John hung his head, shoulders down. "You probably shouldn't. I know—before, I was not to be trusted. Even now, sometimes I feel like the dream is calling me. I feel like I should resist you. But it is fading. Mary quit giving me tea. She noticed that even when the dream was fading, a cup of tea would bring back my—I don't know—evil self."

Laura squinted toward John. "Do you remember anything else the woman told you when she had you smell the gas from her handbag?"

"It fades in and out. I know she told me I would enjoy drinking tea. All Freebooters drink tea. She told me to help the Army. She told me to kill anyone opposing the Army. She said that we could take whatever we wanted from the Unenlightened." John put his head down. "I would have killed you all if I could." He looked at Mary. "I have told you I was sorry. But I had—terrible thoughts about you. And I am a married man." He took a deep breath, releasing it slowly between pursed lips.

"Unenlightened is what Freebooters call us?" I asked.

"Yes! Once initiated, everything changes, and it appears normal people are—ignorant of the truth." John stood up, raising his voice. "I don't know why I am telling you this!" He turned a lecherous eye to Mary. "And you, you curvy sweet thing, I think you should GET ME A CUP OF TEA!"

John waved his arms, snapping his head around, accusing us all. "Your kind are all going to—" He pointed at me. "You! You're that stupid captain kid. The one, the leader of the—"

"John," Mary said, "John, take a breath."

He sat heavily.

"It's OK now," Mary whispered.

"John, thank you for telling us this." I studied his face for a moment and realized his eyes were sincere again. "I cannot let you go free until we have discussed this further. But thank you."

"I don't think I should be unchained—yet. I want to go home to my wife and children, but there are still times, especially early in the morning, when I wake up with the dream in my mind." He rubbed his eyes. "I don't even trust myself yet."

Liam took John out.

"How often does he—revert—go back?" I asked.

"It is worse in the mornings. As the day goes on, he is more docile. It's hard to say. It happens between one moment and the next."

"Like night and day," José said. "I think we can expect the same from Finn."

"What do you think about his story?" Mary asked.

"He is either being honest, or he is a good fake," Nathan said.

Laura folded her arms. "You can shave a fox's fur, but you can't change his ways."

José laughed. "That is a good one. Yes! He may be the fox in the henhouse."

"Well, even he suggests we don't let him go free. He said he isn't to be trusted," Mary said. "I am not sure he remembers his ranting and yelling a few minutes after it happens. These episodes come when he loses his train of thought—is daydreaming."

"John has been here a couple of weeks, but more importantly, today is the twentieth of January," I said. "Mary, when did you notice the change?

"Before the fifteenth, but then one day, he was especially vulgar in his talk—about me and to me. I got mad and wouldn't let him have more tea." There was determination in her voice. "He asked for it more often, begged, but I thought water was good enough for a Freebooter."

"We don't know how powerful the first dose is," Laura said. "But Finn got his on the nineteenth. Maybe with no tea, he will begin to recover sooner?"

"What changes did you first see?" I asked Mary.

"He was more civil. He began to thank us for food. He worked without complaining. He tried to talk to me but—well, I would have none of it." She looked into the fire. "I was pretty cruel to him. I was so angry."

"The question I have is why Finn is not mean, wanting to take things or be evil with women. He seems to be in more of a stupor than most Freebooters?" Dad asked.

"I have been thinking about that," Laura said. "The instructions José was given, and I assume Finn was given, are different than what John described. John's instructions seemed to give him a feeling of superiority over... well, the rest of us. He also was told to join the Army." Laura fell silent for a moment. "Could it be that there are levels of instruction? The Freebooters are to be aggressive and attack. Finn is supposed to stand aside. Wolves and sheep."

"Laura, I think that is it, exactly," I said. "Whoever is behind this wants to cut down resistance. That woman in the town may be only creating sheep. The ones given wolf instructions are probably already Army men or men of some influence."

"What about the Mortimers and the Thomases?" José asked. "They drank tea all day."

The group was silent. "Hard to judge," Laura said. "It could be that they were simply rich and spoiled. Maybe they are sheep."

"Benny, bring the parasol out to the fields by the greenhouse, please." I asked. "We need to look at it, but we should be in the open air. Remember, be very careful. Don't breathe in when looking at it, especially the tip."

It was a beautiful winter day with a few fluffy clouds. Laura and I walked hand in hand to where Benny stood.

I held my breath, carefully took the parasol, and looked at the end. There was a pinhole for the air or gas to puff out. The handle was typical, with a crook to allow it to hang on the arm. Laura pointed to the shaft above the crook. It was wider and appeared to be made of soft material. "A squeeze ball, like for perfume?" she wondered.

I turned so that the wind was at our backs. "Everyone, hold your breath." I pointed the parasol away and squeezed the bulge. We all jumped when a hiss could be heard. We stepped back so that the wind carried the gas away.

"Well, we know how they do it," Laura said.

I held the umbrella at arm's length. "Yes, and different props are used to attract the victims—flowers, a bag, a parasol."

"In town, when I grabbed the umbrella, I did not breathe again until I was across the street. I do not think I am under the effects of the gas." José wrinkled his mouth. "If nothing else, I think the new tea is horrible, and Finn tries to fill my cup every time it is half empty!"

Laura gave José one of her looks. "You keep drinking it. It's for a good cause. But don't let anyone outside Eagle's Crest offer you anything close to your face. Like Mr. Salsbury, anyone can change."

We decided to have Mary hide the parasol in the women's bunkhouse.

Ed led us out to the point to show us the drawbridge project. It was impressive. I expected a high set of crossbeams and a winch to lift the bridge, but Finn planned to use Levitrite. Cans at the end of the bridge would lift the bridge with power from the Eagle Crest dynamo.

"Let's don't have it take off and fly away," I joked.

I was surprised when Minnie rang the bell for lunch. The lodge smelled terrific, and Mrs. Rodriquez, Minnie, and Addy were carrying in bowls and platters.

After we offered grace, Minnie said, "Addy mashed the potatoes."

Addy had taken a seat opposite José. She glanced at him and then looked away quickly. José stared down at his potatoes, but he was smiling. Laura nudged my ankle with her foot.

We spent the afternoon digging a ditch for the drawbridge electric cables. It was cool, perfect weather for hard work. I found my spirits lifted and remembered Mary saying digging in the dirt was healing.

29

That evening, we sat by the fire in the lodge when Dolph slipped in from the kitchen. He came close and said, "Will, Finn has destroyed the message that came a little while ago. He was mumbling that he needed to tune a transmitter so he can *tell the Army* we will give them the ships."

"Benny, can you please go and keep an eye on Finn? We don't need him overhearing us."

"On my way."

"This isn't good," I said. "We missed the message tonight and can't allow Finn to send the Freebooters any information."

Dolph waved a piece of paper in his hand, as we all had done in our school days. "I know the message."

He stood tall and straight, his round face glowing.

ENGINE TEST SUCCESSFUL STOP FIRST TEST FLIGHT TOMORROW STOP

"Then the other end got mad!" Dolph squinted in the air, and we waited for him to be ready to go on.

"The leader was not happy. He said if this happens again, heads would—roll?" Dolph looked from me to Laura. "How do they roll heads?"

I covered my mouth, and Liam coughed.

José ruffled Dolph's hair and sat down. "English is a funny language. It means they will chop off some heads." José glanced at Hannah talking to her doll. He mouthed sorry to Minnie.

Dolph concentrated hard. "Oh! When they chop—"

"That's enough, Dolph," Minnie said. "Little ears." She pointed to Hannah and Maria.

"Only for the adults. I see." Dolph sat, watching José, leaned back, and put his hands behind his neck.

"That's right, Dolph. You did a good job tonight," Laura said. Minnie looked pleased.

"We have to go down to the Freebooter Army camp tomorrow. That ship cannot be allowed to fly," I said.

"I will have steam up by early morning," Liam said.

"There is one other task," I said. "I want to go get Mr. Salsbury. We may have to kidnap him, but he must be rescued from this fog and sobered up. If he knew he was like this, he would hate it."

The group was quiet.

"It takes more time, but he's stood by us. He's like family."

"It is not that we disagree, Will. But we have to plan carefully." José gave me a thoughtful nod. "But yes, we will bring him to Eagle's Crest."

"Jobs are piling up," I said. "We must redouble our efforts. When we tested the *Silver Seed,* it needed adjustments. Some Liam can do, but it is like a stone skipping on water when we try to fly at more than Half speed.

"I am sure there is something that can be done," Liam said, "but Finn would be the one to handle these adjustments."

"I think I can get him to make the changes," Laura said. "Finn wants to please the Adjunct Leader. I will talk to Finn when he is drinking tea in the morning. He—" Laura stopped. Finn had come into the lodge.

Benny, following Finn, held up his hands, shaking his head.

"I am going to have a cup of tea," Finn announced. "Here is the first radio. I think I deserve a little dessert with my tea." He looked at Laura.

"I would like a cup, too," Laura said with a big smile. "It is good to enjoy a cup of tea. I bet Minnie has something good in the kitchen."

Finn sat at the table with a contented look.

Laura slanted her big eyes toward José.

José put a pretend smile on his face. "Yes, a cup of tea sounds good. I especially like this new tea."

Addy covered a laugh. "I'll take a cup, too."

"I have a kettle on the back of the stove. It can be hot in a couple of minutes," Minnie said. "I also have one more pie to enjoy with your tea. Finn, come to the kitchen, and I will let you choose how big a slice you want."

"Should we all sit at the table?" I asked when they were gone.

"Yes, but let me do the talking," Laura said.

When Finn came in with the teapot, Benny brought cups, and Minnie carried the pies.

After Finn poured the tea, he sat down and sighed. "This is nice—sitting here enjoying our tea." He took a bite of pie. "Excellent pie, Minnie. As always. You should enter your apple pie at the fair next year."

The hypnotizing gas had given Finn a gift of gab!

"Thank you for the first radio." Laura looked at the box. "I don't see a crank."

Finn brightened. "Yes. This will connect to the electricity in the airships, like the radio in the shop." He took a sip of tea. "No cranking."

"Finn, you are so clever," Laura said. "I think the Adjunct Leader will be pleased."

"We should always please the Adjunct Leader. I wish he could be here to enjoy this tea." Finn took another bite of pie and sat back, sipping his tea. "It is good to sit and enjoy a cup of tea."

Laura leaned forward. "Speaking of pleasing the Adjunct Leader, Will and I took the *Silver Seed* up for some tests, and there were some problems we need to fix before we turn the ship over to the Army."

"Oh?"

"When we tried to fly faster than Half, the ship became difficult to keep level. I used the elevation rudders, but the tiniest correction suddenly made the ship dive up or down. It's unstable."

"This sounds like we don't have enough throw on the control surface rods." Finn twisted his fingers in the air as if tightening a nut.

"Do you think it can be fixed? It would be a shame to present the Army with our best airship and have the Adjunct Leader be displeased."

Finn stared into the fire. "We should always please and support the Adjunct Leader and the Army of the United States of America."

"Yes, that is why I thought we should talk about it while enjoying our tea," Laura said.

"Yes, I will think about it. Right now, I am going to sit and enjoy my tea."

"Finn, why don't you show me how the radio is to be connected in the *Cloud Queen*? Will is taking her out tomorrow. We could test the radio."

Finn looked intently at me. "Why are you going out tomorrow? You are not going to attack the Army, are you? We should not fight the Army. The Army of the United States of America only does good for us."

"Yes!" Laura leaned closer. "Will and José are only going to see their new ship." Laura winked at me. "They may need help with it."

"I should go along. I could improve their designs if it is like the wreck out there. The engine mounting was inadequate, and the propeller drive system put unnecessary force on the bearings."

"Finn, we need you here. Will can check on their progress. You and I need to work on the *Silver Seed's* problem."

Finn seemed undecided, looking from face to face.

"Finn, let me pour you a little more tea," Minnie cajoled. "You haven't finished your pie. Wouldn't it be good to enjoy a little more tea?"

Finn leaned back. "Yes, thank you, Minnie. It is good to enjoy a cup of tea."

"I will have a little more, too, Minnie," Laura said. Finn watched Minnie pour his tea as fascinated as if she were wiring an instrument for the *Silver Seed*.

After we finished our pie, Finn stood. "I think I am going to head off to bed. I have been working too hard. I must get my beauty sleep." He stared at Mary for a moment and tried to wink. After a moment, he wandered toward the door. Liam followed him.

Laura waited until they were gone. "You see how careful we must be. Finn is still open to suggestion, but he is getting cagey—his suspicions are easily aroused. We must be careful—very careful."

"He sleeps a lot," Benny said. "I will go keep an eye on him."

"John used to sleep all the time," Mary said. "After supper, Liam would take him out to the wrecked ship, and he would be sound asleep in minutes. In the morning, it was a battle to roust him out."

"And now?" Dad asked.

"He still is pokey in the morning, but he has been reading in the evenings," Liam said.

"What about their ship? Do we plan to follow them to their

'rendevoice'—meet with other ships?" Dolph asked.

"Listen, young man, you're growing up, but it's time for you to get to bed," Minnie said.

Disappointment flickered on Dolph's face, but he brightened. "I will be ready to help Finn in the morning. If you need me, just call."

"Good fellow, Dolph," I said. "We will all be turning in soon."

After Minnie, Mrs. Rodriquez, and the children were gone, Paul said, "Dolph brings up a good point. We need to rethink all our plans."

"We will break into three teams," I said. "One, we lead the Freebooters on a wild goose chase. Two, the *Cloud Queen* will get Mr. Salsbury, and three, José and I will go down to stop the progress on the Freebooter airship. Liam and Benny, you take over the *Cloud Queen* engine until Finn has recovered."

"Mary will have to fly you down," Laura said. "I need to oversee Finn's adjustments on the *Silver Seed*."

I was unhappy about being separated from Laura, but it was clear that Finn looked to her for instruction.

"When you get to Mr. Salsbury's, have a cup of tea with him to get on his good side," Laura said. "Convince him the new tea is better."

"I believe Will and I should check on the Freebooter ship before we nab Mr. Salsbury," José said. "We do not know what commands Mr. Salsbury was given. He will need to be watched."

"I think he is one of the sheep," I said. "He didn't try to stop us. He simply would not help our cause. But you are right. No sense having him wandering around the ship while we are spying."

Laura caught my eye and tipped her head toward the door. I mouthed, "I'm coming." She slipped out into the night.

I threw two logs on the fire and stood by José. "Addy is sitting over there. Maybe she would like company."

José turned ever so slightly, but when he met Addy's eye, he quickly looked away. "Maybe you can come with me. To help me start."

"Sure. I will get you started. But then you are on your own."

I got up and moved toward Addy. "Where did your family come from?" I wasn't sure I was much help in the conversation department.

"Fred and I were born in Missouri. We had a farm there. Our mom died there—childbirth. Dad wasn't the same. When he suggested California, Fred and I agreed."

"Sorry about your mom. Me, too. Childbirth seems to take

women."

José moved closer, and I stepped back slightly so he was closest to Addy.

"I have never moved. Well, until now. I have known José all my life. Laura, too." I looked at José, and he shifted his feet. "Tell Addy about the farm, José."

Addy looked up. She had a sweet smile.

"We grow field crops. Corn and we planted potatoes, but Papá has started growing oranges. It is the crop of the future." José lifted the corners of his mouth and then got serious. "Until the Freebooters came. Now, nothing is for sure."

"Where did you get the ship?"

"Will's uncle invented the *Cloud Queen*. He conceived of the ship and built it."

"I like your accent," Addy said. "When your family speaks Spanish, it sounds like music sometimes—to me." Addy paused and wrinkled her brow. "Bwenes Dees, José," she said.

José brightened. "Sí. Buenos dias!"

"Did I say it right?"

"I understood," José laughed. "It is good enough. But it is later in the day. In the evening, we say buenas tardes."

"Tardes—oh, like tardy. Late." Addy's smile was radiant. "Oh, I think I could learn this language. Buenas tardes. Good late time?"

"Good late time," José agreed. "Yes."

I started for the door.

"Good night, Will." Addy turned back to José. "Tell me about oranges."

In our cabin, I told Laura José was telling Addy about growing and picking oranges.

Laura laughed. "Maybe they will fall in love. Like us." She put her arms around my neck.

It snowed that night, and the pilothouse was cold even with the register on. The sun peeked through for a moment, but as we flew South, the clouds became thicker. Occasionally the hills below appeared in the mist. Mary and I took turns steering by the compass.

It was not an ideal time to be in the air, and I wondered if we should have waited a day or two. But time was not on our side, and our enemy was at work in ways we could only imagine. The weather would not hinder completing their airship.

"I think I will go down and get a cup of tea. Would you like one?" Mary asked.

"Sounds good. Bring the real tea—not that swill we are giving Finn."

Her eyes danced. "Isn't that stuff horrible? But Laura has convinced him it is the best tea ever."

I peered down through breaks in the low clouds. Glimpses of the mountains appeared and disappeared. With the snow, the countryside all looked the same. As we worked our way south, the snow disappeared, and I recognized a flat. I rang for Slow.

We were further down the canyon than I anticipated. I rang for Stop and called for us to hide in the clouds.

Mary brought two cups of tea and some warm bread. "Did you see a landmark you recognized?"

"We are an hour ahead of schedule. Unless I am mistaken, the meadow we use is ahead." I hesitated. "Flying in this weather can be tricky. Do you think you can navigate while José and I do our work? We could risk staying on the ground."

"There is more wind than I would like," Mary said. "We'll have to keep the engine running regardless. What if we used the anchor and floated above the meadow?"

"We'll look for another flat spot further up. I don't want to take any chance of the enemy knowing you are here."

I set the engine order telegraph for Slow and steered north. José and Benny kept a close watch as we slipped out of the clouds. We had drifted east, and ensuring we were over the right canyon took time.

In the pilothouse, Mary said, "Up here, all the canyons look alike."

José was on the bow, pointing. I used the telescope as a compass needle.

"This meadow will do, Mary. Take some time to look at your surroundings in case you break loose at night."

José and I checked our pistols and packs. I went to the telegraph to send a message to Eagle's Crest.

ARRIVED STOP GOING VISITING STOP
MR STOP BE CAREFUL STOP

José tied a clever knot and attached it to a smaller rope. "If you have to get loose in a hurry, pull hard and quick—we can always get another anchor."

"We'll keep an eye on the telegraph," Liam said.

On the ground, we looped the anchor and rope around a healthy oak and watched the *Cloud Queen* drift upwards. The rope was still slack when the ship disappeared into the mist.

José gestured at the thick brush. "The canyon floor will be faster."

We kept quiet, each in our own thoughts. We reached the canyon floor in the late morning, walking quickly along the creek.

José put out a steadying arm. "Our trail is up ahead."

The clouds were back, and I turned up my collar and pulled my coat close.

We sat at the bottom of the trail, munching on cheese. José broke the silence. "I would like to take a look from above."

We followed the deer path until we reached our lookout. The first ship had been moved out of of the workshop. I pointed at the one guard. "He might go to sleep like the last guard," I joked.

"Yes, I will help him take a nap."

"José! They've had steam in the boiler. The fire is probably banked, but that's smoke! Do you suppose we could fly that thing out of here?" The excitement was overpowering.

"We would need time."

"Yes. But what if we could steal their ship out from under their noses?"

"We will be taking a big chance."

"Let's check the pressure. Maybe try the engine. If we could get it to fly, we take it. Then wreck it or crash it."

José looked doubtful. "I suppose if we could get to the meadow, we could take their Levitrite."

My watch said five minutes until eleven. "If we capture the ship, we need another person. Let's call for Benny."

José walked the wire out, and I stepped the ground stake into the damp earth. I hooked the insulator stake in the crook of a tree.

CLOUD QUEEN STOP ALL IS WELL STOP SEND BENNY WITH RIFLE STOP BE READY

BENNY COMING STOP

COME BY CREEK STOP JOSE WILL MEET HIM STOP MR

I lay on my stomach, watching the airship. The guard had kindled a small fire with a kettle hanging over the flames. He spent much of his time huddling with his hands toward the heat. He was only drinking tea, which disappointed me.

The air had a bite, but I could not chance a fire. I wrapped in my blanket, hoping for a break in the clouds.

At noon, a replacement guard came wandering out. The two men talked and drank tea.

When José and Benny arrived, Benny grinned, rubbing his hands together. "We're going to steal their ship?"

"We don't know if it flies, but if it will lift off—yes, we steal it."

José did not look convinced but said nothing.

"José, we can at least look. If there is some pressure, this might work!"

"Then we will have a look." José put his hand on his brother's shoulder. "We will need a little diversion. I am going down to distract the guard. If he sees me, you know what to do." He patted the rifle Benny held. "Can you do this?"

"Not a problem."

At the canyon floor, José pointed to a copse of trees on the bank. Benny moved behind the biggest trunk.

"OK, I am going to make a little noise. When the guard leaves, you check the pressure."

José slipped away.

I measured the distance to the ship, planning my path around the boulders. A rock landed in the dirt beside the guard. Two followed, and one hit the kettle, making a tinny clank. The guard looked toward the shop. "Hey, come on, you guys."

Three pebbles flew in quick succession, the third bouncing off the man's hat. "Hey, cut it out. Is that you, Pete?"

Two more rocks flew. "OK, I am going to whup you good." The guard scooped up several stones and threw awkwardly toward the building.

José answered with a rock that caught the Freebooter square in the stomach.

"Oh, I'm gonna to give you a beating you ain't gonna forget." The renegade ran behind the shop building. I sprinted, dodging the biggest rocks, and jumped onto the deck. The boiler was an upright with a simple gauge near the top. Twenty-eight. The throttle was at the side, and a flat belt went from the engine to a dynamo. I opened the damper.

I ran hard, hair standing up on the back of my neck. I made the deer trail a moment after Benny.

"Where's José?" I gasped.

"Already on top. He was gone the second that guy started running."

José sat near the packs, not even out of breath. "That guy does not have a lick of sense. I was up the side aways, and he ran right under me and partway to their camp."

"Twenty-eight pounds. We can do this."

"Yes, but we must lead the Freebooters away," José said. "Benny can take dynamite far down the canyon." He reached into his pack and pulled out a coil of Finn's slow fuses. "Two minutes per foot. This may give us the time we need."

"Two explosions," Benny said. "One first and another further down a couple of minutes later. One blast is something. Two makes them think there is trouble. They'll send lots of men."

"We'd better get started. We don't want to try to fly that ugly thing after dark," I said.

After Benny left with the charges, I couldn't sit still and paced to the bluff's edge and back.

Thirty-seven minutes had passed when Benny pushed through the brush, breathing hard. "It was easy. The guards are close to the bunkhouses. I set a quarter stick about a mile down and another further yet.

"How much time do we have?"

Benny looked at his pocket watch. "I figure, five minutes."

31

Men spilled out of the bunkhouse and buildings when the first charge rumbled through the canyon. Even the Freebooter guarding the ship ran around the workshop and followed the others. There was confusion in the ranks, and men hustled down the canyon.

An officer attempted to organize the other men, and soon, the entire camp double-timed along the creek. When the second charge exploded, two or three stragglers came out. I had to chuckle watching a man stop to fix his suspenders when his pants fell to his knees.

"Benny—keep watch from here," José said. "Give us a towhee call if anybody comes back."

José and I didn't bother with the trail but bounded and slid to the canyon floor. We threw our backpacks on the ground near the ship. José waved to Benny and then went to check the workshop. At the airship, I found the pressure at twenty-seven. I jammed wood in the firebox and left the door ajar for air.

José sprinted back. "We are just in time. On the table, with the radio, there is a message for tonight telling the Adjunct Leader that the test liftoff was successful."

My hands trembled as I touched the controls. The throttle for the engine was obvious.

"Will it fly?" José asked.

"I think so. Keep checking with Benny." A clutch controlled the connection to the dynamo. The water injector was straightforward, but I couldn't see anything resembling a lift lever.

José was back. "No sign of them." He threw two handfuls of wrenches on the deck. "This will slow them down."

I waved my hand at the mechanism. "I see no adjustment between the dynamo and the Levitrite above. Do they control the lift with engine speed?"

"Who knows what they think?" He stacked wood closer to the

firebox. "The fire does not draw." He pointed to a crank on a blacksmith blower. "This is not connected to the engine. Do we crank that the whole time?"

"I suppose." Prickles ran up the back of my neck.

"I will check Benny."

I cranked the blower and studied the simple controls. A second pulley went to friction disks, a rosin bottle sitting near.

There was a wheel for steering, but when I turned it, the rudder didn't move. A quick look showed that it had not been connected. A tiller had been fashioned between the propeller and the rudder.

José threw a toolbox on the deck. "Still no sign of the Freebooters."

The pressure rose to thirty pounds, and I put my back into the blower. The flames flickered feebly, smoke kicking out of the firebox door. The makeup water tank was only half full.

I pulled at the throttle, but the bushing was tight. I leaned back, jerking it with all my weight. The throttle opened a crack, and the engine rocked but did not start. It was on dead center! Which direction did the engine turn?

José returned with a hatchet and put his muscle into the blower crank. "I put sand in the bearings and stuffed rags up the chimney. I snapped a pipe on the boiler."

I leaned into the throttle, trying to close it. "The bushings are too tight. I can hardly move the throttle." I rolled the flywheel counterclockwise, a quarter turn. "Anything from Benny?"

"He was not there. I will look again."

I gave a mighty pull on the throttle, and it opened halfway. The engine started, giving a loud chuff of steam up the short chimney, and I threw my chest against the throttle to close it. The sound echoed off the building. I had heard trains that made less racket.

José leaned against the hull. "They are on their way!"

Benny scrambled down the hill. "They're double timing—they know it was a trick."

I pulled the throttle again, and the engine began to turn, smoke and steam billowing into the air.

"It sounds like a train," Benny exclaimed. "They're gonna hear us! We need to take off now or run."

José pointed up. "Now!"

I jerked the throttle three times, using my body's momentum.

The rods that went to the Levitrite above us twitched. The box was perched on a long pole, like the mast of a sailing ship. The box quivered.

"Hurry, Will!" Benny shouted.

"The throttle's stiff," I panted and pulled harder. The engine turned faster, but we did not lift off. "We need more pressure." I wasn't sure they heard me.

The ship gave the eerie feeling it was getting lighter, and the turnbuckles quivered.

"I will slow them down," José called. He ran into the workshop. Benny slipped around to the east side of the building.

I disconnected the dynamo to idle the engine. A clunking above made me flinch. The box of Levitrite teetered, ready to topple down on me. I engaged the clutch lever and glanced at the pressure gauge. It hovered at thirty-two pounds.

I needed to conserve steam and eased the throttle closed, watching the Levitrite. The awful chuff lessened, and the engine spun easily.

A bullet whined off the rocks against the bluff, followed by a dynamite charge echoing in the hills. Our backpacks flopped on the deck, and José jumped aboard. "If we are taking off, we better do it now."

Benny ran hard, pulling himself onto the deck. "Go, go!"

"Help me pull!"

José grabbed the handle, and jerked the throttle. The ship began to rise, swinging beneath the Levitrite. We inched up. The airship hovered at ten feet. I cupped my hands. "Too heavy! Lighten the load."

"I am not leaving their tools." José went to a box of cannonballs. As strong as he was, he struggled to get a grip on a ball. He rolled it to the edge and tossed it overboard. José rolled cannonballs across the deck, and Benny lifted them over the side. We were as high as the eaves of the shop.

The steam chuffing up the chimney made a terrible racket, creating a draft. Fire shot out of the short stack.

Benny threw several more balls over the side, and we were finally rising. The pressure had increased, and the firebox was burning a lusty blaze.

A bullet tore into the Levitrite pole. Benny went to the ship's port side, ducked down, and shot several times, smoothly working the rifle's lever. He stood, took careful aim, staggered back, and went down hard. Blood oozed from his shoulder.

"Benny!" José's mouth screamed, the sound lost in the chug of the engine.

Benny looked up, eyes not focusing. He touched his shirt and stared in wonder at the blood on his hand.

José dragged him closer to the boiler. He took dynamite toward the stern and lay on his stomach.

We were drifting in the breeze, and the branches of an oak clawed at the side of the airship. A long three-inch limb surrounded me, twigs rattling against the spokes of the flywheel. I willed the ship to rise when the explosion rocked the ship.

I tried to push the limb away, but the afternoon breeze held us against the tree. Benny's eyes closed.

José joined me. "Push it toward the stern!"

I buried my head in leaves, putting my shoulder against the branch. I scrambled, fighting to keep my footing on the deck. The clumsy craft slowly rotated, and the limb let us go. We bobbed and drifted as high as the bluff, scraping the manzanita.

José sliced Benny's shirt open with one quick motion. He put the heel of his hand on the wound, pressing down hard. Benny grimaced.

I ran around the cabin and found a second box of cannonballs lying near the bow. I slid to my knees, heaving the ammunition overboard.

A bullet splintered the railing above my head. I ducked and ran to the engine. I bent close to José's ear. "We have to control this thing."

"What do I need to do?"

"I'm going to start the propeller. The steering is not connected. Go back to the tiller and bring us to port, hard over." I eased the propeller clutch in, and rosin dust flew from the leather-covered disks. The propeller shuddered, beginning to turn, and I was able to push the lever over center.

José worked the tiller, the propeller wind plastering his shirt to his back. Benny watched me with vacant eyes.

32

The leather disks were beginning to slip and smoke. I shook rosin on the two wheels, and the engine dug in with the added load.

The pressure had risen to thirty-five. I jammed as many logs as possible into the firebox and got the transmitter out of the backpack. The ship floated toward the meadow where we had left the *Cloud Queen,* and I signaled for José to come forward.

"We have to send a message," I yelled. "I'll put the wire out and—"

The deck rolled. I lost my footing and flopped onto my side. I staggered to the railing. The tree tops were dragging heavily on the ship. I disconnected the propeller, and the engine picked up speed. "We can hardly fly, and the propeller takes what little power we have," I yelled.

José covered Benny with our coats. We were free of the tree but hardly fifty feet above the hilltops. I managed to jam one more log in the firebox.

José stood. "He is not bleeding as much. We need help."

"Radio. Put out the wire. I'll connect the ground."

José let the antenna hang over the side and turned the crank. All sound blanketed by the engine, I watched José send, CLOUD QUEEN STOP NEED HELP STOP BENNY SHOT STOP FLYING ENEMY SHIP STOP DO NOT SHOOT STOP TURN ON LIGHTS STOP REPLY SLOWLY STOP ENGINE NOISY STOP WE HAVE TO WATCH THE CLICKS

José cranked the little dynamo, eyes on the key.

EMERGENCY OR DO WE PULL ANCHOR

EMERGENCY STOP MEET US AT DROP STOP CAN NOT CONTROL SHIP STOP WILL LAND WHERE WE LAND

José laid down the box and rolled Benny on his side, examining his back. "The bullet did not come out! We have to get it out," he shouted.

It was going to hurt.

If only the engine would be quiet—stop its endless hammering. I needed to think.

José yelled, "We have to do it on the *Cloud Queen*,"

We were slowly drifting up the canyon. If the Freebooters came on horseback, they would catch us.

"We need to run the propeller." My voice was hoarse. The pressure held at forty-three pounds, and I hoped to engage the propeller without falling out of the sky.

With the clutch engaged, I shook rosin powder onto the driving disk, and the propeller picked up speed. The concussions of steam blowing through the stack told us the engine had slowed. José and I jerked hard moving the throttle a little more, and the engine gained speed. At the tiller, I brought us on course and lashed it down.

The pressure dropped to forty. "José, can you figure out how they get water up to the Levitrite box?"

José followed a small tube to a pump under the water tank. When he worked the handle, water dripped from a pipe coupling leading to the Levitrite. After several minutes of pumping, water misted down on us.

I went to the port side. "That gave us more lift. We are at least a hundred feet above the trees."

"We should not press our luck. This machine is not safe." José went to the tiller. The ship was poorly designed—the cabin blocked all view of what was ahead. I risked a peek over the starboard. The Freebooters were either under the trees or had fallen behind. The terrain below was rough, and horses wouldn't do well in the thick manzanita and scrub.

We continued to climb. I pulled the lever, increasing the speed of the propeller. Rosin made a cloud around the disks.

The water level in the boiler was low, and I started the injector pump. The tank holding the makeup water showed one-third. I cupped my hands toward José. "We need more water!"

José came close. "Benny is asleep or passed out. Nothing I can do for him right now."

"Watch for the *Cloud Queen*."

I worked the Levitrite pump handle twenty times.

José came back smiling. "I can see their smoke." He knelt over Benny.

I released the propeller clutch and studied the mountains behind us. We'd been flying at a snail's pace and had blown northeast across rough hills and steep canyons. I eased the throttle, bumping it with my shoulder.

"Can we make it to the mine?" I shouted.

José looked doubtful. "Benny needs the bullet out soon."

"Can you do it if I hold him?"

The *Cloud Queen's* whistle cut the air. I ran to the bow. Liam had the bow gangplank out and was standing on the end. He tossed me a rope, and I tied it to the cannon pulleys.

"Must get Benny to you," I yelled.

Liam cupped his hands. "You're sinking. Can you fly level?"

"I'll try!"

Before opening the throttle, I found a wrench in the clutter of tools. I eased the nuts on the packing flange until the throttle lever moved smoothly. In our excitement, we had not stoked the boiler. I used a poker to stir the fire and threw in several logs.

By the time I came forward, the *Cloud Queen* had bumped us bow to bow, and Liam jumped down onto our deck, moving past me. Mary appeared in the pilothouse. She ran up and down the stairs, adjusting their altitude and trying to steer. The *Cloud Queen* nudged us again, and we swung like the pendulum of a clock. Mary pointed up.

I nodded and went to the throttle, easing it open.

Liam and José had Benny and struggled toward the bow. The *Cloud Queen* gangplank was ten feet above us.

I increased the engine speed and gave the Levitrite pump six quick strokes.

I went forward, waiting as we inched higher. Liam tugged on the rope, keeping the ships together.

"I can't go up faster." I cupped my hands. "It's hard to control."

When the gangplank was several feet above us, José made a quick jump and pulled himself up. Liam and I lifted Benny chest high, and José dragged him onto the gangplank. Liam followed.

Mary was there, looked at Benny, said something to Liam, and disappeared.

Liam came to the end of the gangplank. "Can you stay in the air by yourself?"

"For an hour. We need water for the boiler!"

Liam gestured and the gangplank began to retract. "Watch the rope. We're going to tow you."

Liam walked along the side of the deck, keeping the rope from tangling as the *Cloud Queen* glided past. The airscrews stopped, and Liam climbed the propeller cage, working the rope along. He jumped to the deck and made the line fast at the stern. "You keep that thing in the air. We will adjust the speed!" Liam's voice thundered.

I checked my knot and watched the rope play out between us. The air screws churned, and the rope rose between us as the *Cloud Queen* pulled ahead. I held onto the side as it became taut, the bow moving left and right.

The *Cloud Queen* wagged her tail in a slow dance, the airscrews spinning at Flank speed. My stomach protested as the hull of the renegade ship bobbed like an apple swinging in a stiff wind.

I tended the firebox and the engine. An oil can hung on a nail. I oiled the big engine bearings that I had poured sand in before. I hoped the Freebooter repairs were sufficient. The dynamo oilers were half full. I threw two more logs into the firebox and went to the front of the ship.

I was below the *Cloud Queen,* and the rope was at a steep angle. Mary was not in the pilothouse. They were working on Benny. I nudged the throttle further open and gave the Levitrite water pump several brisk strokes. I said a prayer for Benny.

I looked at my watch.

It was thirty-four minutes before José came out on the deck. His hands and arms were red when he held up the bullet.

Mary had changed course, and I started the airscrew. For the next few minutes, I ran between the water pump for the Levitrite and the bow, trying to maintain an even altitude.

The rebel ship was losing altitude when the pump handle went limp in my hand. The bolt connecting the handle to the plunger had chewed through.

The cabin had a small toolbox with several wrenches but no bolts. I scrabbled around under benches, having no luck. Nails much smaller than the original bolt were scattered in the carpentry box. I grabbed several. My low altitude was pulling the rope tight. I hurried to the pump. The nail flopped around in the hole but allowed me to pump twenty strokes before it bent and fell to the deck. The water brought the ship to the same height as the *Cloud Queen*.

The propeller turned briskly with rosin on the drive wheel, but the makeup water tank was well below one-quarter.

José came out on the rear deck, and I tried hand signals to tell him about the water problem. When he didn't understand, I found a bucket and made pouring motions. He nodded.

The airscrews of the *Cloud Queen* stopped, and José and Liam hauled on the rope.

I stopped my propeller and nudged in the throttle. I brought a handful of nails, pumping water until it misted down. I jammed in two new nails at a time after each filling. With the injector running every few minutes, the water level in the tank was below the sight glass.

José and Liam continued hauling on the line and had cut the distance between the ships in half. From time to time, Mary came behind the pilothouse to check our elevation. Keeping the ships level when tethered closely together would be tricky.

When we crunched together, Liam lashed us with a few feet of rope to allow for the differences in altitude.

"How is Benny?"

"He is resting, but he is not awake," José said. "The bleeding has stopped—so, now we wait."

"Should we let this ship crash and get him to Eagle's Crest?"

"He is comfortable. There is nothing more we could do at Eagle's Crest. It is a matter of time. We have come this far. If we can get this contraption to Eagle's Crest, we will have their Levitrite, the engine, and cannon."

We passed buckets. The job was awkward as the ships were rarely level. Pouring the buckets into the Freebooter's tank was difficult as the fill hole required climbing a ladder. I spilled water, making the ladder rounds slippery. I lost my footing once, landing awkwardly, the bucket rolling on the deck. I took it forward, favoring my left ankle.

Mary started the airscrews and the wind whipped our shirts and hair. The spigot on the *Cloud Queen* water tank was small and buckets arrived slowly.

Mary gestured for me to come closer and handed me a piece of bread with apple butter. "Will, we are falling. Can you try to go up?"

"I'll try. Keep a close watch. This thing may go up too fast."

Hobbling back to the engine, I stoked the boiler and pumped five strokes of water. The makeup water level was back to one-third.

Searching the deck, I found what remained of the original bolt for the hand pump and took it forward.

I had floated above the *Cloud Queen,* straining the rope. Liam and José could no longer pass buckets. Mary was skilled at her task and the *Cloud Queen* matched my climb.

When the ships were level, I tossed the broken bolt to Liam. "I need a bolt this size!"

After emptying a bucket, the Levitrite pump and boiler needed tending. Liam came aboard with another bucket and a bolt and nut. He surveyed the boiler and engine. "Are you sure we shouldn't leave this thing? It's jury-rigged at best." He touched the leather driven wheel, pulling his hand back. "Ouch. That thing is about to catch fire."

"I'm going forward to talk to Mary. Then we'll decide," I said, glad to let Liam take the bucket up the ladder.

Mary stepped close to the stern. "We are drifting. I need to run at Flank!"

I stepped across to the *Cloud Queen.* "How far do you think it is to the mine?"

"We are close, but the air is moving up canyon, making me steer at an angle."

"I ran the propeller for a while. Do you think it helped?"

Mary laughed. "Well, it wasn't as if I was afraid you would ram us from the stern."

The bucket brigade continued until Liam said, "That's as much as we dare give you. The *Cloud Queen* tank is at one-third."

I took the last bucket and stepped back onto the Freebooter ship. "Let the rope out again."

The new bolt allowed water to be pumped briskly to the Levitrite. Even with my propeller running, the *Cloud Queen* walked away from the Freebooter ship. The rope played out and tightened, jerking the bow.

I fell into a routine of checking pressure, looking around the cabin, stoking the firebox, adding rosin, and pumping water to the Levitrite. My ankle began to feel better.

The first stars were out when the *Cloud Queen* hovered over the clearing at the mine. She was down canyon, the rope holding my ship over the clearing. José stepped out of the pilothouse and motioned for me to start down.

I stopped the propeller and nudged the throttle until the engine slowed. The *Cloud Queen,* slightly above me, followed my descent.

I tapped the throttle closed in increments and watched the ship slip between the canyon walls. I stepped around the cabin. The *Cloud Queen's* airscrews were speeding and slowing, the rudders swinging left and right. At the throttle, I couldn't see the pilothouse of the *Cloud Queen* or the ground. I ran back and forth, making adjustments.

A board fell off the cabin when she hit the ground. She bounded up only to hit again. When the throttle closed, a terrible groan came from above. The Levitrite box tipped, bending the stay rods. I left the engine turning slowly and watched the *Cloud Queen* settle gently to earth.

José jumped down and met me on the deck. "You fly a funny ship, Captain Will."

"I know. It's exhausting. I can't keep it level."

I pointed to the Levitrite container. "I have the engine running to keep that box from coming down on us. We need to level this ship."

I struggled to raise the ship off the ground. Liam and José pulled and tugged, trying to move it to even ground. One moment the hull was dragging, and the next, it was ten feet high.

I couldn't hear them calling to me, and Mary came aboard, watching over the edge, giving me hand signals. At last, the ship was level enough for the Levitrite to balance. I closed the damper.

Mary shaded her eyes, gazing at the Levitrite. "This is the silliest machine. It looks like a toadstool flopped upside down."

I grinned. *Toadstool* might be a good name.

We went to the *Cloud Queen*, my ears still holding the concussions of the plagued steam engine.

José hung his hat on the levitation lever. "Benny says, 'Tell Captain Will he has done a good job with the enemy ship, but I will not be bringing him any tea today.'"

When I smiled, José smiled as well.

TOWED ENEMY SHIP TO MINE STOP HOPE TO BE HOME TOMORROW STOP

DOLPH HERE STOP WONT TELL FINN STOP HE GETS GRUMPY WHEN HE THINKS OF FREEBOOTERS STOP

TELL LAURA I AM BEING CAREFUL STOP

I MAY NOT TELL HER ABOUT STEALING THE SHIP STOP

Dolph was right; Laura wouldn't think I was being careful.

34

The creek was full, but we were not as close as we would have liked. Liam and Mary passed buckets, José running to meet Mary and setting them on the deck. I found myself counting my trips up the ladder. The advantages of a water recovery system like the *Cloud Queen's* became more apparent each trip. We hadn't filled even a quarter of the tank at one hundred buckets.

José started the *Cloud Queen's* engine and turned on the lights.

We stopped when the tank was half full. José and I prepared supper while Mary redressed Benny's wound. He ate a couple of spoonfuls of chicken soup.

After eating, we worked our bucket line again. It was late when we had three-quarters of a tank. If the wind cooperated, we reckoned it would be enough to get to Eagle's Crest. We primed the *Cloud Queen's* pump and dropped the hose in the creek. The makeup water tank filled quickly.

"We have to get Salsbury," I said.

"We cannot fly this evening," José said. "It could be dangerous."

"The moon will be well up by midnight," Mary offered.

"Then it's settled," I said. "We need wood for that plagued machine while we are at it. After we get Mr. Salsbury, we will take a chance and get wood at Dad's house. There is still a cord there if someone hasn't stolen it."

"If the Freebooters haven't stolen it, you mean," Liam grumbled.

It was like old times, with José and I in a rear cabin. Liam stayed in the engine room to keep an eye on the pressure. My legs ached when he shook me awake. The oil injector was running, and the pressure was at sixty pounds. "I jammed a couple of logs in that wretched firebox out there," he said.

"You are a good man, Liam."

"I untied the rope," José said.

I probably would have forgotten.

It was warm in the engine room, and Mary looked tired when I went to the pilothouse.

"Did you sleep?"

"A few minutes. Benny was restless, and I sat with him. I don't think he has a fever, but there has been a shock to his system. He's a bit dim."

I laughed. "Benny is never dim. Would you please go to the back cabin Laura and I use and sleep? We will need you awake in the morning."

Mary looked as if she were going to protest. "Yes. Knock if you need me."

I called down to ask Liam if he was ready, and José answered, "I sent Liam to our room. He has not slept."

"Good. Let's go up quick. I am ready up here."

The *Cloud Queen* lifted straight up. I never grew tired of the feeling of power. The bluff disappeared below us in the moonlight, and I rang for Full. José answered, and the airscrews churned.

The eastern sky behind me began showing the first shades of dawn color. We had slept longer than I realized.

"What's your plan, José?" I asked on the speaking tube.

"He gave us no trouble last time—he just would not help us."

"What if we land and try to be nice? Maybe offer him some tea?" I suggested.

"I think we grab him. He is strong, but Liam and I can handle him."

In the gloom, a rock formation appeared, marking where we usually turned down canyon. I thought of all the times we had gone to get supplies in the past four years. How would we get what we needed without Mr. Salsbury's help?

I rang for Half, following the canyon. "Time to wake Liam and Mary."

"It has not been two hours."

"It's time."

Mary came up. "I was dreaming of my little girl," she said. "She was so sweet."

"I am sorry we woke you."

"No. It was lovely. She even smelled like she used to. Her big eyes looked right at me and said, 'I love you, Mama.'" Mary tilted her head as if looking down at a small child. "It was the best dream."

I turned, clenching my fists, eyes filled with tears of great sadness and rage.

Mary pulled gently on my coat sleeve, turning me back. "No. It was a good dream. I haven't dreamed of her." She sighed. "I held my little girl again. I feel like she visited me moments ago. She's right here." Mary tapped her forehead. "Right here."

"I..." I wanted to say I was sorry. Or should I be glad for her? I made myself stand straight. At a loss, I settled for, "Can you ring for Slow and tell them we are starting down?"

Liam went out on deck with a pistol. The air still moved up the canyon, making the approach easy. I hovered over the yard in front of the barn, and we settled to earth.

Mr. Salsbury came out on the front porch with his rifle.

"No need for a gun, Mr. Salsbury. We brought you a tin of tea. I know you enjoy a good cup of tea."

Mr. Salsbury hesitated and then stood the gun by the door and waited.

"Mary, be ready to take off. Lash the wheel, and keep the engine spinning so we go up hard if necessary."

I went down the stairs and handed José the tea.

Benny lifted his head from his cot by the boiler. "What is going on?"

"We are getting Mr. Salsbury," I said.

"Oh, I should—" He sank back onto the pillow.

I put my head out. "I will be there in a minute, Mr. Salsbury. Some cake we brought would be good when enjoying a cup of tea."

Mr. Salsbury nodded. "I always enjoy a good cup of tea."

José started to hand the tin to Mr. Salsbury but let it fall between them. When the old fellow started to stoop over, José had Mr. Salsbury's hands behind his back in one quick move. Growling, he tried to resist, but José had him on the ground, and Liam held his legs.

Mr. Salsbury wiggled like a snake under a boot, but Liam had a firm grip. I ran with the rope and wrapped it around his ankles. The fight seemed to go out of him. I tied Mr. Salsbury's hands behind his back, and Liam and I carried him to the *Cloud Queen*. José ran down the canyon.

We had tied Mr. Salsbury to the fuel tank stand when José jogged into the yard with the dog. We spent no more time on the ground.

"This ain't right." Mr. Salsbury swung his shoulders left and right against the ropes. "I have my duty to support the Army of the United States of America!" he growled. His dog licked his face.

"I'm sorry, Mr. Salsbury, we have orders from the Adjunct Leader to take you."

"I never heard of no a-jinct leader."

José beckoned with his head, and I followed him down the hallway. "Mr. Salsbury's commands are not the same as Finn's. He only wants to honor the Army."

"This keeps getting more complicated. Get him a chair so he can sit. No sense being mean—he's addled by the gas."

When I got to the pilothouse, Mary had set a course directly east. We were climbing, and I didn't think we would attract much attention in the early morning light. I called for three thousand feet.

"Your dad's house?" Mary asked.

35

The wood remained ricked as Dad had left it, and we landed a few yards away. We ran back and forth with our arms full, tossing it on the deck, José running a wheelbarrow. We took the time to go around to the port side to keep the ship balanced. I kept an eye on the driveway with each load.

When we had half of the rick loaded, we launched.

At the mine, we landed as close as possible to the Freebooter ship.

"I can't lift all the wood," I told Liam. "We barely got this thing off the ground at the rebel stronghold."

My arms ached by the time we had some wood piled by the boiler of the *Toadstool*. Anxious to get in the air, José cranked the blacksmith blower. I ran the engine slowly, steam chuffing up the chimney, echoing against the canyon walls. The pressure gauge slowly climbed.

Try as we would, the *Toadstool* would not rise. In the end we had to transfer part of the wood back to the *Cloud Queen*. Water dripped from the Levitrite box as the ship creaked and groaned, finally breaking free of the earth.

"You are all tied on," José said. "It is time."

I nodded, watched him jog to the *Cloud Queen,* and felt very alone.

Mary pointed a thumb up. I pulled the throttle back, and she matched my height perfectly. I swung like a bell clapper as the *Cloud Queen* began the pull. The rebel engine drummed in my ears. I longed to hear the chop of the *Cloud Queen's* airscrews and the whine of her blower.

I started the propeller and began my trips to the bow and back, pumping water, feeding the boiler, and dusting rosin on the drive wheel. I talked to myself under the engine's din and fell into a rhythm. Mary gave me up or down hand signals.

One time the throttle closed further than I wanted, and my feet felt light. I bumped it open again and hurried to the front. I was thirty feet lower than the *Cloud Queen,* and the rope had stretched tight. I waited for Mary to match my elevation.

I missed the revolution counter and altitude gauge. Mary signaled that I should stay level. I made no changes for the next hour, adding water two strokes at a time.

My head throbbed in cadence with the engine. We passed over a ridge that was halfway to Eagle's Crest.

Mid-afternoon, José appeared on the rear deck of the *Cloud Queen* with Benny. I gave an enthusiastic wave which José returned. Benny raised one hand, giving me a weak smile. They only lingered a moment, and José helped him back. Mary was on the upper deck, pointing to Benny and smiling. It was good news, indeed.

I had ten logs left and went to the front, holding a piece. José had rigged the towline to a block and tackle. The *Cloud Queen* airscrews slowed, and they tied me close. The wind whipped around, reminding me to have Laura cut my hair.

They tossed logs onto the front of the *Toadstool,* and I let the pile grow. Mary indicated I should rise, but my throttle was wide open, water dripping from the Levitrite. I shook my head, and the airscrews began to churn. José let the tow rope play out.

I began the repetitious task of checking my elevation, carrying two logs to the boiler, and working the pump lever three times.

The sun was moving west when the Levitrite hose clattered on the cabin's tin roof. The connection had come loose from the coupling leading to the Levitrite. I checked my watch. I had been adding water every four minutes.

I didn't take the time to signal to the *Cloud Queen.* There was only one Stillson wrench on board. The makeshift cabin was tall, and the steel rods holding the ship in the air were too far away.

I swung the Stillson like a club, bashing out every other board on the side of the crude cabin, creating a ladder of sorts. I tossed some of the splintered pine in the firebox hoping for a quick hot fire. Three minutes had passed.

I couldn't get a grip above the eave and resorted to burying a hammer claw into the thin roof and pulling myself up. Standing on my tiptoes, I could just touch the steel pipe. The hose reached but didn't have any length to spare.

The *Toadstool* hung below the *Cloud Queen,* and Mary stood on the upper deck, shrugging her shoulders in wonder. I pointed to the pipe and made a chopping motion.

I couldn't work on the fitting properly and climbed down. The cannonball box was well made, and I threw it on the roof.

Mary kept the two ships level, but my ears told me we were losing altitude. The bushing hadn't been correctly installed, and the threads were chewed. I brushed out the filing with my finger and got a metal sliver as a reward. I fumbled with the connection until the threads caught and gave it a turn.

We were no more than twenty feet from the top of the pines. I tightened the connection until the whole pipe leading to the Levitrite began to turn. The union threads started easily, and I tightened it as much as I dared. It would have to be enough.

I dropped the wrench on the roof and swung to the deck. I gave the handle twenty quick strokes and ran forward. Mary was at the pilot house door. I nodded, and she went inside.

The tip of a pine caught the *Toadstool,* and the ship bobbed fore and aft. I gave the pump six more strokes. The connection wasn't leaking any worse than it had before the break.

For the next hour, I pumped, stoked the fire, lugged wood, and checked with Mary. Hitting the rosin bottle with the palm of my hand, I shook out the last crumbs. I let the propeller run until the disks smoked with heat and disengaged the clutch.

Mary continued to run at Flank, and we wallowed on into the late afternoon. I wanted the flight to be over but thought of our success. If Finn recovered, we could cannibalize this ship.

I had three logs left when the *Cloud Queen* gave two blasts of her whistle. Eagle's Crest had never looked so good.

Mary signaled down but gently patted the air in front of her. The following minutes were comical. Getting the throttle set for a slow descent was tricky. I bobbed up and down until Mary gave me the OK sign.

A crowd waited in front of the workshop. Ed and Dad had a stretcher.

Mary had us over the open area, but I was falling too fast. I waited until I was no more than fifty feet from earth and gave the pump three strokes. My fall finally slowed.

The *Cloud Queen* followed me down, stopping her descent a few feet off the ground. The rebel ship crunched hard on level ground, every joint protesting. When the engine slowed, the Levitrite box sat firmly on its perch. I turned, and Laura had me in her arms.

"You silly, silly man. What were you thinking, flying in this contraption?" She smelled wonderful; I doubted that I did.

"I want to put this 'Tea Drinker,' Freebooter nonsense to bed," I said. "We have their engine, boiler, *and* their Levitrite!"

"Don't get me wrong, capturing their ship is wonderful. But, you are a silly man." She held me at arm's length. "A brave, silly man."

I had never thought of myself as brave but didn't argue. José and his father carried Benny toward the lodge on the stretcher, Mrs. Rodriquez trotting alongside.

We stepped off, and Paul and Liam helped Mr. Salsbury down. He was not resisting, but when he saw me, he glared. "Ain't right!" he yelled.

Mary joined us. "We did it," she said.

"Yes. Safe and sound. Well done, Mary. I couldn't keep that contraption level with the *Cloud Queen*. You handled it perfectly."

She took off her hat and ran her fingers through her hair. "I'm going to get out of this coat and hat and check my crops. I will see everyone in the lodge. They say Minnie is getting food ready."

Dolph held out his hand. "Welcome back, Captain Will."

I took his hand and gave him a sturdy shake. "Dolph, we have to keep Finn from seeing any messages tonight. We stole this ship from under their noses. Has there been chatter?"

"I keep him distracted. It's not hard. Sometimes Finn stands in a daydream. He forgets things." Dolph stared toward the workshop. "I miss the old Finn."

"We all do, Dolph." I shook myself. "Report to me if he's doing things we don't want him to do."

Dolph ran toward the workshop with the strides of a young man. The men were already towing the *Cloud Queen* into the big building, and I started that way.

Laura pulled my hand. "No, Mister, you are coming to the lodge to eat. They say you have not eaten much for two days."

We walked easily together. "Let me handle Finn," she said. "Remember, we brought their ship here to make improvements for the Adjunct Leader." Her dark eyes sparkled.

"You will use your beguiling ways, I am sure."

"Works on you!"

There was no doubt of that. I could not remember when I hadn't loved Laura, but at that moment, I loved her more than ever.

"I have to wash and change," I said. "I will run."

The first star, Venus, stood in the sky like a crystal. It would be a cold night.

36

The lodge was warm, and wonderful smells drew me to the kitchen. Mrs. Rodriquez carried a bowl of chicken soup out the back door for Benny.

I reached for a slice of chicken, and Minnie batted my hand away. "Get out of my kitchen!" She winked and handed me a bowl to carry. "Go sit down like a gentleman. You can wait one more minute!"

"Captain Will!" Dolph called. "Finn has seen the Freebooter ship, and he's upset. He says having their ship here is—'reasonous'".

"Treasonous?" I hid a smile at his excitement.

Dolph looked up. "Yes, that's what I meant. He's upset. I tried getting him to talk to you, but he won't listen."

"Thanks, Dolph. When we get out there, hang back, and we will see what we can do. Minnie, you'll have to hold supper."

Laura was already out the door.

The three of us walked quickly toward the Toadstool. A cutting wind crossed the yard, and I wished I had a heavier coat. Finn stood on the deck, arms crossed. He had turned on the yard pole light.

"I'll try to handle this," Laura said. "Follow my lead."

Dolph nodded eagerly.

Finn had his hand on the throttle. I moved closer to the boiler, glad for the heat.

"Finn, what do you think of the ship? Can we fix it for the Adjunct Leader?" Laura asked.

"Adjunct Leader? It is good to support the Army of the United States of America." Finn brightened. "We are fixing it for him?"

Laura's big eyes were wide. "Do you think it could be upgraded?"

Laura hadn't directly answered the question. A white lie, as she called it.

"It is poorly constructed," Finn said. "It's a wonder it even flew."

Laura tilted her head toward me, eyes wide.

"Yes," I said. "There is no way to control the elevation other than with the engine's speed. There is no water recovery, so we had to stop at the mine."

Finn turned quickly, his eyes unblinking. "Why would you be at the mine?"

"For water. We had to stop and get water. From the stream."

Finn was not convinced. "Why didn't any of the Army crew come with you?"

"Finn, we didn't get a chance to discuss this," Laura said. "The Army men tried it once and then were afraid to fly." Laura gave him a big smile. "Will brought it here because if anyone could make improvements, it's you. The Adjunct Leader said so."

Finn inflated, his smile widening. "I am honored to be of service to the Adjunct Leader." He looked at me. "You flew it here?"

"Yes." I improvised. "It is good to support the Army of the United States of America."

I tried for the blank stare Finn had. "I flew it. The propeller mechanism is crude. I had to keep dusting rosin on this drive wheel to keep it from slipping. The *Cloud Queen* had to tow me."

Finn ran his fingers over the scorched leather of the friction disk. "I thought the Adjunct Leader would have better plans. This is no better than their first ship."

I blurted, "Finn, that is why you are important to the Adjunct Leader."

Laura's look told me to stop. She touched Finn's arm. "The Adjunct Leader said you need to take care of your health. You are too valuable to risk getting sick." She cocked her head. "You have had a long day, haven't you? I know Will has. Minnie has supper. Why don't we eat and have a nice cup of tea?"

"I enjoy a good cup of tea." Finn seemed uncertain. "I need to get to the workshop and see what the Adjunct Leader's exact orders are."

"I will watch the telegraph and bring messages right away," Dolph volunteered. "I am not hungry anyway."

Finn continued to stare at the mechanism, not hearing. I motioned for Dolph to go.

Laura touched Finn's arm. "Come, Finn. You look tired. I am under strict orders to keep you healthy."

"Yes. Tea will help me not be tired."

The three of us walked to the lodge in silence. I asked Maria to take supper to Dolph.

Finn walked around the table, to the fire, and back. Laura came to his side. "Finn, why don't you see if Minnie has a warm kettle?"

He brightened. "Yes. I will make some tea."

When Mary arrived, she and Laura had a quiet conversation at the side of the fireplace.

Finn returned with a pot of tea and went straight to Mary. "I am so glad you are back. I've missed you." He put his hand on her shoulder for a moment.

Mary didn't wince. "It is good to be back."

"I was thinking that after supper, we could go for a little walk. Under the stars." Finn gawked at Mary, eyes traveling up and down.

"Oh, Finn. Perhaps another time. I am tired from the trip, and I have a headache. But perhaps we could sit by the fire and have a cup of tea."

Mary looked at Finn as if he was a small child. She put her hand on his arm as he reached for her shoulder again. "Now, Finn. We have talked about this." Mary's voice was calm and kind. "I know you like me, but—a man should never touch a woman unless they are special to each other."

"You *are* special to me. I think about you–"

Mary turned her head to one side and raised her eyebrows.

"I–" Finn stopped mid-sentence, frozen in time.

"Finn?" Mary said.

"I'm sorry, Mary. What were we talking about?"

Mary glanced at Laura. "You were telling me how you would make sure the Silver Seed radio is ready."

Finn looked puzzled. "Radio? The *Silver Seed*?"

We all waited. Finn rubbed his eyes. When he looked up, his wolfish grin had returned. "I think you and I had better take a little walk." He reached toward her again.

Mary made a quick turn and looked over her shoulder. "I thought you were going to bring me a cup of tea. I'd like to enjoy a cup of tea."

Finn obediently poured a cup of tea and gave it to Mary. When she moved toward the fire, Finn followed like a puppy.

"How long has this been going on?" I hissed. "Maybe Finn needs a good talking to."

Laura turned her back to Finn. "Will, relax. Mary didn't want to worry you. She is handling Finn. I don't think he needs a talking to from you." She gave me a knowing smile. "We ladies can handle men better than you men handle yourselves."

I nodded sheepishly. "Probably so."

José came in and stood by the fire. He wore a new shirt Letty had made for him. Addy brought in a platter of chicken, and they exchanged glances. He caught my eye and joined us. "What is the news?"

"Finn is infatuated with Mary," I said. "He wants to take her for a walk!"

"Mary? I doubt she wants to go for a walk with Finn."

"So far, she is able to distract him." Laura helped Miguel climb into his chair.

José lowered his voice. "This is hard. How does a man know?"

I was confused. "Know what?"

"About a girl—a woman—if a young woman wants to go for a walk?" José shifted, crossing and uncrossing his arms. "Addy. How do I know? I do not want to be like Finn and do it wrong."

"José, I think Addy would love to go for a walk—or talk. But if you go outside, make sure she has her coat and doesn't get cold. Just walk. No hand-holding until she seems ready. Take your time."

José looked over my shoulder, and his gaze told me Addy was back at the table.

"If you sit by her at dinner, hold her chair when she sits down. Help her scoot closer to the table."

José rubbed his hands together. "I can clean a gun, ride a horse—I can set dynamite charges. But this—I do not know what to do."

I laughed. "That's how things are. We men rarely know what to do. Follow along, and you will be fine." I slapped his shoulder. "She likes you, my friend. She likes you."

José helped Addy with her chair, and she blushed. I had seconds and then thirds.

After supper, Finn leaned back. "I'm enjoying a cup of tea. I think I can rework the Army airship's propeller system if I use the pump motor from the greenhouse."

"Finn," Mary asked, "do you want our crops to die?"

"We probably won't be here that much longer, do you think, Will? We should move to one of the Army camps so we can help them build bigger and better ships."

"Well, that is a possibility, I suppose." Mary looked across the table at Finn. "But, what if the Uninlightened were to attack the Army's food supplies?"

"Yes, Finn, we might need the stronghold for a while longer," Laura said.

"Well, I guess I could use–" Finn turned his teacup around and around on the saucer.

Laura held up her hand, and we all waited. Other than a log popping in the fireplace, the room was silent. A minute or two passed.

"—one from the shop." Finn moved in his chair. "I could—I'm sorry—what did you ask?" He looked at Mary wistfully.

"Finn, I think you might be coming down with something. You look pale," Mary said. "I wish you would rest more."

Finn turned to me. "Will, why did you bring that wretched ship here? That ship is a piece of junk. The Army doesn't know what they are doing."

I looked at Laura, and she shrugged. I took a chance and said, "I brought it so they wouldn't use it to drop fire on us."

"Well, the Freebooters must be stopped, that's for sure." Finn took a deep breath and let his cup drop onto the saucer. "I wish I had some decent tea!" He raised his voice. "I don't like this stuff."

Mary came around to Finn's side of the table. "Finn, you are tired. Won't you please go rest? You will do it for me, won't you? You'll feel better in the morning. We can have a nice cup of tea at breakfast and maybe go for a walk."

Finn smiled. "You are so pretty. I would like to go for a walk now. I want—I—"

We waited.

"Let Liam help you to bed, Finn."

Finn gave Mary a sly smile. "Why don't you come tuck me in?"

"Oh, Finn, I know, but please go with Liam for now."

"Finn, I can make you a cup of tea in the bunkhouse," Liam

said.

"I always like a cup—" Finn slapped his palm on the table. "I don't want a cup of that swill. I think I'll go to bed. I have a headache."

Liam walked Finn out.

"That is a good sign," José said. "For a minute, the old Finn was back."

"He'll be back in the fog in the morning," Mary said. "We're not done with this yet. John's been in and out for ten days after we stopped giving him regular tea. And yet when I was in the greenhouse earlier, he was an absolute gentleman. I believe he is close to being trustworthy."

Dolph came in. "Captain Will. This message came in—this is different. The signal was weak. I think whoever sent this is far away."

"What makes you think it's so different—not just a weak radio?"

"This is not the usual coding. There are no spelling mistakes. Look."

YOU LOST A SHIP TO THOSE KIDS STOP YOU WILL BE DISCIPLINED STOP UNACCEPTABLE STOP YOU ARE ALL TO HAVE A SPECIAL PASSING OF THE BLUE VIAL TONIGHT STOP HAVE TEA AFTERWARDS AND LISTEN TO THE DIRECTIVE STOP THEN PREPARE FOR BATTLE STOP ADJUNCT LEADER WILL SET SAIL IN TWO DAYS WITH A COMPANY IN THE GRAND BALLOONSHIP FALCON STOP THESE KIDS WILL NOT FOIL MY GLORIOUS PLAN STOP

I read the message aloud and passed it around. "This sounds ominous. This is a much bigger operation."

Laura was thoughtful. "And these orders are for the Adjunct Leader. This sounds like it came from on high."

"Let's piece together what we know," I said.

Nathan paced back and forth. "Grand Balloonship with a company of men bothers me. This is a battle plan."

"They will sail down the big valley from Sacramento," José said. "We have to find out more about this balloonship."

Nathan continued to pace. "What if we could get a look at this thing? We know it is coming south, but we don't know where it is going."

"Can we be sure they are not coming to Eagle's Crest?" José wondered. "For all we know, they could be headed here."

I made a decision. "We will start north in the *Silver Seed* in three days. We'll take a small scouting crew: Laura, Liam, José and me. The others must finish the drawbridge."

Dolph laid another message on the table. "This one is for Finn." He could hardly contain his enthusiasm. "SPECIAL MESSAGE FOR FINN RYAN STOP FINN YOU ARE TO WORK ON A MORE POWERFUL RADIO FOR THE SILVER SEED STOP YOU HAVE CREATED A MARVELOUS SHIP STOP IT WILL BE A GLORIOUS ADDITION TO MY FLEET STOP DO NOT REPLY STOP WE MUST NOT LET THE ENEMY KNOW OUR PLANS STOP

Dolph looked from face to face. "Too much?"

"No, Dolph. This is perfect," Laura said. "Very clever."

Mary stood. "I will get Finn to connect the *Silver Seed* radio to the main dynamo," she said. "He will do it for me. We will get some work out of Finn yet!"

"I don't like an Army on the south and this balloonship to the north," Paul said. "It's never good to have the enemy on two sides."

"What do you suggest?" I asked.

"I think we finish the bridge and set up the Freebooter cannon. We cannot be caught by surprise."

"We need to get some rest," Laura said. "There's much work ahead."

I stood. "I'm going out to the spare cabin to see Mr. Salsbury. I'll be along in a minute."

I found him stiff-backed on the bed, scowling at me.

"Is there anything I can get for you?"

"You can get me loose!" He shook the shackle on his ankle.

"You know I can't do that." The dog curled up beside the bed and yawned.

"What's your dog's name?"

"Pal. Least he's loyal. Does it ever get dark in here? That thing up there glow twenty-four hours a day?"

I pulled the string, exchanging the electric glow for white moonlight stretching across the floor.

"Have a good night, Mr. Salsbury."

"Humph."

The *Silver Seed* rose in cold air, and we took her high.

"Shall we try some speed?" I asked Laura.

Laura glanced away from the elevation rudder wheel. "Yes, but in stages. A little at a time."

I set the blower tubes to Half. At this high altitude, movement was imperceptible.

"I am trying Full." The horizon remained steady in the window.

"Finn may be addled from the gas, but he knows what he is doing," Laura said. "The elevation rudders work perfectly."

"I am going for Flank speed."

I pulled the lever all the way back, and the whine of the airscrews increased. "José, take the wheel, please."

In the salon, I watched Eagle's Crest shrink in the distance. We were flying at least four times faster than the *Cloud Queen* could fly, and we were bucking a slight headwind.

Back in the helm room, José and I took turns practicing with the elevation rudders. Then, Liam came forward to try his hand.

We were flying at eight thousand feet, but the heaters throughout the *Silver Seed* kept us comfortable. Flying west, we slipped over Tehachapi and down into the vast valley. We scanned the forward horizon with the telescope. An occasional settlement passed and then the patchwork of Bakersfield. Far below, men toiled in tar pits.

"This ship flies so well now, it's almost boring," Laura said.

And it was. We sailed into the night.

In the morning, we scanned the valley floor and reckoned that we were passing over Fresno.

A noon, I fixed lunch, and we ate in the helm. Fresno was far behind us when Laura said, "Come look. I think I see something. It's a tiny spec, but I am sure something's out there."

José went to the telescope. "Yes, a speck. I cannot see it with the naked eye."

I tried the hand scope but saw nothing.

We watched for the next hour and became convinced we were seeing the balloonship.

"Will, that ship must be huge. Immense," Laura said. "We have been sailing toward each other, and only now is it big enough to identify."

I went to the telescope. Huge bags of lifting gas forming a cigar gleamed in the sun. Under the bags was slung a long boat-like hull. "Do you suppose it would float if it landed on water?"

"It looks like a boat, but who knows what they plan?" José said.

We flew at Flank speed for another half hour when Laura spoke. "Fellows, that ship is more than immense. It must be five or six hundred feet long."

Smoke billowed from a stack, and four large airscrews, two on each side, beat the air. "Yes, but it is slow. Those airscrews are tiny compared to the size of the gas bags."

Liam came for a look and whistled. "How high do you think they are?"

I pulled the speed lever to stop. "They can't be at more than a thousand feet. I don't think they see us."

"They probably think they are on top of the world," Laura said.

"And they do not think to look up," José remarked. "They only expect enemy from below."

Laura continued to study the craft with the telescope. "There must be a hundred men on that ship. They are packed in the hold or whatever you call it."

"What are they planning?" I wondered. "We have to assume the directives they have been given are nothing good."

"How do we take it down? Can we shoot a hole in it?" José asked.

"A bullet would make a tiny hole. I doubt much gas would escape," I said.

"Ram it, and we might get tangled in the lines. We don't want it to take us down," Laura said.

José gestured with his chin. "Look, they are turning."

"I don't think they are turning," I said. "The wind has changed. They are being blown northeast, toward the mountains. With such small airscrews, they are at the mercy of the slightest breeze."

Laura pointed to small clouds scudding below us. "They are in for a big storm. Look to the west."

Storm clouds filled the sky.

"They are losing altitude!" José exclaimed.

In the next few minutes, we watched the men throwing wood, boxes, and weapons overboard. The ship gained some height, only to start down again. They hit the ground, the hull tipping, men and supplies spilling out. The Freebooters tried to hold the ship with ropes, stumbling and rolling in the dirt. They were forced to let go, one by one, and the wind carried the craft away.

José chuckled. "Those men will have a long walk to wherever that ship ends up."

The wind buffeted the *Silver Seed* as well. "I think we should go home. They won't be able to fly until this storm passes. I am going to Flank speed."

When we landed at Eagle's Crest, Finn met us, Dolph following at a distance.

"Be careful," Laura cautioned, "we don't know what mood he'll be in."

When I opened the door, Finn smiled. "Good to see you, Will. How was the flight?"

Unsure of his mood, I gave a vague answer. "We had a good flight. It is a beautiful ship."

"Did you see the Freebooters?"

Dolph made the OK signal with his thumb and finger.

"Yes, we saw a huge airship. It didn't have enough power to battle the wind and was carried away in a squall."

Finn stared at nothing.

"Finn? Finn!" Laura stepped closer. "What are you thinking we should do with the *Silver Seed*?"

Finn snapped out of his reverie. "We must use it to stop them. Destroy their airships."

Laura wrinkled her brow. "But, how? Their airship is huge. It has a series of balloons that suspend a hull that can hold a hundred men."

"I have been thinking about Airships. Ramming them is not good—the first attempt almost took us down. I have a plan to rip their bags open. We—"

"He gets stuck," Dolph offered sadly.

"We—" Finn rubbed his temples. "Will, where have you been?" There was another long pause. "It's like a fog. I can't seem to think straight."

"You were saying you had a plan to rip the Freebooter ship's gasbags open."

Finn brightened. "Yes! Come and see. We have the weapon started in the shop."

Dolph nodded. "Finn showed us what to do."

Finn and Laura started for the shop, and Dolph towed me aside. "Finn has been himself most of the morning. Yesterday he was only part good. In the morning, he was grumpy and mean. But by noon, he was the old Finn."

"How was he early this morning?"

"He was confused. Like just now. He stops and then—like—wakes up from a nap. John says he had a terrific headache and couldn't think straight for days."

A giant saw blade was laid out on the shop floor. Five angry steel teeth a foot across glimmered in the lights.

Finn was excited. "It bolts to the underside of the *Silver Seed's* rear frame and swings down for an attack."

Dolph brought a drawing of the jagged shark-like fin under the *Silver Seed.*

Finn pointed to the plans. "If the blade were to get caught on something, a lever inside will pull these pins—releasing the blade."

Dolph's eyes were wide. "I would hate to lose the blade. All this work."

Finn ruffled Dolph's hair. "If we lose it, we will make a better one." Finn went to the shop table and stared at a box of gears.

Dolph cautioned us with his hand and whispered. "He does this. It's better if we don't talk to him. He calls it the fog. He doesn't like it, I mean later. After."

We waited. After several minutes Finn picked up a set of gears.

"I will install these in the rear of the engine room to unlock the blade and lower it into position.

It was difficult to watch our friend in such a state.

That evening we intercepted a message from Sacramento. The Freebooter's ship had been blown back up the valley and landed in the foothills east of Sacramento. Wagons with supplies were being sent with repairs.

The meeting of the airships was postponed until the *Falcon* was again ready for battle.

38

"We'll have a jousting contest!" I said. We were at the big table, and Minnie and Mrs. Rodriquez had outdone themselves.

"With horses, like the knights?" Dolph asked.

"I have another idea in mind. We are going to have a cutting competition with the *Silver Seed*."

Several sat forward.

"We tie a light rope between two trees." I held my index fingers up. "Then we take turns flying the *Silver Seed* in a rope-cutting contest!"

"We can have a trophy," Laura laughed.

"I will make a winner's cake!" Minnie said.

"But the winner has to cut it." Addy was serious. "No ramming it down."

José was smiling and winked at Addy. I had never seen José wink, and Addy blushed.

The *Cloud Queen* hovered over trees on the west point, stringing the line between two tall pines. Laura had made a chart on the big chalkboard. José and Addy put out chairs so everyone could watch. Benny came and sat with Maria.

It was decided that Finn would fly with each team.

José and Addy wanted to be a team, so Addy flew with Laura and me to become familiar with the elevation rudder system. Over the fields, I made a wide circle and then aimed between the two trees. I pulled speed to Flank. "All good there?"

"Steady. No problems."

The *Silver Seed* gained speed. "I'm too high," I said. I eased the lift lever, and we bore down on the red cloth in the middle of the rope.

The *Silver Seed* porpoised and heard Laura say to Abby, "Did you feel that? Watch. I am turning the wheel in tiny increments to keep us level—keep your eye on the bubble."

As we closed, I had the altitude right and held the wheel steady. The elevation was perfect, and the rope passed under us.

"Did we get it?" I asked. "I didn't feel anything." I brought us around. Below Dolph pointed at the line still strung between the trees.

Addy whispered something to Laura and turned aside, her shoulders shaking.

"Will, did we forget anything?" Laura laughed.

"Were we too high?"

"I should get some extra points for José and me," Addy said.

When I hovered over the area in front of the spectators, it dawned on me—we hadn't swung the knife into position.

When I opened the door, Dolph was there grinning. "Good flight, Captain Will. Good speed."

"I felt like they had perfect aim," Paul said.

Dad patted my shoulder. "You make a father proud."

Minnie brought me a glass of root beer with one swallow in the bottom. "Here's something for your trouble," she said.

Laura put her arm around my waist. "Well, apparently, we gave them quite a show." She wrote a zero on the chalkboard.

Letty came with her baby, Lucy. "I thought it was a beautiful flight—not very effective, but you missed very well."

There was more laughter.

"I think we should get another try," I joked.

Mary stepped forward. "I think it is time for a woman to try this! Come on, Nathan, let's show them how it's done."

Dolph brought me a chair. "Here, Captain Will, this will help you rest after your embarrassment."

I sat down, and Laura sat on my lap. "Well, at least we went fast," she said.

"And level," I added.

Mary took the ship up, and the knife swung down. She came to the center window and made a muscle with her arm. Laura waved.

The *Silver Seed* was beautiful to watch as it went out and began its turn. The tube fans began to whine, and the ship picked up speed. The rope caught on the plating below the helm windows and broke loose.

Laura put ½ on the chalkboard.

When they landed, Mary was the first out the door. I got up as she strode over. "Will, I may have spoken too soon. This may not be as easy as it looks." She tipped her top hat and gave me a little curtsy.

She and Nathan laughed as Minnie gave them each a half glass of root beer while the *Cloud Queen* reset the rope.

Laura and Mary flew with José and Addy. The *Silver Seed* flew level but missed the rope and circled back for a landing. They too were laughing as they came out. Minnie gave them their glasses with one swallow. They gazed at each other as they drank, hardly noticing the rest of us.

Dolph stepped forward. "Captain Will, I want to try. Laura could run the elevation rudders?"

I looked down at Dolph's earnest face, and several were nodding behind him. I thought of when we took turns carrying him to the lodge four years before and what a fine young man he had become.

"OK, Dolph. You steer, and Laura and I will assist. Is that all right, my friend?"

"Proud to have you aboard, Captain Will." Dolph's round face showed no emotion, but his eyes danced.

Finn announced the engine room was ready, and we took the ship to 100 feet.

"Lower the knife and go to Half Speed," Dolph said. He stood on his tiptoes and turned the wheel. We came around quickly, and he tried to spin the wheel back but overdid it.

"It's OK. Go around again and get a little further away. We want to have time to get some speed," I said.

Dolph's tongue peeked out the side of his mouth.

"Are you holding your mouth right, Dolph?" I teased.

Dolph only nodded slightly. He came out of the turn and had us lined up. "Full speed ahead," Dolph said.

Dolph didn't blink as he homed in on the flag. "Ramming speed!"

I tweaked the lift lever, and we rushed forward. The speed indicator read eighteen knots.

I didn't correct Dolph's steering, and we flew over the rope with a few feet to spare. I saw it flick past in the glass port at our feet and heard a faint clunk at the back of the ship. Dolph brought us around, and below, our friends cheered. The line was down.

"You are quite the pilot," I said. "We're proud of you."

Dolph bounced on his tiptoes. "That was the most exciting thing I have ever done. Thanks, Captain Will."

When we opened the door, the group sang, "For he's a jolly good fellow." Minnie started to put her arms around Dolph and then thought better of it, settling for a pat on the shoulder. Hanna handed her brother a brimming glass of root beer.

We ate a leisurely lunch under the trees, and then Laura and I won a second round. Minnie and Mrs. Rodriquez gave it a try, and we were proud of Mrs. Rodriquez for overcoming her fear of flying. They missed the rope but came out laughing. By late afternoon several teams had three cuts in a row.

We held a meeting that evening. Minnie let Dolph stay up, and Benny sat by the fire. He said the heat made his shoulder feel better.

"There is another ship because the Freebooters are talking about a rendezvous. How do we handle that?" Finn asked.

"The best would be to fly high above the ship from Sacramento. Let them lead us to the others," I suggested. "Strategically, we have two advantages—the ship from the North is easy to see at a distance, and we are much faster."

"I believe we can fly higher and rise faster," Finn said. "We don't know how the balloonship operates—but—"

Mary had gone to stand by the fire. Finn shook himself. "Someti—I don't know what I am thinking—what was I saying?"

"How the balloonship operates?" Dolph offered.

Finn pulled his eyes away from Mary. "Right—gas bags are slow to rise compared to either of our ships."

"Do we take the *Cloud Queen* out?" Laura wondered.

Mary slipped on her duster, but there was no disguising her shape. She sat in a chair on the far side of the fireplace, eyes glistening. José casually moved in front of Finn, blocking his view of Mary.

"I think we use one ship at a time for as long as we can," I said. "I don't want to put all our eggs in one basket."

"The *Cloud Queen* is easier to spot in the air," José said. "It would be sad to lose her."

39

Mr. Salsbury made a double jump and kinged the red checker. His game had improved as he came out of the fog.

"You're a good man, Will. What you do is important. Everything, the last month or so, seems like a dream. I remember what I said and what you did." Mr. Salsbury stalled, staring into space. "But it seems like it was someone else that was there. Like I was watchin' it all."

It wasn't time to let Mr. Salsbury go free, but he was only a week or so from being himself. "What do you want to do?"

"I would like you to let me go home. Take me home, I guess is what I am saying." Pal licked Mr. Salsbury's hand. "I can help. I can help supply your efforts again. We have to put a stop to this nonsense."

"We'll take you home in a week if your condition continues to improve."

"That is all I can ask. You have always been fair. More than fair." He stretched and made a triple jump. "I'll miss the cooking here."

"We're going to teach you to send and receive code. Simple messages. Dolph will help you."

"I don't spell so good," Salsbury mumbled.

Dolph took his job seriously in the days that followed, creating a picture dictionary in a notebook with shortcuts. XXX stood for Freebooters. They were laughing together by the end of the week, and Dolph called him Papa Salsbury.

Laura, José, and I flew Mr. Salsbury and Pal back. Dolph promised to listen for a hello message every day at sunrise. It had been raining hard all night, but there was a break in the weather.

Before returning to Eagle's Crest, we flew to Glendora Canyon.

We hovered high above the Freebooter camp and watched with the telescope. If they were working on the third ship, we could see no sign of any progress, and no guard was posted at the back doors.

"Let me go down," José said. "I can be in and out in minutes."

Laura brought the *Cloud Queen* low to the ground further up the canyon. José made a rope fast and tossed it over the side. He pulled on gloves and shinnied down. He sprinted, dodging brush, and jump-slid down into the canyon.

We lifted higher, and I stood at the bow with the rifle steadied on the telescope mount.

José was in the building and out again. He hightailed it along the creek and scrambled up the bank. Watching through the drop port, I kept us just above the manzanita.

José stuck his head through the engine room door. "Why are we not starting home?"

He wasn't even breathing hard.

I leaned toward the speaking tube. "If you can believe it, he is up the rope and already aboard." I pulled the lift lever to eighty percent, and Laura rang for Full.

"I do not think they have touched the ship," José said. "I got the feeling only a skeleton crew is left at the camp."

At Eagle's Crest, we made preparations and waited. It was ten days later when Dolph came with a transcribed message.

REPAIRS MADE TO THE ADJUNT COMMANTERS AIRSHIP FALKUN STOP WILL SAIL WITH THE WIND ON FEBURY FIFTEEN.

"The reply originated from a third transmitter," Dolph said. "LOADING SUPPLIES. GAS BAGS FUL STOP TWO UNITS OF SOJERS READY TO BORD. WILL BE AT RENDUVIOUS ON THE 28."

"Good work, Dolph."

"They sure can't spell."

"No, Dolph. The Freebooters aren't picky about who they give the gas to."

Dolph stood tall. "I want to come, Captain Will."

"I know you do, but who will man the telegraph and watch the generator while we are gone?"

"Mom knows code. Hannah knows code. I can operate the radio in the *Silver Seed*. I am twelve. Benny was ten when he started flying. You always say he did a good job. I can do a good job."

"I will talk to your mother."

I thought it best to seek the counsel of José and Finn. "I think Paul and Ed should stay. Paul can tend the generator and help defend Eagle's Crest," I said. "Ed needs to care for the greenhouse and start the planting." I paused. "Dolph has asked to come."

"Dolph has been my right-hand man," Finn said. "I would have gotten into a lot of trouble if he had not been there to—guide me in my time of confusion."

José nodded. "Dolph is not much younger than we were when we started our first flights and battle. He is as smart as a whip."

Minnie wasn't thrilled, but agreed that Dolph would be a strong addition to the crew. It was decided that we would take a double crew. The original *Cloud Queen* crew made up the first team with the addition of Dolph. Mary, Liam, and Nathan were the second crew.

Before dinner, José and I sat watching the fire. "I want Addy to come with us."

"She wants to come?"

"You took Laura on our first flight out of the canyon. I did not argue. Laura was important to our victory."

"But does she want to come? Is she ready?"

"She is ready." José poked at the fire. "It is not just because I—we—"

"You love each other?"

"I think she is the one. She—I want her with me. I trust her to take care of what needs to be done." He watched Addy carrying food to the big table in a flowered dress Letty had made for her. "She is hurt, too. Like Mary. She lost a brother and father to the Freebooters. She deserves to be a part of this."

I put my hand on his shoulder. "Then she comes, my friend."

The *Silver Seed* was fueled and loaded with supplies. We waited a day after the balloonship left Sacramento, anxious for it to lead us to the other ships.

"We can fly for fourteen days if we don't run at Full," Finn said.

"Can we take extra cans of oil?" José asked.

"Good thinking, as usual," Finn said. "We can lash several barrels next to the tank."

We lifted the *Silver Seed* onto some high blocks of wood. Benny and Addy painted all day, creating a dull finish on the underside.

We lifted off before the sun rose, and I took us high. We took turns at the controls at each station, flying at different speeds. Finn had written an instruction book for the engine room and explained it in detail. But mostly, we were bored.

The following morning, Laura stood at the forward windows. "It is beautiful up here. So peaceful."

"High above the troubles, down there." I was tired of the fight. Tired of not having time to simply live.

"I see nothing." José was disgusted. He had been at the telescope for thirty minutes.

"This is the hard part," Mary said. "The waiting."

Finn brought out a small box. "I got these during our last supply run." He proudly displayed a set of darts. "Dolph and I made a board. It's tucked under my bed."

Dolph was grinning. "I painted a bulls-eye. Finn showed me how to scribe a circle."

"Let's have a contest," Laura said.

Liam brought out a sheet of plywood. "If you miss the whole piece of backing and hit the wall, you get to paint over your error." He pointed at Dolph and winked.

"I've been practicing," Dolph bragged. "Finn says I am pretty good."

"We'll take turns operating the ship," I said. "Let the darts begin."

We laughed. We teased. We won and lost. On the third day, Laura spotted the balloonship.

Benny was at the telescope, watching the ship wallow along, belching smoke. "At this rate, we will have to go back to Eagle's Crest and refuel before they get to the mountains."

"It is like watching corn grow," José said. "Maybe not as fast."

"Should we get closer?" Laura wondered.

"I think we should wait for them," I said. "No sense using fuel going north if they are coming south."

After a half day, we could see the Freebooters crowded in the hold. A small raised area in the stern allowed the men fifteen minutes to exercise. They rotated back row by row, stumbling over wood for the boiler, and I did not envy their trip.

"They won't be in any condition to fight after this trip," Finn said. "I doubt they are being fed well."

"I think this calls for a checkers contest," José said.

Addy's eyes flashed. "Yes, but let's make it a good contest. Winner gets to skip a duty of their choice."

We played until I didn't care if I won or lost. As predicted, the balloonship turned east at the mountains, rose to clear Tehachapi, and wallowed toward Cajon Pass.

I was disgusted. "If we had known they were going this way and not straight south, we could have waited thirty miles from home!"

José called us to the helm. "They are trying to go over the Pass in the afternoon. Apparently, they have not studied the winds."

We took turns watching. Buffeted, the Freebooter ship attempted a landing.

Finn lingered at the telescope. "They are heating whatever gas they are using. As it heats, it expands and gives them more lift, but the process takes time. I don't think they took into account they are in the high desert."

The Freebooter ship dragged to the ground and bounced along, kicking up dust.

I came to a decision. "It is two o'clock. We can be at Eagle's Crest by five. We'll find them easily in the morning."

Finn went to the helm, calling for Full.

40

The moment we landed, Mary headed directly to the greenhouse. We filled the *Silver Seed* with fuel, and Minnie restocked our food.

That night, at the big table, we waited anxiously for messages sent by the Freebooters.

When Finn and Dolph came in, he let Dolph deliver the message.

"The first message said, FLIGHT FROM SACRAMENTO SUCCESSFUL STOP PERFECT LANDING AT CAJON." Dolph snickered. "'Perfect, if you think bouncing along in a boat being dragged through the desert is perfect."

"After they crashed in the foothills, this probably looked like success," Mary remarked.

"Is there more?" I asked.

Dolph became serious. "Yes. Sorry, Captain Will. I was—" He squinted at the rafters. "Distracted!"

WILL RENDEZVOUS AT RIVERSIDE STOP ALL MUST BE READY STOP

"Then the other ship sent a message."

RED HAWK LANDED AT RIVERSIDE AT NOON STOP THE GULL ALREADY HERE STOP

"Riverside." I was relieved. "At least we know where they are headed."

"Three ships," Paul said, "could mean two hundred men."

"Can we make Riverside in four hours?" I wondered.

Finn stood. "Cutting across the highest mountains, I think three should be plenty of time."

"Could we get them to chase the *Cloud Queen*," I wondered, "if they thought it was damaged?"

"Why not just bring them down?" José wondered.

"The men in the ship are puppets," I said. "What if we brought their ships down in the desert—kept the Freebooters there until they come out of their fog?"

"We are talking two to three weeks with no tea," Finn grumbled.

"I know that is a long time, but those men deserve a chance to become themselves again."

John cleared his throat. "Do we know when they passed the vial?"

Dolph raised his hand, waving wildly. "I didn't get to finish. It says WE WILL CELEBRATE OUR RENDEZVOUS BY PASSING THE NEW VIAL STOP WE WILL BE STRONG FOR VICTORY STOP"

"Which ship sent that message? Can we tell?" I wondered.

"Easy," Dolph said, "the big ship has the strongest signal."

"How do we stop them from delivering the vial?" I asked.

"By stopping the rendezvous," Paul said simply. "The two ships at Riverside must feel they are under attack. They must see the *Cloud Queen*, feel threatened, and give chase."

Finn sat and stood again immediately. "The *Cloud Queen* will have to leave early if we are to make Riverside before the ship from Sacramento."

I agreed. "We should start getting up steam immediately."

José said, "We must be careful—we do not know what kind of weapons they have."

Finn pulled on his fingers. "Staying above them will be part of the trick. The balloons will shield us from the hold."

"They wouldn't want to shoot a hole in their gasbags," Dolph chuckled.

"The *Silver Seed* will stay above, keeping careful watch. If the *Cloud Queen* is in danger, it swoops down to take out their ships," I said.

There were nods of agreement.

"All right," I said. "First things first. We need to get the *Cloud Queen* ready."

"I will get started right now," Finn said. "I have slept enough lately."

"I can help," Dolph offered.

"You have been a big help today," I said, "but we need you to be rested. There will be plenty to do tomorrow."

Minnie gave Dolph her "I'm your mother" look, and Dolph headed upstairs.

"The original crew will fly the *Cloud Queen*," I decided.

"Mary, can you handle the *Silver Seed*?" Paul asked.

"I can handle the ship, but I need Finn. She's a new ship."

"She's right," Finn said. "If the *Silver Seed* needed some adjustment, it's best I'm aboard."

I chafed at not having Finn on board the *Cloud Queen*. "Then Liam can tend boiler for us."

Ed stood. "I'll check the guns and dynamite and put them aboard."

"Yes, but you should stay. Someone has to keep the farm running, and if Freebooters come, you are an excellent shot."

Ed looked as if he were going to protest but shook my hand. "I will keep the farm and Eagle's Crest safe."

I knew he would.

I stopped by the workshop on the way to bed. "Finn, is there any chance you could have a receiver on the *Silver Seed* tuned to the Freebooters?"

"The silly fools have not thought of sending messages while flying, so it wouldn't be that much help. But, no, there isn't time." Finn sighed. "We need someone here to relay any messages. I'm afraid Dolph has to stay."

"He won't like it. He's going to be heartbroken."

"Let me handle Dolph. I have a project he can work on in the shop. He'll be alright."

At our cabin, Laura packed extra clothes. "It will be like old times, being on the *Cloud Queen*. Except for Finn."

"Yes. You and I and our friends." I loved this woman. "If we can't have Finn, his dad is the next best."

Finn knocked on our door at four, but we were already awake. We hurried out into the cold and went to the engine room, where José and Benny joined us. Ed had rifles and ammunition neatly stowed away.

"We will follow you at dawn," Finn said. "You better get moving."

We stood in a circle, and José put his hand out to Finn. "Take care of yourself."

"You too," Finn said.

Addy came into the engine room. "I want to come, Will. I can watch gauges. I can shoot. José's papa has been showing me some techniques." She crossed her arms. "Will, they killed my brother and my father. I am seventeen years old. I'm not a child."

"You can come," Laura said.

"I want to hear it from Will."

José gave me a helpless look as if to say, "I did not put this in her head."

"Addy, you are a welcome addition to our group and flight."

"Give me a minute." Laura hurried out of the room. When she came back, she was out of breath. "Here, Mom just finished this coat." She handed Addy the duster, hat, and goggles. "You are one of the women pilots, now."

José watched Addy put on the coat and cinch the belt tight. She put the hat on and stood straight.

"Perfect," I said.

Finn stepped off, and we tested the balance.

"Be gentle with Dolph," I told him. "He's going to be disappointed."

"He is already in the shop at the radio. Dolph is fine. He is growing up and knows we all have different jobs in this quest."

When Dad and Paul came alongside, I said, "You two and Ed are in charge here. Keep Eagle's Crest safe. I believe John can be trusted with a gun if you should need him." I felt uneasy leaving our home with no airship.

"We'll be fine." Dad jumped up and patted my back. "I'm proud of you, Son. Very proud."

Dad and I didn't often say such things to each other. I wanted to tell him I loved him but felt my face grow hot. I settled for patting him as well.

Laura went to the pilothouse with Addy. As we rose, the engine order telegraph rang for Full, and José set the airscrews.

I went out on the stern and watched our friends waving. Dad had his hands clasped together like a winning boxer in a ring.

In the pilothouse, Laura had turned on the heat, and Addy was steering, eyes on the compass.

41

THE BIG SHIP IS GETTING READY TO TAKE OFF STOP SO IS SILVER SEED

I tapped out, THANKS DOLPH STOP WE ARE PAST BALDY

MR was the reply with BON VOYAGE tagged on the end.

When I showed it to the crew, Laura said, "He's quite a guy—he doesn't miss much."

I watched the engine running at high speed, confident we would be ready to draw the enemy away well before the clumsy balloonship arrived.

Addy and Benny made breakfast and brought it to the pilothouse. Addy whispered to José, and they laughed.

"Share, you two," Laura said.

José looked embarrassed. "Addy thinks I should grow a mustache. She says I will look like a pirate in my coat."

"A pirate indeed. But a good pirate, right, Addy?" Laura laughed.

"He's a good pirate," she said. She leaned against his arm. "The best pirate I have ever met."

José and I stood on the bow, scanning the horizon. Occasionally we swung the telescope north but did not expect the big balloonship to be making much progress. It was mid-morning when we spotted two smaller balloonships moored in a field outside Riverside.

We gathered in the pilothouse.

"We have a northwest wind," Laura commented. "Let them run with the breeze."

"Right," Liam laughed. "Otherwise, they would never be able to give chase."

Laura had pinned a map on the wall. "The winds are cooperating, and I have been studying the area. This place—Anza Borrego is here, with steep mountains to the west. It might be easier to keep them corralled there."

"We know some of the terrain on the way," Benny said. "Even if some men escaped, they would have a long walk."

"Good work, Laura," I said. "Now, how do we best get their attention?"

José was firm. "First, we watch—find out what kind of weapons they have."

After sailing over both ships, we were high, shivering on the front deck. Clouds were gathering in the east.

Each craft had a cannon at the bow. The westernmost ship was the *Red Hawk,* her gasbags half collapsed.

"Cannon may work for forts and ships, but they are no good for fighting in the air," José commented. "They cannot aim up or down well or be turned from side to side."

"So," I raised my eyebrows, "we don't get in front of them."

I motioned for Addy to join us. "Everyone, take a look. Study both ships carefully. We don't want to be surprised by anything once they know we are here."

"They're certainly clumsy things," Laura said. "The second ship is the *Gull.* It's a single gasbag ship—smaller."

"She has a single propeller in the front." I wondered if that made it more agile in the air.

Benny adjusted the focus. "Lots of men with rifles around."

Addy watched for a long time. "There are no more than twenty-five men at each ship."

When Benny took another turn, he said, "We better do this now. They are firing their boilers, and men are assembling."

"Dynamite," José said, "but we miss. They will think we do not know what we are doing."

"Drop it so it goes off when we are overhead," I said. "Then we do our wounded bird act."

José went to the telescope again. "The cannon are the bad part."

"We'll watch as they load the cannon," Liam said. "Cannon roll back when fired. Then they swab, put in the powder, ram down the wadding, and then the ball. The last thing they'll do is run the cannon back out. That's when we change altitude."

I took off my hat. "This is taking a big chance. Everyone should get a vote on this."

One by one, we all agreed.

"José, ready the dynamite."

Laura and Addy went to the pilothouse. José began laying out the charges in the engine room.

"Benny, let's bring the pressure to one-twenty," Liam said.

José and I returned to the bow, and Laura edged us to the north side of our target.

"How close do we want to get?" I asked.

"We want them to pay attention," he said. "I will make it pretty close."

I took one last look. "Places, everyone."

In the engine room, José worked with absolute calm. Benny had a lantern burning with the globe lifted.

I sighted down the front drop with the rangefinder. "Three hundred feet."

José gave me a slight grin. "It is time." He moved to the back drop, releasing a small stick of wood. He counted and trimmed the fuses. "Now."

Benny brought the lantern close, and José let three quarter sticks drop in quick succession.

The first charge went off, and a puff of wind blew through both drop ports. After a pause, the next two exploded in rapid succession.

"These guys never look up!" José complained. He lit a fourth fuse, spit on his fingers, and pinched out the flame. "Have Laura get closer. I will drop this right where the men are. They need to know it comes from up here."

The *Cloud Queen* inched closer to the *Gull*. Men ran around like ants, but not one looked up. The dynamite sailed down and bounced off a man's shoulder. Rifles came up and pointed at us. I slammed shut the steel door on my port.

Muffled shots continued, but I heard no bullets digging into the *Cloud Queen*.

Laura stopped the airscrews and let us drift to the southeast.

"We'll go out a couple hundred yards and then see what they do. Liam, give us a tip."

The ship groaned as the starboard dropped.

José went out on the back deck with a rifle and lay behind the shield.

Benny closed the air on the boiler flame, and black smoke poured out of the stack. We lit two buckets of oily rags with coals from the cook stove, setting them on the deck.

"One ship is loading men," José called. "I count twenty-five."

Men double-timed to the second ship. A squad ran into the dry desert land, bullets clanging against the shield. José gave me a wry grin. "I guess they know we are here."

The *Gull*'s gasbag had expanded, and men began letting loose the mooring lines. The *Red Hawk's* gasbags were nearly full.

Addy peeked around the back shield in the pilothouse. "The *Gull* is in the air. The *Red Hawk* is letting the lines loose," she reported.

"Don't ever let one of them get behind us at the same altitude. Keep Liam posted."

It took another five minutes before the *Red Hawk* was in the air. It didn't matter; the *Gull* was no closer. We continued to drift, staying above the cannon's maximum elevation. We were well into the morning before we started the airscrews.

"This is like fighting snails," José quipped.

By noon we were at five thousand feet, the wind remaining in our favor. Even at Dead Slow, our shadow snaked along briskly when the sun occasionally broke through.

"The *Silver Seed* says look up," Liam called on the speaking tube. I stepped in front of the pilot house. It took a minute to see them. "Addy, come and admire your paintwork."

She looked along my arm as I pointed. "Oh, there it is. Good disguise! They'll never see it, never guess it's there."

"Show José. Be careful to stay low."

The *Red Hawk* began a wide swing to our port, fifty feet below us. The *Gull* closed the gap but far below.

Volleys of rifle fire came from the *Red Hawk*. I went to the speaking tube. "Everyone alright up there?"

"Fine," Laura replied. "A bullet hit near the pilothouse, but it hardly dented the wood. They are too far below to get a good angle."

"Liam, take us a little higher." The gauge crept toward eleven thousand feet.

"The ship behind us is trying to get the cannon aimed at us," Laura called down. "Addy is watching. So far, they cannot get it aimed high enough."

Our plan sounded simple at the lodge but was doubly hard with two ships. "Benny, get up to the pilothouse and keep an eye on the *Red Hawk*. Addy can use the hand scope for the *Gull*."

I went back and slid in beside José. "What do you think?"

"We are too high for now. They cannot get enough elevation with the cannon."

"I know, but one shot hits the boiler, and we go down."

"Will, come! Quick!" Laura called.

42

Addy handed me the hand scope. The Freebooters tried to run the cannon truck up on boards. The men struggled with the ropes and pulleys. The big gun lurched up on one wheel and swung to the port. Four large men wrestled it back.

They managed to get the cannon's front wheels up and ran the gun forward. The aim was too close for comfort.

"Call for Up, fast!" I said. The deck pressed hard against my feet.

A Freebooter had a torch, ready to touch off the charge when José shot. The man spun sideways and fell. Another renegade picked up the torch.

The cannon fired, but the shot was below us.

"Now we go down. They might think they hit us. Call for Flank and stay behind the shields. The *Gull* will have a good shot at us as we pass." I hammered down the stairs two steps at a time. "Watch our port. Everyone down." I started down the hallway, but José was already coming.

"I don't like this, José. We need a better plan."

The *Cloud Queen* fell quickly and was a hundred feet below the enemy ships when I called, "Level off, Liam. Be ready to go back up. Keep the engine running hard."

Several bullets dug into the walls and roof of the engine room.

"The *Gull* is dropping fast," Laura called. "Very fast!"

Liam reached for the lift lever when the back wall of the engine room exploded, showering us with splinters and wood. The cannonball went straight through the breezeway and tore through the front cabin.

"I'll check for damage," Liam said. "It will take time for them to reload."

Laura was down the stairs in moments. She took one look at the splintered hole in the wall, called, "Pilothouse is fine," and was gone.

I pulled the lift lever to eighty percent and went to the speaking tube. "Hard aport! Hard aport! We're going to Full."

EVERYONE OK EVERYONE OK

YES

Water trickled into the breezeway, and Liam was on a ladder in moments.

"What?" I asked.

"Broke the line going to the aft starboard lifter." He jumped down.

I shouted up the stairs, "Shut off lifter valve number four!"

José appeared with a hacksaw. "Benny, we have to get water to that stern lifter. Now that we pulverize the Levitrite, water evaporates faster. As soon as I get a clean cut in this tubing, I want you to fashion a funnel out of whatever you can find."

Laura came down. "Both ships are well below us. The *Gull* is still dropping fast, but the *Red Hawk* is gaining altitude."

I steadied the ladder as José sawed. He eased the line away from the bulkhead.

Liam poked his head into the breezeway. "The lifter adjustment is at max!"

Benny sat on the deck, boring a small hole in the heel of a boot with his knife. He worked it onto the pipe and poured a bucket of water a little at a time. "Leaks. Some's going down."

José held up the torch. "I have only seen Finn do this once." He worked the pump.

"I can do it." I cut a piece of pipe to bridge the gap. "Slit two pieces of tubing for collars." The deck creaked.

Laura came halfway down the stairs. "They are still rising. Shall we keep pace?"

"Yes, until we reach ten thousand. How's it going, Benny?"

"I'm getting some to go down."

José stood ready with the equipment. "Good enough. Come back down, Benny."

I climbed the ladder two rungs at a time. "The boot was genius, Benny." I tossed it down. "If all else fails—throw it at 'em."

I got the pipe in place, slid the collars on, and liberally painted flux. José handed me gloves, and I applied the torch to the brazing rod. "Where are Finn and Dolph when we need them?" I joked.

The ship groaned, and I turned up the torch.

I used three rods and ended up with two messy blobs and brazing material splattered on the deck. "That's about as good as I can do."

José went to the stairs to the pilothouse. "Addy! Turn on number four, please."

A bead of water formed at the top connection.

"Good enough." I doused the torch.

"Will, José, you need to see this," Benny called.

We followed him to the front drop port. The spectacle was encouraging and heartbreaking at the same time. The *Gull* hit the ground, and the gondola broke into pieces. Survivors pulled the wounded clear of the wreckage. The limp gasbag dragged the empty stern along the rough ground.

When the *Silver Seed* approached, several renegades raised their hands.

NINE STILL CAN WALK STOP MANY WILL NOT LIVE LONG STOP

I sent MR.

Liam set the airscrews to Slow. The remaining ship had fallen behind. She was climbing but too far away to be a threat.

"Meeting," I called into the speaking tube. "Dead Slow and lash the wheel."

When everyone was gathered, I clenched and unclenched my fists, turning in a circle. "I made a big mistake. We should have stayed above them."

"Will, we never dreamed they could drop so fast, and it was the end of them," Liam said. "It was a thousand-to-one shot."

I looked at the hole in our ship. "Yes, but two feet lower and to the center, and the boiler would have been hit. We would be dead. It was not a good decision."

"Will, we all do the best we can. None of us argued," Laura said.

José offered a wry smile. "We knew you were not perfect."

"We survived," Addy said.

"Sure. One ship down. One to go!" Benny exclaimed. "Well—

two left, but we are winning."

Laura took my hand. "Will, this is war. War is dangerous. We all knew that when we got on board."

I let a piece of splintered wood fall through my fingers.

"Hey, it all can be fixed," José said. "Do not worry. We are going to win!"

Some of my starch came back. "Alright. We lead these guys out further, switch crews with the *Silver Seed,* and use her to take out the *Falcon.*"

Benny shook his fist toward the shattered *Gull.* "Your time to bother people has ended," he shouted. His boyish enthusiasm was infectious.

The *Red Hawk* stayed behind us, and we developed a system of zig-zagging while changing altitude. We kept far enough away that gunshots would do little damage, but José spotted a long rifle. One shot put a hole in the chimney of the cook stove.

"I have a plan to make them think they have hurt us," Benny said. "I pretend to get shot. I'll dive onto the deck like I'm dead. Then we go higher. And I'll be protected by the deck."

"Sounds risky. What if a lucky shot comes when you are falling?" I was not comfortable with the idea.

"They must feel some success," José said. "I have been watching. The man with the long rifle is their sharpshooter. That gun shoots farther but is a single-shot bolt action. It takes time to reload. After he shoots, Benny comes out, staggers around, and falls down."

"And we keep just far enough away that their Winchesters won't be effective," Liam said. "This could work."

Benny held up the broom. "Next time we swing to port, I will be ready behind the shield in the breezeway."

José rubbed his hands together. "It is all timing."

Wispy lower clouds made it difficult to judge distances. With the rangefinder, Laura, José, and I agreed we were more than a thousand feet away. The marksman had his rifle trained on the *Cloud Queen,* biding his time.

"Coming to port," Laura called down the stairs.

Benny took off his hat and put it on the broom. Lying in the breezeway, he pushed the hat up a few inches above the shields. Immediately a bullet tore through the hat.

"Go, go!" Addy cried.

Benny was up, put both hands to the side of his head, spun, and collapsed behind the shield. He crawled back to the engine room.

"Tell Benny, good acting—they're cheering," Addy said into the speaking tube.

43

Benny's little trick energized the Freebooters, and they shot with wild abandon. Laura skillfully kept us out of range.

The captain of the Freebooter ship had a hand scope, watching us carefully. Benny cooked lunch out of sight.

"Liam, nudge us a bit above Slow," Laura called down. "I am not sure they are flying at full speed."

Soon smoke boiled out of the Freebooter's stack.

"How much fuel do you suppose they have?" Addy wondered.

"They're going through it fast now." I handed the scope to Laura. "Their men have crowded away from the boiler. It is hot down there."

The *Cloud Queen* had never taken us so far south. On the bow, Laura and I scanned the new horizon, shrouded in cloud.

"I think those mountains ahead are the northwestern edge of Anza Borrego," Laura said. "We'll know soon."

"Food's on," Benny called.

In the forward cabin, Laura said, "You make good food for a dead guy."

We hunkered down behind the shields. I was getting tired of scuttling like a rat.

Liam checked the boiler and returned in moments. "Dolph says the two ships are talking." He shrugged. "I guess they learned to dangle an antenna."

"This is good," José said. "Now we know their plans."

Liam picked up the tape from the code receiver. GULL DOWN STOP FEAR ALL LOST STOP IN PURSUTE OF STEAMBOAT STOP KILLED ONE CREWMEN STOP ARE

ABEL TO KEEP IN SHOOTING DISTINCE STOP.

"That is from the ship out there. Then he sent a second message. PROCEEDING AT FULL STEEM TO ASSIST STOP WE WILL BLAST THEM OUT OF THE SKY STOP."

Liam handed Laura the tape. "Dolph says they aren't learning to spell any better." She caught my eye and winked.

"This may be better than we planned," I said. "I was afraid to take on three at a time, but with two ships and the *Silver Seed* above, we have them where we want them."

"But how long will it take for that scow to get here?" Laura wondered.

"It is slow, but perhaps not as slow as our friends who are with us," Liam said.

I studied the *Red Hawk*. "Let's pull away so it's safe to bring the big telescope to the stern. Liam, take us down so they can't use the cannon if they get behind us. Benny can watch off the stern deck for the *Falcon*. Get a different shirt and hat. You can wear my captain's hat if you want."

Benny grinned. "Captain Benny! I like that. Better than serving rich people."

I chuckled. "Just don't get shot again. Stay low."

José crouched low in the breezeway and trained the hand glass on the Freebooter ship. "They waste a lot of ammunition." José inspected a slug in his palm. "It hit the wall and fell there. It is from the long rifle. The sharpshooter lobbed it high, hoping to get it to us."

"How's our course?" I asked Laura on the speaking tube.

"We are aimed at a low place in the mountains."

"Liam, bring us up another thousand, almost into the clouds. Addy, keep an eye on that cannon."

"Already watching," Laura assured us.

The pressure stood at one hundred-twenty. "Liam, spin the engine faster in case we have to go up fast."

José took the big telescope off its mount and handed it to Benny. "OK, Captain Benny. Get to it. Sing out if you see anything."

Benny had hardly had time to balance the telescope on the shield before he came back down the hallway. "I see the *Falcon*. Hard to tell how far. Miles. They're a tiny speck under the clouds. Don't know if they see us."

I went to the code key. FALCON BEHIND STOP

BEEN WATCHING HER STOP

"Liam, can you let out a big puff of smoke? Something they might see."

He choked off the air, watching the second hand on his pocket watch. He opened the air. "What do you think?"

"Is everything OK down there? We belched a big puff of black smoke," Laura called.

Liam went to the speaking tube. "We're giving the Freebooters a little show." He smiled at me. "I guess we made smoke."

The dark cloud drifting behind us was impressive.

For the next hour, we varied our altitude. Liam worked out a system of letting a puff of smoke followed by us suddenly dropping.

Each time we turned to the side, I tossed the cook stove wood back through the breezeway, and José caught them. He slid them back to me, hidden by the shield. We made a show of moving wood to the boiler using four pieces of wood.

Our efforts were rewarded. BALLOON BOAT THINKS YOU ARE RUNNING OUT OF WOOD STOP

"Almost too easy," José said.

I studied the shattered bulkhead where the cannonball had torn through the ship. "Yeah, almost."

44

We crested the mountains, the steep terrain giving way to a valley. The sun had broken through the clouds beyond. The *Silver Seed* sent a report: FALCON THREE HOURS BEHIND YOU STOP EVEN IF YOU STOP IT WILL BE AN HOUR.

I went to the speaking tube. "Meeting. Have Addy keep us on course."

When we were in the engine room, I said, "I want this crew on the *Silver Seed* when we use the knife."

All nodded. Liam tapped out the message, and the *Silver Seed* replied: FAR ABOVE YOU STOP WILL CHOOSE LANDING SIGHT OUT OF RANGE STOP

"Liam, start taking us down but at full speed. Make them think we are crashing. We need time on the ground to switch crews."

The airscrews churned as we began our descent.

As the Freebooter's ship fell behind, their men rearranged the wood so the cannon was aiming down. Laura began a series of zigzags. After watching for several minutes, I became confident there was little chance of them pointing the gun anywhere but straight and level.

"Don't take your eyes off them, Addy."

At the front drop port, the rangefinder showed we were a thousand feet above the rocky ground. The airscrews were set to Flank speed, the stacks belching smoke.

The *Silver Seed* hovered over a flat piece of ground two miles away. We would not have much time for the change.

"Liam, give us as much speed you can muster. We don't want that cannon being aimed at us."

"The temperature is making it difficult for the Freebooters to cool their balloons," Liam said. He had me stand over the drop port and feel the wind on my face. "Some of the air is because we are going down, but some of what you feel are air currents. Wait a minute, and you will see what I mean."

In a moment, warm air brushed my face.

"With the sun beginning to shine, rising air is holding their ship up. This may give us more time, or they may lose control and crash like their sister ship."

My ears told me we were descending rapidly, but the *Silver Seed* was a half mile ahead.

I went to the code key. AFTER WE SWITCH BE CAREFUL STOP WHEN YOU GO UP GO UP FAST STOP REMEMBER WE WERE HIT WITH A CANNONBALL STOP DO NOT RISE IN FRONT OF THEIR SHIP

MR

In the next few minutes, I willed us to get there faster. The Freebooter ship had begun to descend.

When we hit the ground, the crew of the *Silver Seed* was on the deck in moments. We shouted greetings to each other as we passed. Benny was still in my captain's hat, and Laura had her top hat and goggles. Her cape flew out behind her. I stood at the door of the *Silver Seed*.

The *Red Hawk* descended to three hundred feet and was half a mile away. The *Cloud Queen* went straight up. I was always amazed at how quickly she could rise. The Freebooters fired, but it was a shot of desperation. The cannonball raised a cloud of dust two hundred yards beyond, and the hair stood up on my neck.

I secured the door and made my way to the helm. Pressure stood at one hundred eighty pounds. I pulled the lift and the propulsion levers back hard, spinning the wheel to the port. My stomach rolled as we turned toward the Freebooters, swinging wide. When we were several hundred feet above the *Red Hawk*, I took us far to their flank.

José lowered the knife into position. Laura sat at the elevation rudders as we lined up with the enemy.

"Brace yourselves." I pulled the propulsion lever to ramming speed. The tube fans howled as the *Silver Seed* accelerated. José came and operated the lift lever, tweaking our elevation. I aimed for the center balloon and watched as the ship loomed closer. Bullets rattled harmlessly against the bottom of the *Silver Seed*.

When the knife ripped into the gasbag, we slowed suddenly. I thought perhaps we were caught in the lines that attached the gasbag. The *Silver Seed* continued to move and tore away.

"Good job, Laura, José. Steady as can be." I began to swing around.

Benny came running from the back of the ship. "Sliced the center bag open like melon! She is going down."

When the *Red Hawk* came into view of the front windows, we could see she was in trouble. We followed her descent.

"I think we need to take out at least one more gasbag," I said. "We don't want them able to fly with fewer men."

I brought the *Silver Seed* around and stopped the air tubes. We floated slowly down, matching the speed of the Freebooter's descent.

Freebooters threw wood and cannonballs overboard to lighten the load. Some threw over their rifles.

When the ship hit the ground, she lifted in the air as two remaining gasbags tugged against the weight. She fell again. The men tried to get their footing and jumped off. I pulled the propulsion lever to ramming speed.

We closed the distance, and I aimed for the rear gasbag, bullets rattling under us.

The *Cloud Queen* was a lovely craft, but the speed of the *Silver Seed* was exciting. Laura held us steady, and José set our elevation perfectly. After a slight shudder, we came around, the rear gas bag folding in on the ship. She would not fly again for a long time.

"The *Cloud Queen* reports job well done," Benny said. "They will watch to make sure the men stay corralled."

When we were a thousand feet up, José slid back the shield protecting the floor viewport. The *Cloud Queen* waited sentinel a few hundred yards away from the downed airship. The men were no longer shooting. They were a long way from home, with nothing but desert for miles. Using the hand telescope, we took turns watching a fistfight that broke out between three Freebooters.

I pulled the lift lever. One more ship to go.

45

"I am taking us high," I said. "We will stay directly above the *Falcon* so their gasbags hide us."

José stood at the front windows. "Their ship is overloaded. They have no room to rescue their friends."

"We'll double-check," I said. "We don't want to find they dropped off a squad in Riverside."

"I suggest having the *Cloud Queen* stay low," Laura said. "High enough to be safe but give the impression that they cannot lift out of the valley."

"Yes. Good. We need to talk to them and see how it is going anyway." I went to the telegraph table and sent: HOW GOES YOUR PROJECT STOP

HOVERING OVER THE MEN STOP THEY BUNCH TOGETHER CROWDING INTO THE SHADE WE MAKE STOP SUN IS STRONGER STOP

"That is better than we could ask for," Finn laughed. "I suppose they are hot and thirsty."

"And I hope discouraged," Addy said. "They can see their plans crumbling. Too bad!"

I tapped: USE SPEAKING TRUMPET AND WATER TO BRIBE THEM TO STAY CLOSE STOP

DONE STOP LOWERED TWO BUCKETS OVER SIDE STOP THEY SHOT A HOLE IN THE FIRST STOP MARY SAID IT WAS HER FAVORITE BUCKET FROM THE GREEN HOUSE AND HOW DID IT GET ON BOARD THE CLOUD QUEEN STOP JOKE STOP

Behind me, there was laughter.

"Oops!" Benny raised his shoulders in innocence.

Laura shook a pointed knuckle at Benny's head. "Mary is going to give you a coscorrón."

"Ay." Benny rubbed his head. "Her knuckle hurts," he laughed.

I sent: SOMEBODY WILL GET A COSCORRON STOP

The response was swift. BENNY STOP I KNEW IT STOP

"She's gonna get you, Benny," Addy said. "Nobody messes with Mary's tools."

"Why does everyone think I am the guilty guy? Will borrows things, and he doesn't always put them back."

Laura nudged me with her shoulder.

I took us to eight thousand feet. Our ears ached, but we would be an unnoticed spot in the sky.

Finn came forward. "Makeup water is over three-quarters, and fuel is only down an eighth. We can fly for days."

"What about the *Cloud Queen*?" I wondered.

"They are giving a little to the men below," Finn said, "but Dad says they are good for a while. The extra barrel is half gone."

This worried me. "How do we get water to them? We don't want them to have to land with the Freebooters around."

Laura unrolled her map. "This shows a natural spring. That is the reason there is a settlement. The *Cloud Queen* can get water."

"Not without us to guard." José's voice was firm. "We do not know if the settlement is under the influence of the gas."

"Agreed," I said. "If that pig of an airship ever gets to the valley, we will take it down. Then we get water, and the *Cloud Queen* can go home. Send the message, Finn."

Below, the tortoise of an airship plodded along.

"Will, we must take them down before they get a chance to use their cannon on the *Cloud Queen*," Laura said.

"Way before." I turned the wheel slightly and increased the propeller speed. "It will make it harder to round up the men, but we must slice their gasbags as soon as they are in the valley."

The afternoon breeze was gusting, and the Freebooter airship flew slightly sideways. "They cannot even fly straight." José was disgusted. "The wind blows them like cotton."

"Yes, but at least the wind is pushing them faster," I said.

Finn brought a message from Dolph: FREEBOOTERS TRY TO SIGNAL OTHER SHIP STOP AFTER THREE TRIES THEY GAVE UP STOP

"They are bringing her around," José said. "Are they trying to retreat?"

Smoke boiled from two boilers, but the wind carried them toward the valley.

Finn came to watch. "The fools. They will never be able to fly against the afternoon breeze."

After fifteen minutes of futility, the airship turned with the wind and began moving in our direction. Even with a tailwind, it was another forty minutes before the ship cleared the last of the mountains.

"Are we ready?" I asked.

"This is our moment." José looked again with the telescope. "Take us to the side, and I will count how many men are on board."

I pulled the propulsion lever to Half and moved the ship to the north.

José used the hand glass, but even with the naked eye, I could see the men were packed in the hold.

"They are moving in circles of three and four. I do not think there are as many as before, but I figure at least seventy-five." José handed the scope to Laura. "Hard to count with them milling about. They are miserable, that is for sure."

Laura studied the ship. "They'll soon be over the first flat piece of land. This may be good."

"I want to get them closer to their friends." I paused. "How far do you suppose the cannon will shoot?"

"That looks like a twelve-pounder," Finn said. "It can shoot over a half-mile on level ground."

We were at least three miles from where the *Cloud Queen* hovered over the Freebooters. Too close for comfort. I pushed the lift lever forward, and we began to drop.

"Shields up. Lower the knife." I started a wide circle, putting distance between us and the airship.

The knife rumbled down and clicked into position. Finn came up and gave a brief nod.

At one hundred yards, I swung toward the Freebooter's vessel. "José, Laura, [repare for ramming speed."

The *Silver Seed* began to pick up speed as we came out of the turn. The tube fans whined, and I steered for the fourth bag from the stern.

Bullets rattled against the shields as we hurtled forward.

We were too high, and José adjusted the lift lever. We dropped a few feet, but the knife missed.

The distance to the *Cloud Queen* had diminished. I let the *Silver Seed* run out several hundred yards.

"They are dropping fast," José said, urgency in his voice. "The *Cloud Queen* is rising fast!"

I turned the wheel, and José let us drop. I pulled the propulsion lever to ramming speed, and we began our advance.

This time we were low, and the shields began to rattle again. The knife caught and slowed us but made a clean cut. I brought the ship around as the Freebooter ship slipped away. A gaping hole in the bag rippled as the gas escaped.

Once again, Freebooters began throwing objects overboard. Fear is a great motivator, and they managed to get the cannon over the side.

The hull began to twist, nose low, as the ship descended. When it hit, it tipped and dumped men and supplies on the ground. There was chaos as they scrambled for rifles. Several men shot, but we were too high for bullets to reach the *Silver Seed*.

José pulled back the shields from the windows and pointed at the mountain. "They will not get over that soon. I think we have found a good cage."

"Will, the *Cloud Queen* is in trouble!" Finn called.

46

I didn't want any surprises. "Contact Dolph. See if there are any other messages—other ships."

I swung toward the *Cloud Queen* and pulled the throttle to Full.

Finn came back with a long code ribbon. "Dolph says the enemy is silent. The San Gabriel Canyon group is talking to Sacramento, but only a skeleton crew is there. He says they are like a bee hive without a queen."

I pushed the propulsion to Flank. "What is wrong with the *Cloud Queen*?"

"Levitrite water," Finn said. "The tank went dry."

"Are they down?" Laura asked.

"No. Skimming the ground, staying out of range of the Freebooters. I told them to drain some water from the makeup supply tank and carry it up with buckets."

"That bottom spigot is slow," I said. "They might not be able to stay in the air." Hopelessness crept into my thoughts. "Let's fill pots—anything that will carry water. Addy, help Benny. Fill them from the galley sink."

José had the telescope trained on the downed *Red Hawk*. "The enemy is moving very slowly toward the *Cloud Queen*. The ground is pretty rocky."

"Have dynamite ready; we may need to use it."

I steered directly for the *Cloud Queen*. Flying low, it looked like a steamboat on a river of rocks. As we flew over the renegades scattered, trying to find cover.

The *Cloud Queen* settled in an open area, and we landed beside her. José was out the door with the soup kettle.

"Benny, Liam—get José. Take a look around. We don't need the *Red Hawk* men sneaking up on us."

I paced while Finn checked the *Cloud Queen's* boiler. He turned off the oil burner. "We came close to ruining the boiler. She was nearly dry." He turned. "Do *not* start the injector pump. The boiler is too hot. We could crack the tubes."

Every available container was taken back to the *Silver Seed,* but they returned at an agonizing pace. In the pilothouse of the *Cloud Queen,* I found Mary with the hand scope. To the east, a group of small buildings stood a mile away.

"Company, Will." There was urgency in Mary's voice. "Men from the *Red Hawk* are moving quickly over that rise." She handed me the scope.

José was moving his team in their direction, but on the ground, they would not see the Freebooters.

I went to the speaking tube. "Finn, if we have steam for the whistle, send code. Men coming over rise."

The whistle wheezed out the message, and José turned and waved his hand. They ran for an outcropping of rocks when the back of Benny's jacket tore open. His momentum sent him sprawling awkwardly to the ground. Liam worked the lever on the Winchester in rapid succession.

José scooped Benny into his arms and ran for the boulders.

I put the hand glass on them again and whispered, "Oh, Benny!"

José's mouth was open wide, and I knew he was screaming. He lay Benny on his back. José leaned his cheek close to Benny's mouth. He made the sign of the cross.

I couldn't breathe.

José crawled to Liam at the top of the outcropping. Smoke puffed from the barrels of their rifles.

I offered the scope back to Mary, but she shook her head. "I've seen enough."

"We have to get them out of there! Keep watch."

I ran to the engine room. "How soon can we fire the boiler?"

"The burner is running, but we won't be able to take off for a few minutes."

"Benny's been shot." An awful silence surrounded me.

Rage flooded me, shaking me awake. "Freebooters are coming.

Toward José and Liam. Maybe fifteen with rifles. We have to put the *Silver Seed* in the air."

"We don't have enough crew unless you or I go," Finn said.

He was right. I sent our best boiler tenders to guard us. Now Benny was dead. I felt an inner quake.

"You must stay here—make sure the *Cloud Queen* is restarted correctly. I don't want any more damage. Mary can steer if you can get back in the air. Hopefully, Nathan can keep the enemy at bay. Addy, get any full containers."

I met Laura. "Benny is down. Leave the bucket on the deck. We're taking the *Silver Seed* up."

Finn stuck his head out the door. "Will—the *Silver Seed* doesn't carry as much makeup water as the *Cloud Queen*. Only use the drinking water."

I waved as I ran. In the *Silver Seed,* I met Addy with a cooking pot. "Set it on the *Cloud Queen's* deck and hurry to the helm."

Laura had fired the flash boiler, the pressure rising.

It was my turn to pace. Addy returned at a full run.

I brought the engine up to speed, and Addy plopped down at the elevation rudders, breathing hard.

"Going up," I said into the speaking tube. I pulled the levitation lever, and we lifted quickly.

I turned toward our men and pushed the propulsion to Half.

Ahead José and Liam shot at the Freebooters. The renegades had hunkered in a gully.

"Laura, how is the boiler?"

"Fine. On my way."

With Laura at the wheel, I got a quarter stick of dynamite and opened the drop tube. The charge fell away, and we turned back toward our men.

The explosion was muffled, the periscope showing an impressive cloud of dust. José ran with Benny in his arms to a clearing. Liam followed.

Moments after we touched down, Liam called, "All aboard. Go."

I lifted off and turned the ship toward the Freebooters, bullets pinging off the shields. I went to the speaking trumpet. "Leave your guns and ammunition belts. Go back to your ship, or you will have dynamite on your heads. Wave if you understand."

Men waved and piled the rifles and belts. "Pistols too! We are watching."

The code light came on, and Addy brought forward a message from the *Cloud Queen*. LIFTING OFF STOP CAN'T MAKE THE SPRING STOP WILL PUT DISTANCE BETWEEN FREEBOOTERS AND US STOP

I was about to ask where José was when he came into the helm room. His shirt and pants were soaked with blood. He wiped his nose with a shaky hand.

"My brother died instantly," his voice almost a whisper.

"Oh, my friend! I am so sorry." I wanted to put my arms around him.

I sent Benny to his death. I took a shuddering breath. *No. I did what I thought best.*

The Freebooters started their retreat. I lowered the *Silver Seed* as if to land, and they began to run. "Like herding cattle," I mumbled.

José went to the gun pod and shot three times to encourage the men to hurry. I admired his restraint to not shoot men in the back. Even in the face of tragedy, José only killed when necessary.

When the men were several hundred yards away, we landed with the door near the pile of guns. Liam and I made quick work of loading the weapons.

Addy handed me another message. DOWN AGAIN STOP LIFTER WATER BRAZING CRACKED STOP MAKING REPAIRS STOP LOST WATER STOP

47

I took us up fast and turned toward the *Cloud Queen*. They had made only a quarter of a mile, and she tilted on rough ground. I trained the telescope on the settlement. A water tower proved there was water, but riders were closing on the *Cloud Queen*.

Mary was sprawled on the deck in front of the pilothouse, her rifle a few feet away. "Mary's down!"

"The *Cloud Queen* isn't answering the telegraph," Laura said.

José fired from the pod as we bore down on the *Cloud Queen*. Nathan dragged Mary into the pilothouse as we flew low over the ship.

"José, we need dynamite!"

José laid three quarter sticks on the deck. "Only two after this."

"We are not losing the *Cloud Queen*. We are not losing Mary." I caught Laura's eye. "Come in on them hard."

The *Silver Seed* shifted. "Addy, steady," I said. "I'm going to Full." I pulled the levers, bringing us lower. "After we get these men out of here, we'll load the wooden water barrel from the *Cloud Queen*. José, be ready to get the straps off the barrel. Hurry!"

"I will use the ax."

José dropped two sticks, the second quite close to the townspeople. The shields slid shut, and bullets rattled on the ship's underside.

We came around fast. Laura studied the scene in the periscope. "That slowed them down."

"Do we have time to get the barrel?"

"Yes, but landing won't be easy. It is rough out there."

"Then we will do it like we used to load coal—hover next to the deck."

The *Silver Seed* eased down, and José opened the door. The propeller tubes inched us sideways. José shouted up the hallway, "Good! Can you hold it there?"

"Yes!" Laura swiveled the periscope and made adjustments to the controls.

I went to the side door and met Finn and José carrying the barrel out on the deck of the *Cloud Queen*. "Down a tiny bit! Good!" I shouted.

They lifted the barrel and set it in the doorway. I worried it inside. "How's Mary?"

"Nathan's bringing her," Finn said. "She's hit in the—she's hit in the back of her lap—where she sits."

"Lower, Laura. Lower!" I called.

José jumped up on the *Silver Seed,* and Nathan stepped across easily, holding a pale Mary in his arms.

Addy went aboard the *Cloud Queen* with two pitchers of water.

"I am staying with the ship," Finn said. "I have the leak repaired. Is this all the water?"

"Yes, the drinking water tank is empty."

"Not enough," Finn said. "I'll try for enough pressure to get off the ground if attacked, but it wouldn't be for long."

I handed Finn the third stick of dynamite. "If this goes bad, destroy the ship."

"Mary is OK for the time being," Nathan said. He followed Finn out with four enemy rifles.

When we launched, the men from the village were again closing in on the *Cloud Queen*.

"Have these guys been sniffing the blue vial, or are they just ruffians?" I wondered.

"Hard to say," José said. "We better not take chances."

"Laura, take us high enough to make sure the men on the other side are still moving away. Some may have saved a pistol or two. We can't have the *Cloud Queen* in a crossfire."

Addy came forward. "Mary's bleeding has stopped. I gave her some tea."

"The bullet?"

"In her hip. I don't think it hit the bone."

We would have to take care of that soon.

Below, the townsmen had stopped advancing and were

watching us.

"The others are still moving back to the *Red Hawk,*" José reported as he climbed into the pod.

"We're going to drop suddenly!" I called.

Only two of the men below were shooting. The others tossed away their guns and stood with their hands in the air.

At fifty feet, one of the shooters fell. The other tossed his gun aside.

"On the ground! On your stomachs!" I shouted through the speaking trumpet.

The men stretched out on the rocks.

"That was easy. Keep a close eye on them." I hovered inches from the ground. José was out the door in moments, Addy joining him. She had lengths of rope and made quick knots. José bent them backward, cinching hand to foot.

"Laura, if this goes wrong, take the ship up! You can do more from the air."

I ran to José, picking up weapons.

José went to the wounded Freebooter and dragged him toward the *Silver Seed.*

"José, leave him! We have their guns. Our job is water."

"What was I thinking? Why should they ride?" He tied the hands of the wounded man.

He is in shock from the death of his brother.

We jogged back to the ship, and she rose as the door closed. The men from the *Red Hawk* were still retreating toward the wreckage.

"Time for a water run." I spun the wheel and pulled the power to Full. "Addy, keep us level. We're going fast." I pulled the lever to Flank, and we skimmed toward the buildings.

When we drew closer, I slowed the *Silver Seed,* and we watched and waited. Several were shooting, but we were out of range.

"How many, José?"

"Maybe nine or ten, but there will be more."

Laura put her hand on my shoulder and looked down. "How are we doing? Is there a pump?"

I moved aside so she could get a better angle and pointed. "I don't think we need to. That water tower will do fine."

I turned to José. "We need to evacuate this town. Let's show them some dynamite power."

"Take me close to the big building, and I will put a quarter stick close enough to make their ears ring."

I brought the ship around until we floated above the buildings. José sighted down the drop tube, gestured, and I eased the ship forward. He touched the fuse and let the stick drop. I pulled hard on the lift lever.

The concussion thumped the hull. Men ran out of two buildings. These were not Army men but dirty Freebooters like we fought four years before.

A woman ran out into the open. A burly man knocked her to the ground and dragged her. A single shot put him down. Addy was in the rifle pod.

"Sorry, Will. I can't let that go on. He will live—probably."

"Good job, Addy." I went to the speaking trumpet. "Come out with your hands up, or we will hunt you and kill you."

Several men came out.

"Walk away, toward the east. Don't look back, or we will shoot you."

The men gestured this way and that. José leaned into the speaking trumpet. "Where the sun came up this morning!" He turned in disgust. "Man, these guys are stupid."

The men began walking. A shot from Addy, and they trotted between the buildings.

Several women came out and ran in the opposite direction.

"Stop, ladies," I called in the speaking trumpet. "Go to the water tank."

A man came out of one of the buildings and approached the women. A single shot put him on the ground. I was glad Addy was not after me. The man put one hand in the air; the other held his leg.

"Are there more men here?"

The women huddled near the legs of the water tower. In the spyglass, I could see two holding up three fingers. They pointed to the building where they had been held.

"Any more women or innocents in the other buildings?"

They shook their heads.

"José, let's drop some rocks and see if we can flush out more bad guys."

I put the *Silver Seed* over the building, and we opened the drop door. A large round river rock plowed through the roof. Two men came out.

"Next one is dynamite!" I called.

They put their hands in the air.

"Throw your guns aside. Sit down. Where is the third man?"

The men did as I ordered and pointed to the building. We waited.

"You, in the building. Come out, or the dynamite comes in."

A man crawled out. His legs dragged behind him. He made it halfway to the others when his head dropped in the sand. He didn't move.

"This is going to be tricky. Do we trust the women? Do we go down for water? Do we rescue them?" I looked at Laura and then José.

"Let me off and go back up," José said. "I will settle this."

"I'm going with him," I said. "Lift off and watch."

Laura let us down, and I ran toward the tank.

As I came close, the women cowered. "We won't hurt you. The ship is not magic. It's going to stop the Freebooters."

The women were in wretched shape, with masses of bruises.

"Go there, and the ship will pick you up." I pointed to open ground, but they shook their heads.

José slipped between the buildings, and I joined him. He trained his rifle on the men sitting on the ground. "Go to the water tank. You have work to do."

The men hesitated, and dust kicked up near them. José could shoot a rifle from the hip and come dangerously close. The men jumped into action.

"Stop!" José stood like a pillar. "You are going to fill a barrel with water. Buckets. Where are buckets?"

A thin man said, "There are buckets at the spring."

"You get them. Go fast, or I will shoot you!"

The man ran toward the center of the plaza and returned with four buckets.

48

I twisted and sagged to my knees. Shots were ringing from the *Silver Seed* and José. A man fell from a window in the building near us.

Something hot was burning my collarbone. I looked toward José, gasping.

José's pistol was firing as he charged the building. I slid down against a wall. Someone touched my shoulder. A woman pressed on my shirt. Blood ran between her fingers.

Confusion followed.

I was carried to the *Silver Seed* and put in with Mary. Laura cut off my shirt.

"Are we getting water?"

"Yes. Be quiet."

José was there with his knife. I screamed and vaguely heard the bullet plink to the floor.

I didn't recognize the woman leaning over me. She had a large yellow bruise on her cheek. *We rescued you.* I was shivering. "How long?" My voice sounded far away.

"Five days. Laura is coming."

Laura.

"Hey, sweetheart. Good to see you with your eyes open."

"Thirsty."

Laura lifted my head, and I choked on the water.

Laura was there.

"How long?"

"Six days since you were shot."

Shot. My shoulder's on fire. "Water." I coughed. "Did we get the water?"

"The *Cloud Queen* is at Eagle's Crest. You rest."

"Freebooters?"

"They are fighting each other. Some are sobering up, and others are chasing them. José tells the sober ones to run away, and we pick them up. We have twelve so far."

"Can't trust them."

"José has made a jail cell out of one of the rooms. They are locked in but behaving."

I slept.

"Will?" Laura was calling me from far away.

"Will, wake up." It was Laura. Always Laura. Mary stood near.

"Mary, you were shot."

"Yes, but I am better, and you will be too." She handed Laura a cloth, and Laura wiped my forehead. The rag was cool.

"How long?"

"Only a few hours. The *Cloud Queen's* pipes have been repaired, and she's on the way back to us."

"We've not been home?"

"You wouldn't let us. You demanded, as Captain, that we guard the men on the ground." Laura put her hand against my cheek. "You can be quite insistent when you're delirious."

"I—I don't remember."

"We didn't think you did, but José and I thought you were right, even if you weren't in your *right* mind."

I loved her smile.

"Fuel?"

"We start back tomorrow. José has figured it all out. The *Cloud Queen* will take up guard. We're getting you home."

I struggled to sit up, my head spinning.

"Will, you *must* stay down." She laughed. "For the hundredth time!" She kissed my forehead.

"I really—want to sit up. I need to get my strength."

"Are you hungry?"

"Starving."

I ate, half-sitting, and felt strength coming back.

"Not too much."

"Still hungry." I took a big mouthful. "I'm OK." I leaned over and vomited into a bucket.

It didn't seem like it was the first time. *There is something else.* I could almost remember—*something else.*

"It's the fever. You are keeping more down."

I slept.

Laura wasn't there. Mary was watching me.

"Do you want me to get Laura?"

"How long?"

"Six hours. Your fever broke. You will get better fast now."

"Can I sit up?"

Mary arranged a pillow under me. She was limping.

"You were shot."

"That's what you keep telling me." She gave me a smile. "I'm healing fast. José is becoming quite a surgeon. Hungry?"

"Yes, please." I lay back.

Laura came with broth. "Welcome back!"

"Tell me what's happening."

"We hover, watching. We left the water barrel. There was food in the little town, and we drop it for them."

"How many are sober?"

"There are a number. José says we should arm them and leave them to guard the pass."

"Yes. José knows what to do. Can I see him?"

"He's asleep."

"It's night?" I loved her smile. "I love you."

"I love you too. Rest. It's a while 'til morning." She nestled in beside me. I listened to her sleep.

José came in the morning, which turned out to be mid-afternoon.

"Good to see you, Will." He smiled. "Good that you are not calling me Mother."

"I called you *Mother*?"

"Yes, and Finn and Mr. Salsbury."

I chuckled weakly. "I guess I've been pretty far gone." *Mother died in childbirth when I was three.*

"For four days, we did not know. We did not see any reason to take you to a doctor. I got the bullet out, and the wound was healing. The bullet nicked your collarbone and lodged in the muscle. You had a fever, and it had to break."

I dozed for a moment, coming awake with a gasp. "Benny!!" Tears filled my eyes. "Benny. Oh, Benny—"

José hung his head miserably.

"I'm sorry I forgot. I'm sorry I sent him with you. I'm sorry I —"

José stood over me, giving me the gentlest smile. "Will, we are all sorry, but this was not your fault." He turned away quickly, bringing a sleeve quickly across his eyes.

It feels like my fault.

"There is a cemetery in the little town." José spoke to the wall. "We buried him there. It is a nice spot." Turning back, José raised his shoulders, took a breath and let them fall with a sigh. "We sent news to my folks—no sense waiting—I suppose." A muscle in his jaw flickered.

Memories flooded—Mrs. Rodriquez hurrying to Wolfskill Lodge when Ed was shot—running beside the stretcher when Benny was shot. She would be devastated.

Benny.

I wasn't even there to help bury Benny. I didn't think I could stand the turmoil I felt deep inside.

José shook himself, standing tall. "The *Cloud Queen* is guarding the enemy—your father, Liam, Nathan, and Mary."

"Mary was just here—" *That was last night.* The propeller tubes were howling. *We're on our way home.* "How long to Eagle's Crest?"

"Soon. You rest."

I struggled to sit up. "Tired of resting. Help me up."

"Not yet. Maybe later. I want you to meet someone. One of the sober Freebooters. Captain Simon Smith."

I let my head fall back on the pillow. "OK."

José wore a different shirt. He brought Captain Smith, and they sat near the bed.

"Captain Smith, welcome aboard the *Silver Seed.*"

"Welcome back, Will. I have been on board for a week."

I gave a half smile. *This is going to take some getting used to.*

213

"I was on the *Falcon*—from Sacramento. Things were a mess there. We had the new supply of blue vials and lost most of them on our first attempt south. Men threw everything overboard, trying to save the ship—cases and cases of vials went overboard."

"But we intercepted a message from the *Falcon* that said there was to be a special vial ceremony when you got to Riverside."

Captain Smith pulled back one corner of his mouth. "We lied. So much had gone wrong, the Adjunct Leader didn't want to admit this gross failure."

"Where is this Adjunct Leader?"

"Killed when the *Falcon* went down."

"Someone else, higher up, was sending orders."

"I was never told who, but yes, someone else."

"Do we hear messages?"

José put his hands on his knees. "All communication has stopped. Perhaps he was on one of the other ships and died. Maybe they changed the frequency. Dolph is trying other settings—listening."

I struggled to sit. José propped a pillow behind me.

Captain Smith stood. "Our instructions were to overpower the Army and the government—put them under the influence of the vial."

Captain Smith paced back and forth. "I killed. I killed my fellow soldiers in the beginning. I should be hung for treason. I have tried to turn myself in, but José refuses." He stood at attention. "I appeal to you."

"Captain, you were under the influence of the blue vial. You were not in control of yourself."

Captain Smith looked down. "It's not right. I'm guilty."

I know about guilt. "Sir, we're not soldiers, but we've killed Freebooters. They were innocent—under the power of the vial."

"It was a nightmare," José said. "The world went crazy."

I stared at Captain Smith. "You seem familiar. Have we met before?"

"Yes."

I pushed my hair back. *He seems kind. I need my hair cut. He sounds Southern.* Silver bars glistened. *Gray eyes.* "We've had this conversation before, haven't we?"

"Yes. I have turned myself in to you three times."

José grinned. "You would wake up and want a report." He shrugged. "So, we gave the report. Who am I to deny my friend?"

214

José, dutifully bringing the Captain. Did I ask about Benny?

I adjusted the sling on my right arm. "How long since the men out there have had the vial?"

"Some? Four and a half weeks." Captain Smith sat. "Some will be in twilight. The tea holds the effect. With no tea, twilight comes faster."

Twilight. I have been in the twilight.

I shifted my arm. *Yes—I asked about Benny. Laura and Mary were here. I vomited in the bucket.*

José leaned on his elbows, palms together. "Dolph has been talking to Mr. Salsbury on the telegraph. Men came down from the camp where they built the ship. They were, as Captain Smith says, in twilight. There were not many left. Most were not actually in the Army."

"What about the southern ships? They had no vials?"

"No," Captain Smith replied.

"We won?"

Captain Smith stood. "Yes. Without the vials, all should go back to normal." He stepped closer. Thanks to you, we won."

No, we lost Benny.

49

The reunion at Eagles' Crest was a mix of great relief and heavy sadness. Mrs. Rodriquez put her arms gently around me and held me, swaying slightly.

"I know you tried," she whispered. "You were my Benny's hero, Captain Will." She held me at arm's length and fingered my sling. "I am glad you are getting well." She kissed my cheek.

How does one endure such grace?

Ed stood near. "Welcome back. I would shake your hand, but —" He gestured toward my arm.

We were family, and we had lost one of our own.

I was weak but enjoyed wandering around. One-handed, I helped Ed in the greenhouse. I didn't want Mary to take us to task when she returned.

When the *Cloud Queen* glided over the clearing, we were all there to greet her. There was a wonderful celebration that evening.

We made plans to fly everyone to Benny's grave in early spring. Mr. and Mrs. Rodriquez deserved that. In the meantime, we took Dad and the Rodriquez family back to their homes.

One evening, Laura and I sat by the fire. "A penny for your thoughts," I said.

"I suppose we should go back out and make some money when the *Cloud Queen* is fully repaired. Addy will be a good addition." She didn't say replacement.

"In due time. We have our whole lives to make money. Let's enjoy now."

We stood, and she snuggled into my arms.

Epilogue

The sweetness of victory is fleeting, and it wasn't long before there were rumors of gas being used in Colorado. Reports were slow in coming, but when Freebooters gassed an entire small town northeast of Denver, there was no doubt the engines of evil were churning in the remote mountains of Colorado.

About the Author

George taught 6th grade for years. He now lives with his wife in an old stone house called Graestone.

You can read more about the author at http://graestonewriter.com

Books By George Beckman

Members of the Cast

There is the family you are born into and the family that grows around you.

In 1959, Margo's parents break their promise, leaving her behind for another archaeological dig. She is sent to California to spend her junior year with a great uncle she's only met once. Her parent's interests remain buried in ancient ruins, but Margo begins to discover herself beneath a lifetime of family secrets. For the first time, she has a close circle of friends, a budding romance, and an academic future. But a struggle between herself, the past, and her parents tests all she has learned.

Enter into Margo's world and experience the "California Dream" feel of 1950s Southern California. This is a wholesome book for all ages—a book you can give to your granddaughter or grandmother.

The Ship from Wolfskill

Young Will and his friends are determined to defend the valley from the Freebooters, a band of ruthless Army renegades pillaging and burning their way north.

Will discovers his uncle's last great invention, an airship styled after a Mississippi riverboat, and he hopes to escape with Laura.

When men from the valley are captured, five young friends sail with the prevailing winds to rescue the hostages. Without conventional weapons, they must rely on their wits to battle the Freebooters.

Partway to Wolfskill

Partway to Wolfskill is a collection of poems describing an idyllic childhood in San Dimas Canyon. These lines reflect the beauty of the land and its loss to eminent domain.

Liquid Ambers
They were planted
The year I was born
And we grew there, together...

www.ingramcontent.com/pod-product-compliance
Lightning Source LLC
Chambersburg PA
CBHW071503170626
46811CB00007B/2711